I0690299

A FUTURE DENIED

RAY HOBBS

Wingspan Press

Copyright © 2024 by Ray Hobbs

All rights reserved.

This book is a work of fiction. Names, characters, settings and incidents are either the product of the author's imagination or used fictitiously. Any resemblance to actual events, settings or persons, living or dead, is entirely coincidental.

No part of this book may be reproduced or transmitted in any form or by any means, electronic or mechanical, including photocopying, recording or by any information storage and retrieval system, without written permission from the author, except for the inclusion of brief quotations in reviews.

Published in the United States and the United Kingdom
by WingSpan Press, Livermore, CA

The WingSpan name, logo and colophon are the trademarks
of WingSpan Publishing.

ISBN 978-1-63683-070-4 (pbk.)
ISBN 978-1-63683-942-4 (ebook)

Printed in the United States of America

www.wingspanpress.com

Also by Ray Hobbs and Published by Wingspan Press

An Act of Kindness	2014
Following On	2016
A Year From Now	2017
A Rural Diversion	2019
A Chance Sighting	2020
Roses and Red Herrings	2020
Happy Even After	2020
The Right Direction	2020
An Ideal World	2020
Mischief and Masquerade	2021
Big Ideas	2021
First Appearances	2021
New Directions	2021
A Deserving Case	2021
Unknown Warrior	2021
Daffs in December	2022
A Worthy Scoundrel	2022
Fatal Shock	2022
Last Wicket Pair	2022
Knights Errant	2022
A Baker's Round	2023
Confusion to Zeus	2023
Ways of Gentleness	2023
An Eye to the Future	2023
Stage Direction	2023
Dogs in Daft Outfits	2024
Taking the Stick	2024
People are Like Bottles	2024
A Family Effort	2024

Published Elsewhere

Second Wind (Spiderwize)	2011
Lovingly Restored (New Generation P ublishing)	2018

This story is dedicated in heartfelt thanks to the
surgical, medical and nursing staffs of Sunderland
Royal Hospital and Sunderland Eye Infirmary.

As ever, I am indebted to my brother Chris, who acted as sounding board for my ideas, occasionally offering his own, and who helped fuel my enthusiasm throughout the preparation of the manuscript.

A FUTURE DENIED

1

CATASTROPHE

W hat Walter Charlesworth sometimes referred to as 'dramatic goings-on' were commonplace at his daughter's home in Easingthorpe. Drama was the family's way of life; Sylvia and her husband Freddy were involved in yet another pantomime with Yoredale Players, and *Jack and the Beanstalk* was scheduled to open in two months' time, on the 29th of December. Rehearsals had been far from straightforward, the latest hitch being the indisposition of principal boy Lorna Jenkins, due to acute appendicitis. Happily, Freddy had found the perfect substitute in the chorus. Her name was Wendy Albright and she was a close neighbour. She was an excellent singer and dancer, tall, slender and well-developed; even at fifteen, she possessed the physical attributes that made her an ideal principal boy. Freddy and Sylvia could breathe again, at least for the time being.

Sylvia had just returned from a walk with Nina, the Hinchcliffe family's latest Aberdeen Terrier, when she heard the telephone in the kitchen. Her first thought was that it might be a business call for Freddy and, whilst there was an extension in the studio, he wasn't always immediately available to answer the phone. When he was busy in the darkroom, for example, Sylvia had to field his calls, so she hurried in to pick up the receiver.

'Hinchcliffe Photo Services.'

'Ah,' said the caller, 'is that Mrs Hinchcliffe?'

'Yes, do you want to speak to my husband?'

'Not immediately, Mrs Hinchcliffe. Please don't be alarmed. This is Saint Thomas's Hospital, London. Your daughter Leah has been involved in a road traffic accident, and we've had to admit her.'

Like the caller's words themselves, the surge of adrenalin and its associated rush of blood took Sylvia completely by surprise. 'Leah? How badly is she hurt?'

'It's difficult to say at this stage, Mrs Hinchcliffe. She's still being examined and x-rayed. Are you able to come?'

'Of course.' Thinking quickly, she said, 'We're about two hundred-and-fifty miles away, so it's going to take time. Will it be all right if I ask one of Leah's godmothers to hold the fort until we arrive?'

'That's an excellent idea, Mrs Hinchcliffe. One of the staff from the ballet school is already here. Try not to worry too much. Your daughter's in safe hands.'

Sylvia replaced the receiver with a trembling hand and, biting her lip, she went to the studio, where, to her intense relief, she was relieved to find Freddy free and available.

'Hello, SP,' he said, addressing her by the pet name he'd used since their earliest wartime correspondence. Reading her alarm, he took her hands and asked, 'What is it?'

Struggling to keep her voice level, Sylvia told him, 'Leah's had an accident and she's in hospital. They've asked us to go down there.'

The shock registered in Freddy's eyes. 'Did they say how badly she's hurt?'

'They don't know yet. She's still being x-rayed.'

In his practical way, Freddy switched to coping mode and said, 'I'll ask Reg to take tonight's rehearsal.' Looking at his watch, he said, 'If we're lucky, we might just catch the two-twenty from Northallerton.'

'Okay, will you phone Reg, and then I'll try Joyce and see if she can get to the hospital?'

'Good thinking, SP.' He gave her the quickest of hugs and then dialled the number of Reg Clough, garage proprietor and First Reed, also Deputy Musical Director, and appraised him quickly of the situation. Happily, he was able to stand in for Freddy at the pantomime rehearsal and, having thanked him, Freddy handed the receiver to Sylvia so that she could phone Joyce, her old wartime colleague, who was also godmother to Leah.

'The next job,' said Freddy, when Sylvia had secured Joyce's willing assistance, 'is to make arrangements for Martin and Nina.'

'I'll pack our things and some bits and pieces for Leah while you phone Elaine and ask her to pick Martin up from school, as she's nearest. I'll ask my dad to take Nina. He's got a key.' As an afterthought, she said, 'You'd better phone the school as well, and ask them to let Martin know that Elaine's going to collect him.' She was reasonably sure Elaine Bailey would be available. Caring for a daughter with Down's syndrome kept her pretty-well housebound most of the time. Her husband was sales manager of a car dealership in Northallerton and, although he would be wholly sympathetic as well as anxious about his beloved goddaughter, he would most likely be unavailable for the time being.

* * *

One of the doctors Leah had seen earlier entered the curtained cubicle. He was carrying something in one hand. 'Hello again, Leah,' he said. 'I'm going to give you something to ease the pain.' He drew some concoction into a hypodermic from a phial and squirted out a tiny amount to expel any air.

'I'm very thirsty.'

'I'm sure you are, Leah. When did you last eat?' He gave the injection as he spoke, so that she was hardly aware it was happening.

'About one o' clock.'

'And when did you last have anything to drink?'

'The same time.'

He withdrew the needle, rubbing her arm. 'In that case,' he said, addressing a nurse who had just appeared inside the curtain, 'Leah can have a tiny sip of water to relieve the dryness, but no more than that.'

'Am I going to have an operation?' The whole bizarre procedure was beyond her experience and therefore her powers of understanding.

'That's the general idea.'

'Your mum and dad are on their way here,' said the nurse soothingly, 'and they've arranged for someone else to come and see you. Just lie there and let the injection do its work.'

Mention of her parents caused Leah to sob again. She'd been crying intermittently, whether through fear or shock, since she was lifted into the ambulance, and now she needed comfort. Miss Soames from the ballet school had stayed with her as long as she could, but then she'd had to leave her to attend to matters of duty at the school.

3

It was all so bewildering. She remembered setting off across Duke Street. Miss Selfridge had opened for the first time only recently, and the prospect of visiting the store was terribly exciting. She was almost across the road when she felt herself being hurled into the air. She never felt the impact when the car hit her, just the jarring as she landed on the tarmac. There was a lot of shouting, someone mentioned making a nine-nine-nine call and, amid everything else, Leah remembered feeling completely helpless. The pain came later, unbearable at first, but the injection now seemed to be working. For now, at least, the pain was receding. She just felt helpless, hopeless and very much alone.

She lay in tearful misery, wanting someone, anyone, to come through the curtain, and then, suddenly, her longing was fulfilled by the familiar and welcome sight of her godmother.

'Auntie Joyce,' she sobbed.

'It's all right, darling. Everything's going to be all right.' Joyce bent and laid her face next to Leah's, finally kissing her forehead. 'Your mum and dad are on their way, and everything's going to be fine. You'll see.'

* * *

Walter opened the kitchen door to continued barking, which had begun when Nina heard his footsteps outside.

'What a good girl,' he said. 'That's right, you let 'em know there's somebody here.' He let Nina have a good bark and then took down the lead that hung, as usual, beside the door. 'I know we hardly know each other,' he said, slipping the check chain over her head, 'but I dare bet you anything that, come next trout season, you and I will be seeing a lot of each other at Redmire Falls.'

Almost won over, Nina gave Walter's hand a cautious lick.

'There's someone at my house who can't wait to meet you,' Walter told her. 'He's a cocker spaniel called Adams, and I think you two are going to get on famously together. Shall we go and meet him?'

* * *

4

At about the time Walter and Nina were becoming better acquainted, a boy sharing certain features with Freddy Hinchcliffe, although not his father's prematurely-grey hair, stood alone outside the gates of Yoredale High School, having been told to wait for his lift. The message had resulted in a degree of ribbing by some of the boys in the English class and, ready as schoolboys were to pursue a joke beyond its useful life, one of them had stopped him afterwards on the corridor to ask, 'Is your auntie going to pick up her little nephew every day?' Martin had responded with economy of effort. He expected to hear the stern voice of authority at some stage, but the goading had now ceased, and its perpetrator was crouched in a state of collapse.

A first impression was that Martin was an easy target. He struggled to communicate and had shown no aptitude at all in team sports. His particular *forte* was swimming, but he was only able to demonstrate that occasionally. The PE Department had made it known to Freddy and Sylvia also that, however adept Martin was at boxing, the school neither espoused nor encouraged combat sports. Some boys, then, were foolish enough to tease him and, struggling as he did to read the harmlessness in their manner, Martin seldom responded well to their attentions.

A maroon-and-silver Rover P5B coupé approached almost silently and came to rest by the gate. Its driver, a tall, smartly-dressed man with neat, grey hair and aesthetic features got out and greeted Martin with a smile. 'My dear old thing. Hello, Martin.'

Martin shook his hand. 'Hello, Bailey.'

'I know you were expecting Elaine, but she's a bit tied up.' Noticing that a group of boys was displaying some interest in the car and its driver, he asked, 'What do those characters want, Martin?'

'They thought it was funny that my auntie was going to pick me up. One of them went too far, so I told him to stop.'

'Splendid fellow. How did you phrase it, exactly?'

'A left jab and a right hook.'

'I couldn't have expressed it better myself, dear boy. Anyway, hop in, and we'll make tracks for the Bailey household.' When Martin was seated, he said, 'Janice has been under the weather, you see. She's all right now, but one can't be too careful, and Elaine thought it was better for her not to travel.' He started the engine and pulled out into the road, still watched by the inquisitive few, now clearly impressed by the recently-launched coupé. 'If you open the glove compartment, you'll find something to your liking.'

Martin felt inside and took out a bag of wine gums. 'Thank you, Bailey.'

'Just the usual creature comforts, dear boy.'

'Why are we going to your house?'

'That, my dear old soul, is what I was about to tell you. The fact is, Leah's had an accident. She's in hospital, and your parents are currently hotfoot for London to be at her side. Now, you mustn't worry, because she's going to be absolutely fine, but just for now, you'll be billeted with Elaine, Janice and me.'

That was fine. Bailey had a way of setting Martin at ease, principally because he never said anything he didn't mean. There was never any suggestion of ulterior design; if Bailey said it, he meant it. He'd even carried out his offer, as sometime Royal Artillery Light-Heavyweight Champion, to teach Martin the pugilists' art, much to his mother's dismay, but even she had to admit it did no real harm. Meanwhile, if Bailey said Leah was going to be all right, that was good enough for Martin. He could now concentrate on the Rover.

'Is this the new model, Bailey?'

'The newest, old scout, the P5B, three-and-a-half litres of get up and vroom.'

'What's it's top speed?' Numbers were reliable, Martin knew where he stood with them, so he liked them.

'About a hundred and fifteen miles an hour, they say. This is a demonstrator, and I think we'll use it, you and I, as we go about our day-to-day business.'

'That'll be good. What's the acceleration?'

'Nought to sixty-two in twelve-point-five seconds.'

'Impressive.' Martin was concerned about Leah, but now that Bailey had reassured him, he was looking forward to spending some time at their house. Elaine was nice and Janice was all right. She had her problems but, like Bailey, she only ever meant what she said. Bailey, though, was full-time fun.

* * *

'The cracked ribs and broken collar bone will repair themselves in time,' the surgeon told Freddy and Sylvia. 'The pelvic fracture is a simple one, so that's a blessing.'

'What's simple about it?' asked Sylvia, to whom medical jargon meant nothing.

'There's no displacement,' he explained. 'The two surfaces will knit together. The problem, I'm afraid, is in her legs, where there are several fractures.' Pointing to the x-ray, he said, 'They're going to need quite a lot of pinning and plating – that's rods and screws to reinforce the bones – and the right knee is of particular concern. To begin with, however, I should like to operate on her legs.'

'What about the knee?' asked Freddy.

'It will most likely need to be rebuilt.' Looking at Sylvia's crestfallen face, he said, 'It could have been worse, you know, and we should be able to get her walking again in a couple of months.'

'She wasn't just walking before the accident,' said Sylvia. 'You know she's at the Royal Ballet School, don't you?'

Lowering his voice sensitively, he said, 'Yes, I know.'

'They were talking in terms of a great future for her. This is going to break her heart, never mind her bones.' Unable to control herself further, Sylvia descended helplessly into tears.

'I understand the police are likely to throw the book at the driver,' said the consultant.

Freddy snorted. 'It's a pity they can't throw his bloody car at him, the way he threw it at our daughter.' He squeezed Sylvia's shoulder as he spoke. 'Even then, though, it wouldn't undo the harm he's inflicted on her.'

'I'm sorry, Mr Hinchcliffe. We'll do everything we possibly can for Leah. All you need to do for now, is to sign the form giving me permission to operate, and then you can see her for a while before she goes under anaesthetic.'

Taking their leave of Mr Willoughby, they followed a nurse to the curtained-off bed, where they found Joyce talking softly to Leah. She stood up to draw Sylvia into a silent hug that meant everything.

'Thank you, Joyce,' said Freddy, 'it was wonderful of you to do this.' He made his way to the other side of the bed.

'Oh, I'll be back. Don't you worry, and don't waste money on hotel bills when you have friends in town.' She slipped away, leaving Sylvia and Freddie with their heavily-sedated daughter. Even then, Leah sobbed with relief when she saw them.

'Everything's going to be all right,' Sylvia told her. It was a reflex, and automatic response, because it was the last thing she truly believed.

'Absolutely everything,' said Freddy. Everyone kept saying so. He just hoped and prayed they were right.

2

HELPING HANDS

S ylvia and Freddy eventually fell asleep in each other's arms and, such was the extent of their joint reaction to the emergency and the fatigue resulting from it, that they opened their eyes to find themselves still entwined. Freddy withdrew his arm to chafe it back into life while Sylvia asked, 'What time is it?'

Barely awake, Freddy squinted at his wristwatch as it lay on the bedside table. 'Either ten to seven or five-and-twenty to ten,' he reported sleepily, 'depending on which way you look at it.'

'Is it dark outside?'

'Very.'

'In that case, it's ten to seven.' Sylvia had always been quicker than Freddy to come to life in the morning. After a little more thought, she said, 'I'd phone the hospital, but they said something about shifts, I seem to remember.'

'They said we'd be better waiting for the day shift to come on,' he reminded her.

'When's that?'

'I've no idea. Let's have a bath and get dressed. By that time, it'll be a normal working day.'

'I don't know what we've got in our bathroom, but let's use it, anyway, shall we?'

'Affirmative.'

They discovered that their room was equipped with both a bath and a shower, so they saved time by using the shower and, by the time they were dressed, it was seven-thirty, so they went down to breakfast. After all that, Sylvia phoned the hospital and was connected with the sister on Leah's ward.

'My daughter, Leah Hinchcliffe, was admitted last night,' said Sylvia. 'Mr Willoughby said he was going to operate on her legs. Can you tell me anything?'

'Oh yes, Mrs Hinchcliffe, Mr Willoughby operated on Leah last night and she's now comfortable. You'll be able to visit her this afternoon between two and four-thirty, and this evening between six-thirty and seven-thirty.'

'Thank you.' It wasn't exactly an abundance of information. 'Can you tell me if the operation was successful?'

'I'm afraid that's all I can tell you for now, Mrs Hinchcliffe. Come in this afternoon and we may be able to tell you more.'

'Thank you.' Sylvia put the receiver down, only a little better informed than she'd been before making the call. She asked Freddy, 'Do you remember when it seemed that everything that was worth having was rationed?'

'As I recall, that only ended a dozen-or-so years ago.'

'That's what I thought until just now, when I discovered that the hospital is rationing information. All they'll say is that Leah's had her operation and she's comfortable.'

'Well, that's something to be thankful for, at least.' Reminded of an earlier time, he said, 'They were rationing information when you were in hospital having Leah and Martin. They wouldn't tell me a thing apart from sex, birthweight and the fact that mother and baby were both doing well. They didn't even say what it was that you were both doing so well.'

'You can be obtuse at times, Freddy.'

Looking suitably humble, he said, 'I'm sorry, darling. What can I do to make amends?'

'Let me phone my mum and dad, and then you can phone Bailey and Elaine.'

'Right.'

Sylvia spoke first to her mother and then her father, passing on what little information she had. In return, her father, although intensely relieved that his granddaughter was still in one piece, told her that Adams and Nina had spent a cosy night together and were consequently bosom pals. When she relayed the news to Freddy, he experienced a moment of alarm before reminding himself to his relief that Nina had been spayed, and that they would never be more than innocent playmates.

Elaine and Bailey expressed their relief before passing the news to Martin and Janice, the latter interjecting throughout, as she always did, and demanding more news than was currently available.

Finally, Freddy spoke to Reg, who expressed his delight that Leah was out of danger and assured him that the rehearsal had been quite successful, and that the entire cast of *Jack and the Beanstalk* had sent Leah their love, regards or best wishes, depending on how well they knew her. Freddy came off the phone touched by their concern.

'People can be lovely when they try,' observed Sylvia.

'Some don't even have to try.'

'Who do you have in mind, Freddy?'

'Wendy Albright.'

'Oh yes, the way she stepped into the principal boy role, and at only fifteen, as well.'

'Not only that, SP.' His pet name for her stood for 'Sugar Plum', after the fairy in the ballet, and it stemmed from an anecdote she'd described in one of her letters to him during the war. 'She's told Reg that if you need to spend a lot of time here, you needn't worry about the dance routines. She knows them from being in the chorus, and she's happy enough to rehearse the others.'

Sylvia's eyes filled with tears. 'What a lovely girl. What a wonderful offer. I'd been agonising about that.'

'I took the liberty of accepting her offer on your behalf,' said Freddy. 'You can take up residence with Joyce and Len, now. I have to be back by Monday to keep the home fire burning, but I'm sure you'll be happier down here for now, and so will Leah.'

Still mopping her eyes, Sylvia said, 'Let my mum feed you. She'll be offended if you don't.'

'And I wouldn't dream of offending her.' In truth, he would appreciate the company of his in-laws. The thought sent his mind racing back to 1945 and to his disappointment on arriving home from Germany and learning that Sylvia was overseas. It was good to know he could rely on them again. Otherwise, Leah was quite naturally never far from his thoughts.

His pensive state was not lost on Sylvia, who said, 'A penny for 'em, Freddy.'

'I was only thinking that out of this tragic business, however it eventually affects Leah's dancing ambitions, the mercy is that we've still got our daughter.' Measured against all that had happened, it was the greatest mercy of all.

* * *

Leah had come round from the anaesthetic during the night but, in that uncertain, shadowy world between dreams and reality, she was aware of very little. Now she was awake again, and any doubt she might have had was erased immediately by the pain in her legs, both of which appeared to be entombed in a tent of some kind. She also felt it in the centre of her body each time she tried to move. At one stage, she gave a sharp cry that attracted the attention of a staff nurse.

'Good morning, Leah. You had your operation last night, and all you have to do now is lie still and let nature do its work. Let's pop this under your tongue.' Taking the thermometer from its receptacle fixed to Leah's bedhead, she inserted it into her mouth and held her wrist to check her pulse.

When she could speak, Leah said, 'There's an awful pain....' She tried to point, but that simple action caused even more discomfort. 'It's in... the middle.' In her sixteen-year-old modesty, she found it impossible to describe the location without embarrassment.

The nurse finished entering the temperature and pulse, and said, 'That's your pelvic girdle. Just a minute.' She opened a drawer in the table that stood in the centre of the ward and took out a folder containing x-rays. Finding the appropriate one, she held it up so that Leah could see it. 'Here it is,' she said, pointing to a tiny line bisecting the pubis. 'This fracture is causing the pain, but it'll ease in time.' She replaced the x-rays and consulted Leah's notes. 'You're due for another pain-killer, Leah. I'll be back in a minute.'

Leah was trying hard to accept that life would be a progression from one dose of pain relief to the next, at least for the time being.

* * *

After a second phone call from Sylvia, Jessie Charlesworth said, 'Sylvia's going to stay with one of her old friends she knew in the

Wrens. She lives in Streatham, wherever that is, and it'll be handy for Sylvia to get to the hospital.'

'Oh, good.' Walter was relieved by the news.

'Obviously, Freddy will have his work to do, but he and Martin are going to eat with us, Walter. That's when Martin's not at school. He'll have lunch at school, as usual.'

'Excellent.' Emergencies apart, Walter and Freddy had been close friends since Freddy's homecoming as an ex-prisoner-of-war. Martin had never been the easiest of companions, but Walter would make the usual effort to accommodate his difficulty.

'If there's anything we can do, Mum, just say the word.' Audrey, their elder daughter, had called in for news, while she was in the area, personal contact being preferable to a phone call at such a time.

'Thank you, Audrey. I'll bear that in mind.'

'I don't suppose they've any idea how long she's likely to be at St Thomas's.'

'I imagine it's impossible to say,' said Walter. 'She only had the operation last night.'

There was what seemed a natural compulsion to make what, on the face of it, were pointless observations, such was the bewildering effect of the impact the news had made on the family. 'I suppose this doesn't augur well for a career in ballet,' she said, thinking aloud.

'Let's not concern ourselves with that,' said Walter, unconsciously echoing the sentiment his son-in-law had expressed earlier. 'Let's just be thankful that Leah is alive and in capable and caring hands.' Addressing Nina's enquiring look, he said, 'Yes, Nina, you haven't met Leah yet, have you. I expect you'll be good company for her when she comes home.' He underlined his remark by tickling her behind both ears, while Audrey looked on in detached bemusement.

'I don't know why you keep dogs,' she said. 'They only bring germs and parasites into the house.'

'There are no parasites in my house,' protested her mother, who regarded cleaning and housekeeping as a religious observance, and who resented any comment she saw as even remotely critical.

A man of reason, Walter was less inclined to be fiercely defensive. 'It's not all they do, Audrey,' he said, 'in fact, they don't even do that. Our dogs are clean and free from fleas, worms and stowaways of all kinds. Far from bringing unpleasant things into the house, they bring companionship, sympathy and affection.'

'I suppose so.' Audrey had been brought up with dogs and had previously accepted them as part of family life, but her husband David was a doctor, a local GP, with strong convictions, and she now found it difficult not to share his uncompromising stance on household pets. Fortunately for Adams, and now Nina, Walter was a dog lover to the very core, and his home was as good as an animal sanctuary. He just had to remind himself that, in spite of her uncharitable attitude towards dogs, his elder daughter had some excellent qualities, which might yet prove valuable in the developing circumstances.

* * *

'I love you, Martin!' In addition to being as affectionate as most people with Down's Syndrome, Janice was a creature of impulse, which meant that her utterances often came *à propos* of absolutely nothing, but were no less genuine.

Retreating behind his mental barricade, Martin pretended not to have heard her. Such a display of affection would have embarrassed most fourteen-year-old boys, but his inadequacy in matters of communication created an impossible situation. Fortunately, Bailey was on hand to play the diplomat.

'Martin loves you, too, darling, but he's concentrating on mending your doll's pram.'

'What's consupating mean?' Janice's tone seemed to suggest that an acceptable explanation had better be forthcoming, or else. Whilst a year older than Martin, she was said to have a mental age of about eight, with the added difficulty that she struggled at times to manage her frustration.

'Calm down, Janice. It means that he has to put all his effort into doing it. Be thankful you've got someone as clever as Martin to mend it.' Bailey's practical ineptitude was a byword within the family circle, whereas mechanical problems posed no challenge for Martin.

That signalled another protestation from Janice, who declared loudly, 'I love you for mending my doll's pram, Martin!'

'That's all right, Janice.' He tightened the wheel nut and set the wheel spinning, wishing she'd think about something else. Satisfied with the balance of the wheel, he righted the pram and ran it back and forth. 'There,' he said, reluctant to waste words.

'Thank you, Martin,' said Bailey. 'Say thank you to Martin, Janice.'

'I love you, Martin!' she bellowed.

'Just "thank you" would be nice.'

'Thank you, Martin! I love you!' She seized the pram by its handlebar and rammed the sofa with it enthusiastically.

'That's all right.'

Elaine came in from the kitchen and said, 'Thank you, Martin. That was very kind of you.'

'You're welcome, Elaine.'

'Your mum's on the phone. Come and talk to her. I'll stay with you if you like.' She knew about Martin's reluctance to use the phone, and she was quite sympathetic towards him without really understanding the nature of his difficulty.

'All right.' Dutifully, he followed her into the kitchen and took the receiver from her.

'Are you there, Martin?' asked a voice that sounded like his mother's, although he could never be sure on the phone.

'Yes.'

'Is everything all right?'

'Yes.'

'I just wanted to tell you that Leah's had her operation, and she's going to be all right. Isn't that good news?'

'Yes.'

'We're going to see her this afternoon. We'll give her your love. Would you like that?'

'Yes.' Some prompt from within, possibly a salient memory, emerged in time to make him modify his response to, 'Yes, please.'

'Good boy. Your dad's coming home tomorrow, but I'm going to stay with Auntie Joyce and Uncle Len so that I can be handy for the hospital. Your dad'll be in touch with you. Is that all right?'

'Yes.'

'Okay, will you put Elaine on again?'

'Yes.'

'Good lad. I'll talk to you soon. 'Bye.'

'Goodbye, Mum.' Gratefully, he handed the receiver back to Elaine, his ordeal over for the present. Returning to the sitting room, he found Bailey ready to leave for work.

'Are you still coming in with me this morning, Martin?'

'Yes, please.'

Janice asked, 'Can I come?'

'No, darling. Stay here and play with your doll's pram.'

'Why are you taking Martin away from me?'

'Because he wants to look at some motor cars. Isn't it good that he was here to mend your pram?'

An unusually sly thought occurred to Janice. 'What if it breaks again?' she demanded. 'He won't be here to mend it.'

'Be gentle with it and it won't.'

Elaine came in after speaking to Sylvia. 'They operated on Leah last night,' she said. 'It's likely to be a long job, as we thought, but she'll be all right.'

'Thank you, darling.' Bailey waited for Martin to don his coat, and then kissed Elaine and Janice. 'We'll see you both later,' he said. 'Come along, Martin. I like to think that Rovers sell themselves, but I'd just as soon not put it to the test.'

* * *

Sylvia looked down both sides of the ward and spotted Leah. Taking the nearest seat beside the bed, she kissed her and asked, 'How are you feeling, darling?'

Tears started immediately. 'It's horrible. They keep giving me things for the pain, but it's still awful.'

'It'll get easier.' At least, she hoped it would. Memories of her spell in hospital in Valetta during the war gave her at least some encouragement. 'Your dad's gone to find a doctor. He says there must be somebody in charge. They can't leave it all to those in the after cockpit.'

The reminder of one of her dad's silly expressions made Leah smile momentarily, and then she confided uneasily, 'I have to... you know... go to the loo... in a potty, you know, like the one Martin had when he was a baby.'

16

'You had one as well, darling. In fact, if I remember rightly, it was the same one that we'd kept. It was a time of shortages.'

'Mum!'

'Well, we're none of us fairies, love, so it's no use pretending. Anyway, what's wrong with using a bedpan?' She was afraid she already knew the answer to that.

'It's too embarrassing for words.'

'I know, darling, but what's the alternative? You can't walk to the loo, so you have to use a bedpan. It's either that, I suppose, or do it in your knickers. At least, you could,' she teased, 'if you were wearing any.'

'Mum!' It was an anguished whisper.

'It's like anything else, Leah. You'll get used to using the bedpan, and then, one glorious day, you'll be able to walk to the loo. Think of the excitement. I think we'll have a party to celebrate the event. We'll call it Leah's Loo Day. Everyone will come to that.'

'Mum!'

'What, darling?'

'Stop making me laugh. It's agony.'

'I'm sorry.'

After a little thought, Leah said, 'It's only Saturday, isn't it?'

'The twenty-second of October,' Sylvia confirmed.

'So you don't have to go home yet?'

'I'm going to stay with Auntie Joyce and Uncle Len, so that I can come and see you as often as you like.'

Reassurance gave way to concern. 'What about the pantomime?'

'Do you remember Wendy across the road, the girl who forgets to close her curtains?'

'Yes, of course.'

'Not only did she take over the part of Jack when Lorna went into hospital, but she's going to oversee dance rehearsals for me as well. Isn't that good of her?'

'Incredible.' Reflecting on the first part of the sentence, she asked, 'Why did Lorna go into hospital?'

'Acute appendicitis. She had to have an emergency operation, and now,' she whispered, 'she has to use a bedpan, too. You'll be able to compare notes with her when you meet.'

17

'Don't be rotten, Mum. You know it hurts when I laugh.' As an afterthought, she said, 'I don't know why I'm laughing. There's nothing funny about it.'

Freddy pulled a chair up to Sylvia's to join her. 'How's my little flower?' he asked, kissing Leah whilst carefully avoiding contact with any part of her that might be fragile. It left him few options.

'She's feeling shy,' said Sylvia.

'Mum!'

'All right, I'm not going to tell him.'

'Mr Willoughby wants to see us before we go,' said Freddy, realising that his daughter was embarrassed, presumably about something fathers weren't generally allowed to hear about.

'Good.' Seeing that Leah was still eyeing her nervously, Sylvia changed the subject again. 'I've been telling Leah about Wendy coming to the rescue,' she said.

'Yes, she's surprised us all, and she's not the only one. Everyone's been more helpful than we could ever have expected.'

3

December

A Welcome Diversion

With the plaster casts off and Leah making her way gingerly on crutches, she was finally allowed to leave St Thomas's on Friday, 15th December, her case having been transferred to St John's Hospital, Keighley.

After taking her tearful and grateful leave of Mr Willoughby and the nursing staff, she left the hospital building with her parents and joined Bailey, who was waiting in the carpark. Mindful of Leah's immediate needs, he had arranged to borrow a Rover saloon from his employers in order to give her the transport he felt she deserved. Neither Freddy nor Sylvia could argue with that; in any case, they knew there was seldom any point in disagreeing with Bailey, so they accepted the arrangement gratefully.

'You've all had to give up so much,' said Leah, when the realisation came to her of how close Christmas was.

'Not a bit of it,' said Sylvia, joining her on the back seat. 'Christmas will happen but, because of the way things are, your Grandma and Grandad have invited us to spend it with them, this year.'

'Yes,' said Bailey, 'I must remember to return Martin to his rightful owners. I must say, these last few weeks, it's been almost like having a son of my own.' It had been agreed at the outset, that it made more sense for Martin to live with Bailey and Elaine than with his grandparents, as they lived closer to his school and, whilst Martin had no objection to staying with his grandparents, he regarded time spent with Bailey as a treat.

'I hope he hasn't been difficult,' said Sylvia as they entered St Marylebone.

'Martin? Difficult? The very idea. For six whole weeks and the price of a slice of bread and dripping a day and a bed in the coal shed we've had the services of a mechanical genius. What reasonable person could ask for more?'

Whilst she realised he was less than serious, there was something Leah had to know. 'What's bread and dripping?' she asked.

Freddy shook his head and said, 'You really don't want to know, darling.'

'Dripping,' said Sylvia, who was less inclined to be delicate about the matter, 'is the fat that falls from a joint of meat when it's roasted. In the absence of anything better, people used to spread it on bread for breakfast, or sometimes take to work for lunch. I never had to eat it, but I knew people who did.'

'Yerk!'

'There were times in Poland and Germany,' said Freddy soberly, now that the secret was out, 'when Bailey and I would have given all our chances for a slice of bread and dripping. Isn't that right, Bailey?'

'I could still eat some now, old man.'

'When we stop for lunch,' said Sylvia, 'we'll give you something an awful lot better than bread and dripping, Bailey. I think you deserve champagne and caviar at least, for your kindness, although I can't promise you that.'

'You flatter me, dearest one.'

The journey continued with scarcely a break between conversations. Then, when they stopped at the George Hotel in Stanford for lunch, Leah told them about one occasion during the past month when she'd felt particularly dejected. 'I was more miserable than I've ever been in my life,' she said, 'and then, with no warning at all, Auntie Dorothy arrived from Ipswich.'

'I knew she was coming,' said Sylvia. 'I thought it would be a nice surprise for you.'

'It was a wonderful surprise. It really bucked me up to see her. You know what she's like.'

'Yes, she can be a wonderful tonic, and she was just that for me when we were in Malta. Mind you, I remember a time when she was the one who needed support.'

'Go on, Mum,' urged Leah, 'Tell me one of your war stories. History's one of my favourite subjects.'

'You cheeky thing.' Nevertheless, she obliged. 'It was when we were at HMS *Wasp* in Dover. Dorothy had only recently become involved with the hulking great marine you now know as Uncle Alf.'

'Is a marine like a sailor?'

'Not even remotely,' said Freddy, 'whatever they try to tell you, but I'll make a special allowance for Alf, who's a modest sort of chap in spite of being an ex-bootneck.'

'Anyway,' said Sylvia, keeping her story on course, 'Alf was drafted to the battleship HMS *Howe*, and although Dorothy tried to be brave about it, she couldn't keep it up indefinitely. I woke up in the night and heard her crying, so I went over to her bunk to give her what comfort I could. It was freezing in our cabin, but she was so upset I got into bed with her. Bed-sharing was strictly forbidden in the Wrens, although I hadn't the foggiest idea why.'

'Hadn't you, Mum?' Leah sounded incredulous. 'It was to discourage unnatural relationships. It's the same at ballet school.'

'I know that now,' said Sylvia, suddenly embarrassed, 'but I didn't then. Honestly,' she said, 'it's come to something when my sixteen-year-old daughter knows more than I did when I was twenty.' Freddy and Bailey shook their heads in sympathy, sorrow and not a little shock.

'It's the same with the boys, in fact more so, really, because it's still illegal for them under the age of—'

'Thank you, Leah,' said Freddy. 'I think we should talk about something else.'

Again, they found no shortage of topics to discuss, although they now realised that some were best avoided, if only for the sake of their own equanimity.

* * *

Eventually, after the most comfortable journey, Bailey dropped them at home, where Walter, Jessie, Martin, Adams and Nina were waiting.

Jessie had aired and made up a bed for Leah in the studio because it was on the ground floor and handy for the downstairs cloakroom.

'How did you get the bed downstairs?' asked Sylvia.

'There are firms that make a business of moving furniture,' her father reminded her.

There was no answer to that. Indulgence in Walter's generosity, like Bailey's, was compulsory.

'Hello,' said Leah to a new and enquiring face, when she'd greeted everyone, 'who are you?'

'This is Nina,' Freddy told her. 'She's two years old and quite keen on rabbits. She hasn't caught one yet, but hope springs eternal, as they say in Aberdonian canine circles. Meanwhile, she's developing a passion for music and a keen interest in photography.'

'What a beautiful face. Can she get up?' She made room for her on the sofa.

'I'd no doubt she'd break the rules sooner or later,' said her mum. 'They always do.'

When Walter and Jessie had gone, Leah sat with Nina on one side and Martin on the other. 'I hear you've been mending things for Bailey and Elaine,' she said.

'And Janice.'

'Hm. Mending things for Janice is like painting the Forth Bridge, isn't it?'

'Is it?' Like most figures of speech and abstract references, it was lost on Martin.

'When the painters get to the end of the bridge,' she explained, 'they have to start again at the beginning, so the job never ends, like mending Janice's toys.'

'Oh.' He watched Leah stroke Nina behind her ears and decided to give it a try. Nina's affectionate response both surprised and pleased him.

'It's good to be home,' said Leah. 'How's the pantomime coming on?'

'That was going to be my next question, too,' said Sylvia.

'Better than I could have hoped,' Freddy told them, 'but with only eleven days left, it should be promising, at least.'

'And right on cue,' said Sylvia, looking out of the window, 'here comes Jack Trott. Now I can thank her properly.'

'Jack who?'

'Jack, of Beanstalk fame.' She went to answer the door, and Leah heard her say, 'Wendy, come inside and let me thank you for everything you've done. It was ever so good of you, and I'll see you get a special mention on the last night.'

'It were no bother, really, Mrs Hinchcliffe. I just thought I'd come to see how Leah is, if that's all right.'

'Come through, then. Leah, you have a visitor.'

'Oh, Leah,' said Wendy coming into the sitting room, 'you have been in the wars, haven't you? You poor lass. Hutch up, Martin. No, don't go away, there's room for us all on here.' In her usual matter-of-fact way, Wendy picked up Nina and sat with her on her lap, seemingly oblivious to Martin's red-faced unease. As she chatted easily, Leah felt an unusual kind of admiration for her. Wendy wasn't the brightest of people, but she was talented and confident, and she seemed to go through life bestowing kindness and goodwill as a matter of course. It was apparently a family characteristic, as everyone who knew Wendy's mother agreed.

'Will they let you go back to ballet school, Leah?' As she spoke, she put her hand to her mouth. 'I shouldn't ask you that, should I?'

'Don't worry, Wendy,' Leah assured her. 'I won't know until the surgeon's seen me in Keighley after Christmas. He'll send a report, and the school will make their decision. To be honest, I'd rather not think about it.' As ever, the worry of it brought tears to her eyes.

'Oh, Leah,' said Wendy, 'don't let it get you down.' Taking a clean tissue from Sylvia, she offered it to her. 'Do you know what you need to do? You should come to the rehearsal tomorrow afternoon. It'll take you out of yourself, an' it should be good for a laugh.'

* * *

Wendy was right. From entering the hall uncertainly on crutches and receiving the ovation of the whole cast, Leah was relieved of her worry and preoccupation and for the whole of the rehearsal she was able to share in some of the fun the pantomime had to offer. One of its diversions was Daisy, the cow. The costume had been recently completed, and the two boys who were to wear it had only ever rehearsed their dance connected by a cord. The cow costume would test their coordination to its limits, so they were fortunate in having Wendy as their dance partner, although she was not about to tolerate any nonsense, as they soon discovered.

'I'm sorry, Freddy,' she said, pausing the dance routine to coach the two within the cow. 'You both lead with your left, remember? Right, let's try it again.' Looking down at her ballet slippers, she said, 'It doesn't feel right in these things. It'll be better in tights and heels.' Sounds of enthusiastic agreement from within her bovine partner prompted her to say, 'Behave yourselves in there.' Turning to those around her, she said, 'Right fair, is it the only thing lads ever think about?'

Her observation earned spontaneous laughter among the cast, and Freddy played her into the end of the chorus of 'Daisy Bell' once more.

'It won't be a stylish marriage,' sang Wendy,

I can't afford a carriage,

But you'll look sweet upon the seat

Of a bicycle made for two. Ready, you two? Left, right, left, right, left-left-left, right-right, left. That's better. You're getting the idea, now.'

Further along the row, Leah's mum smiled to herself, no doubt satisfied that dance supervision had been in safe hands in her absence. Two seats beyond her, Martin watched, apparently bemused by the whole spectacle. Fiction of any kind failed to win his interest, but he would read science textbooks by the hour and with total engagement. Another subject that appealed to him was that of cybernetics. Leah found the thought of a machine that made decisions and arrived at conclusions highly disturbing, but Martin read avidly whatever information on the subject he could find, and he was still on the lookout for more. His father, whose inclination was reassuringly, at least from Leah's point of view, creative and expressive, took the line that he had 'that sort of brain', probably inherited from his maternal grandfather, and put his communication problems down to shyness. Leah continued to wonder. For the time being, however, the rehearsal continued to serve as a diversion from her worries. The giantess was hiding Jack from her husband. Leah could remember nothing about a Mrs Giant, but was prepared to be enlightened. She watched her push Jack into the oven, standing guiltily in front of it when the giant came into the kitchen.

'Fee, fie, foe, fum,' he observed somewhat predictably, 'I smell the blood of an Englishman, and be he dead or be he alive—'

'Hold it,' said Freddy. ' "Dead" rhymes with "bread", so it has to be "be he alive or be he dead".'

'Sorry,' muttered the shamefaced giant.

'Okay, it's easily done. Let's try again.'

'Fee, fie, foe, fum, I smell the blood of an Englishman, and be he dead... bugger!'

Twice more, he tried the lines, and then Freddy was obliged to offer the advice, 'Write "alive" on the palm of your hand, Stan, and please try to mind your language. Remember we're in mixed company and there are children present as well.'

The giant took a breath and made another attempt. 'Fee, fie, foe, fum, I smell the blood of an Englishman, and be he...' He looked nervously at the note on his palm. 'Be he *alive* or be he dead, I'll grind his bones to make my bread.' Seemingly unable to believe his success, he said, 'Bugger me, I got it right that time!'

Freddy cut to an earlier scene, in which Dame Trott was inevitably found in her kitchen creating mayhem and disorder. It was a well-worn formula, but it was likely to have children helpless with innocent mirth. Leah remembered that whenever Bailey and Elaine brought Janice to a pantomime they had to sit at the end of a row, so that Elaine could get Janice to the loo before her laughter proved too much for her bladder control. The kitchen scene didn't affect Leah in quite the same way but, like the rest of the rehearsal, it proved to be a glorious distraction. The next diversion would be Christmas but, lurking in the background was the spectre of more x-rays and examinations, and the crucial report that would be sent to the Royal Ballet School.

4

A TIMELY VISIT

After six weeks in hospital, Christmas was a time of bliss, with Leah's parents and grandparents doing everything they could to make it special for her. The excitement continued to the weekend with the pantomime.

Leah sat with Bailey and Elaine, with Janice safely in the aisle seat and, for the next couple of hours, she reverted to childhood, enjoying all the silliness of Dame Trott, Daisy the Cow, and the clumsy and half-witted farmhands. The giant wasn't supposed to get laughs, but he did, especially when he got his rhyme wrong, as he had in rehearsal, and the line, 'Be he dead or be he alive…. Bugger!' was implanted permanently in the minds of his audience along with more traditional memories of the pantomime.

At the end, Leah was pleased to see Wendy and her mother presented with flowers, and was surprised at first to see her father hand something up from the pit to her mother, but then she realised what it was. During a discussion about Wendy's remarkable contribution to the production, Martin had mentioned that the stitching of Wendy's battered school satchel was about to give up the unequal struggle, and that she'd been admiring his leather briefcase. Now, in a special presentation before a capacity audience at Easingthorpe Town Hall, Wendy received her own briefcase, a gesture that left her quite emotional. Leah found it more than touching that a girl who lived by kindness was overcome when it was repaid.

The New Year brought with it an appointment at St John's Hospital, Keighley, with Mr James Finchley, an orthopaedic surgeon. It was to be an extended visit, involving exhaustive x-rays of her pelvis and her plated limbs as well as her damaged knee.

A natural optimist, Leah changed into the operating gown provided and followed the radiographer happily into the x-ray room, where she followed instructions as closely as she could. By this time, she was familiar with the process and able to take the changes of position, if not in her stride, at least without serious discomfort.

'Thank you, Leah,' said the radiographer. 'That's everything Mr Finchley asked for. You can get dressed again.'

'Thank you.' It was good news, as the open back of the operating gown was less than conducive to confident movement, and particularly while she was still coping with crutches. That was something that had come as a fresh reminder. Thankfully, she donned her clothes and made her way back to the waiting area, where she found her parents.

'That was quicker than I expected,' said her mum. 'Let's go to the cafeteria.' She made the suggestion without obvious enthusiasm.

'I'll take you for a treat tonight,' said her dad. 'I expect you'll be ready for one.'

'I left a beef casserole in the oven for tonight,' Sylvia told him, 'but we'll see how it goes.'

They followed the signs to the cafeteria, where they had a very ordinary lunch that failed to impress Leah's mum, although her dad found nothing wrong with it. It was a standing joke that both he and Bailey welcomed food of even the most questionable quality, having been half-starved as PoWs. For her part, Leah was less interested in food than she was in knowing how soon she could return to the Royal Ballet School, and she had to endure almost an hour of waiting until two o'clock, the time of her appointment.

Back in the waiting area, she read all the posters, translated them into French and then into German. She even tried setting one of them to music, a task made almost impossible by the insensitively loud conversations of other patients.

Eventually, a nurse came to the waiting area and asked her and her parents to follow her to the consulting room.

Mr Finchley was a balding man of about fifty. He wore tortoiseshell-framed half-moon glasses and what appeared to be an habitually-serious expression.

'Good afternoon,' he said, addressing Leah's parents. 'I've been looking at your daughter's x-rays. The pelvic and leg fractures have healed remarkably well, but she is, of course, young, and young bones tend to heal more easily than older ones.' He referred to his notes and said, 'She's sixteen, I believe.'

'And a half,' added Leah.

Mr Finchley ignored her and said, 'The main concern is the right knee, which was very badly damaged in the accident.' Again, he consulted his notes. 'A traffic accident in London, I believe, Mr Hinchcliffe.'

'Leah can confirm that, Mr Finchley,' said her dad, 'as she was there at the time.'

The consultant's serious expression faltered for a second as he considered the information, but he made no immediate response.

'She's here, in this room, Mr Finchley. It's her injuries we're discussing, and I think she might appreciate being drawn into the conversation, if only once in a while.'

Leah could tell that both her parents were less than pleased and, whilst she found her dad's observation a little embarrassing, she was grateful he was there to champion her cause.

'The chief concern,' said Mr Finchley, 'is the knee.' Turning to address Leah for the first time, he said, 'I'm going to refer your case to a colleague who specialises in the knee joint.'

Leah had to ask the question that had dominated her thoughts almost since the accident. 'How soon can I go back to ballet school?'

Mr Finchley looked at his notes, at the x-ray still illuminated on the screen, and then at his hands. Eventually, he said, 'Without consulting my colleagues, I am unable to give you a straight answer to your question, but I can tell you that ballet, or any other form of dance, will be out of the question for at least four or five months, and that even then there is no guarantee that you will ever regain your former facility.' Perhaps feeling that he'd made his prognosis less than clear, he said, 'The most helpful advice I can offer you is to adopt the commonsense view and consider an alternative career.'

* * *

Leah walked out into the carpark in a numbed state of disbelief. It wasn't until she was about to get into the car that she said in an unnaturally level voice, 'Can we have that treat another time, Dad?'

RAY HOBBS

'Of course we can, darling.'

'I don't think I could face it tonight.'

'I'll ride in the back with her, Freddy.' Her mum closed the front passenger door and joined her on the back seat. Almost immediately, Leah fell into her arms and gave way to a series of anguished sobs. The future she'd envisaged almost for as long as she could remember had been snatched from her. After more than two terms' absence, the Royal Ballet School would give her place to the next rising star, and Leah's dancing career would never be anything more than a cruelly stolen dream.

* * *

With Leah in bed and Martin attending to other matters in his room, Freddy was inclined to be sceptical. 'Honestly,' he asked, 'what do these people really know? The man's an expert on bones, muscles and so on, but what does he know about ballet? It was the same when we saw the specialist about Martin's difficulties, and he told us he most likely had a form of juvenile schizophrenia. The bloody charlatan actually told us to be thankful they no longer put such children away in mental institutions.' In a burst of impotent frustration, he said, 'I still say there's nothing wrong with him but shyness, and he'll grow out of that. For all we know, and for all Mr Finchley knows, as well, Leah might make a complete recovery and dance again.'

'It's not the same, Freddy.' Sylvia's eyes were red and swollen. It was impossible to witness Leah's anguish without feeling it herself and, with her passion for ballet, she had encouraged her daughter's ambition. 'As far as Martin's concerned, there must be lots of grey areas in psychiatry and an awful lot they don't know, but in the case of orthopaedic surgeons, it seems to me that bones, muscles, nerves and tendons are depressingly straightforward, and there's no escaping the fact that ballet calls for the highest level of athleticism. I'm afraid we have to accept Mr Finchley's prognosis.'

'I don't know, SP. Let's reserve judgement, at least until someone's taken a fresh look at her knee. Doctors have been proved wrong in the past, you know.'

Sylvia was unconvinced, and for what seemed to her the best reason.

29

'I don't want her to build up on it, only for her hopes to be crushed again. It would be too cruel. She's only sixteen, Freddy, and already she's had to suffer a level of emotional torment that would challenge someone three times her age.'

'All right.' After twenty years of marriage, he knew how far to press his argument. 'Let's leave it there.' Hopefully, a visit from Elaine, Bailey and Janice might serve as a temporary distraction. They were due to arrive the next day.

* * *

'Don't cry, Leah. There's no future in it.' One of Janice's more entertaining habits was that of picking up odd phrases and throwing them haphazardly into a conversation. She didn't always understand them, but anything grown-ups said had a kind of mysterious gravitas that made them worth saying for their own sake. 'It'll all be the same in a hundred years' time,' she assured Leah.

'That's true, Janice, because we won't be here. Anyway,' she said, forcing herself to think of other things, 'what have you been doing lately?'

'Knitting,' Janice told her, triumphantly brandishing the result of her handiwork, which included a great many dropped stitches. 'I keep making holes in it,' she admitted.

'Yes, you've made a feature of them, haven't you?'

'Well, how are you supposed to do it, then?'

'Do you want me to show you?'

'Yes.'

'What does Brian say?' Brian was one of Janice's long-suffering dolls, who came in useful, thanks to some creative thinking on Bailey's part, as an example of good manners.

'Yes, please.'

'All right. What do you want to knit?'

'*I* don't know.' It sounded like the answer to a silly question.

'Do you want me to suggest something?'

'Yes.'

'Yes what?'

'Yes, *please*.'

'All right. Here's my suggestion,' said Leah. 'A scarf would be useful in this cold weather.'

'Yes, it would.'

Leah surveyed the mess of dropped stitches and asked, 'What do you want to do with this?'

'I don't want it.'

'I don't blame you, Janice. Let's make a fresh start.' It was time to summon her resources. 'Have you any spare wool, Mum?'

Smiling at the welcome development, Sylvia took two balls of bright orange wool from a drawer and handed them to her.

'Thanks, Mum. Just look at this wool, Janice. Won't it make a lovely scarf?'

'Yes, it will.'

'Okay,' said Leah, scooping Janice's earlier efforts off the needles and taking a new ball of wool, 'You'll have to be patient while I cast this on for you.'

'I love you, Leah.' The protestation came from nowhere, but it was no less welcome for that.

'I love you, too, Janice. Let's see if you can make a really pretty scarf to wear.'

'No, you can wear it.'

'That's very kind of you.'

* * *

Later that evening, Sylvia said, 'There's nothing like other people's problems for taking your mind off your own.'

Freddy looked up to ask, 'What made you think of that, SP?'

'Leah was quite happy helping Janice with her knitting. It was the perfect distraction and, while she was doing it, she thought of another.'

'Go on.' Good news was always welcome, especially in the light of recent events.

'She wants me to find a reading book for Janice. It seems to her that, in short and easy spells, a little bit of reading shouldn't be beyond her.'

'That's my girl.' He smiled happily. 'Do you remember how I got Bruce started with a book about Scotties?'

'I'll never forget it, it was so dramatic.' Their nephew had been a reluctant reader until Freddy tapped into his passion for their dog Thea. With no pets allowed in his own home, Bruce spent every moment he could with the object of his affection, and reading about dogs like her became a new and fascinating pastime.

'Let's hope Leah is as successful with Janice. She's always been very good with her.'

'I'll be happy if it takes Leah's mind off her troubles, even if it's just for a little while,' said Sylvia. 'She was very wobbly when she went to bed tonight.

* * *

Martin lay awake, trying to make sense of the situation. Leah was more upset than he'd ever known her, and nothing seemed to work for very long. She'd been all right when she was helping Janice with her knitting but because Janice could never concentrate for very long, that was all too short-lived. With his logical mind, he was never happy when he failed to understand something, and he turned the matter over repeatedly until he arrived at what seemed like the most obvious solution. It was cold in his bedroom, so he pushed his feet into his slippers and pulled on his dressing gown.

Quietly, he made his way downstairs. Nina stirred when she heard him, wagging her tail when he crouched and stroked her. She felt gloriously warm, and that was good. Warmth was always good when you were miserable. 'Come on, Nina,' he said. 'Come with me.' Obediently, Nina left her bed and together they went to the studio. Martin listened at the door. He could hear Leah crying quietly, and that wasn't good, but he had the answer. It seemed to him that stroking Nina made Leah happy. He wished he'd thought of it earlier, but now he could do something about it. He turned the knob quietly and picked Nina up.

Leah stirred in the darkness. Unable to see who was there, she asked tearfully, 'What's the matter?'

'Nothing,' said Martin. 'I've brought Nina,' he told her, laying her gently beside his sister.

'Oh, Nina,' she sobbed, burying her face in her soft, warm fur.

'Will you be all right now, Leah?'

'Yes.'

She was still crying, but she would be all right, because she'd said so. 'Good.'

'Thank you, Martin.'

'That's all right.' With the satisfaction of an important job carried out, he went to the door.

'Good night, Martin.'

'Good night, Leah.'

5

AN ACT OF KINDNESS

Freddy addressed his family after breakfast because it always seemed better to let them eat. He could claim their attention later. 'Each time a new dog comes into this house,' he said, 'I say the same thing, and each time, I find everyone doing the opposite. I'm talking about dogs and furniture. Already, Nina's been up on the sofa – it happened when we came home from London – and this morning, I found her on your bed, Leah.'

'*I* did that,' said Martin, like a knight shielding his *protégée*. 'Don't be cross with Leah, because it wasn't her fault.' Somewhat redundantly, but possibly for emphasis, he repeated the information, 'I did it.'

Leah reached across the table to squeeze Martin's hand gratefully, much to his discomfiture.

'I'm not being cross with Leah, Martin. I'm just saying that there's no point in making house rules, only to have them broken.'

'Martin brought Nina to me last night,' said Leah, because he knew I was upset, and he thought it would be nice for me. He was right. It made all the difference.'

'So it was an act of kindness,' said Sylvia, 'and we know a thing or two about that, don't we, Freddy?' She gave her husband a meaningful look that found its target.

'Yes, it was a very kind thought on your part, Martin. Forget what I said about dogs on furniture.' He adopted the look of a man outnumbered and defeated on his own territory. Still, he had to admit that theirs was a telling argument, and he was as keen as either of them to alleviate Leah's distress.

'That's right,' said Sylvia, happily picking up the used dishes. Her daughter had spent on the whole, a pleasanter night than of late, and that was her primary concern, too.

Martin put on his coat and picked up his case. 'Dad,' he asked quietly, 'can I ask you something?'

'Of course.' Something in Martin's manner appealed for discretion, so he closed the inner door so that they wouldn't be overheard, and asked, 'What's on your mind, Martin?'

'Can you see your way to making me an advance?'

'You want your pocket money in advance?' Experience told Freddy that his son was either tongue-tied or that he expressed himself in precociously formal English. There were occasions, however, when he needed prompting. 'What do you want money for?'

'I'd like to buy a present for Leah.'

As ever, Martin was poker-faced. Words were all Freddy ever had to go on, as his son usually delivered them with neither cadence nor expression. 'Where will you go for that?'

'A toyshop....' He faltered. 'I don't know.'

Clearly, Freddy had to take the initiative. 'I'll tell you what, Martin,' he said, 'don't get the bus home this afternoon. I'll pick you up from school and we'll go into Northallerton to get what you want. How's that?'

'Yes.' Martin sounded almost relieved. As always, it was difficult to tell.

'What does Brian say?' It had become a family custom.

'Please. Thank you.'

Freddy laughed lightly. 'That'll do,' he said. 'Off you go, and have a good day at school.' One of them needed a good day. Even the substantial cheque from the insurance company for Leah's injuries had made no difference to her state of mind, not that any sum of money could ever compensate for her shattered dream.

* * *

Freddy arrived at the school gates by three-thirty and waited. Before long, the doors opened to allow a horde of grateful youngsters to emerge. The first one Freddy recognised was Wendy, who stopped to exchange a word with someone, and then spotted Freddy and his car. She came over to speak to him.

'Hello, Wendy,' he said. 'I'm taking Martin into Northallerton to get something he's got his eye on.'

'Oh, lovely.'

'We'll still be home before the bus, so do you want a lift?'

'Yes, please, Freddy. That would be fantastic.'

It was good that Wendy never needed a Brian to remind her of her manners. 'Jump in,' he told her, 'he should be out soon.'

Martin came via the pedestrian gate, as he always did, even though the main gateway was clear. Seeing Wendy in the front passenger seat, he let himself into the back.

'Hello again, Martin,' said Wendy. 'How's Leah?'

'Hello, Wendy.'

'She's going through a difficult time,' Freddy told her after greeting his son, now rendered laconic by the presence of an agreeable girl. 'It's almost certain that she'll lose her place at the ballet school, and the man we saw at the hospital wasn't at all encouraging about her future as a dancer. As a matter of fact, he left her feeling very down in the dumps.'

'Oh, that's rotten. Poor lass, 'cause ballet's all she's ever wanted to do, isn't it?'

'Martin's going to buy her a present to try and cheer her up.'

Martin said nothing, but looked uncomfortable.

'That's a lovely thing to do, Martin,' said Wendy. 'Do you know something? If I had a brother, I'd want him to be just like you.'

Freddy ignored the illogicality of that statement, taking the line that it was at least well-meant, whilst Martin tried even harder to shrink, tortoise-like, into his coat and blazer. They continued to the outskirts of Northallerton.

'Right, Martin,' said Freddy, pulling into a large carpark, 'what are we looking for? Will Beaumont's do?'

'Yes.' His voice was muffled, coming as it did through three layers of clothing.

Freddy parked and, mindful of his woeful sense of direction, made a careful mental note of the nearest landmarks so that he could find the car again. Having done that, he bought a parking ticket and stuck it to his windscreen.

'Can I come as well?' asked Wendy.

'Of course you can.' He locked the car and led the way into the largest toyshop in Northallerton, if not the whole county. Whatever Martin wanted, he was as likely to find it there as he was anywhere.

Once inside the ground floor, Freddy asked, 'What are you looking for, Martin?' He crouched so that his son could whisper in his ear. 'That's all right,' he assured him. 'Wendy understands these things. She might even help you choose something. Girls' point of view and all that sort of thing, you know.'

'I very likely would,' agreed Wendy, 'if I had a clue what you were looking for.'

Freddy pointed discreetly to the sign that read *Soft Toys*, and Wendy nodded her understanding.

When they arrived at the counter, the choice seemed limitless; there were teddy bears, pandas, monkeys, dogs, kittens, squirrels, donkeys, hedgehogs, penguins and polar bears, among others. It seemed an impossible decision until Wendy pointed excitedly to an affable, if gormless-looking camel, and said, 'That's the one I'd have, Martin.'

The assistant picked it up and showed Freddy the compartment in its hump. 'This one doubles as a pyjama and nightie case,' she explained carefully.

'That won't stop her enjoying it,' said Wendy, 'and she can keep her nightie in it until bedtime if she wants to.'

'Is it for a little girl?' asked the assistant.

Yet again, Martin was trying to disappear, so Freddy said, 'Yes, my little girl.'

'Lovely. Well, if you're sure, I'll wrap it for you.'

Freddy looked questioningly at Martin, who nodded mutely. 'That,' said Freddy, 'would normally set you back three weeks' pocket money, Martin, so shall we just write off the debt and call it a generous thought on your part? After all, it's the thought that counts, not what it cost.' He paid for the camel, and then, taking the carrier and its contents from the assistant, he thanked her and said to Martin, 'As far as Leah's concerned, it's your present to her. All right?'

'Yes.' Then, remembering Brian's excellent example, he added, 'Thank you, Dad.'

Wendy kept both her travelling companions entertained on the way home with stories of soft toys she'd known and her experiences with them. She explained that she was talking about a period before her dad's untimely demise, which had naturally curtailed the money available for toys, and for anything else, for that matter. Still, she maintained in her usual, chatterbox way, she had only another two terms to do at school – her mother had insisted that she stayed on for the extra year until she was sixteen to get some CSEs – after which she would be able to find employment and add to the family income.

They arrived in Easingthorpe with Freddy secretly saddened on her behalf, and Martin still trying to make himself invisible.

As they entered the house, Freddy greeted Sylvia and Leah with a kiss and said, 'Wendy's come to see you, Leah.' Martin hung back, carrier in hand, while Wendy enquired after Leah's health and commiserated with her in her misfortune.

'Right,' said Freddy, 'it's Martin's turn.'

Leah looked from one to the other, wondering what was afoot, and then Martin shyly handed her the bag and its contents.

'Martin's been shopping for a special present for you, Leah,' Freddy told her.

'I can see that.' She stripped the wrapping paper off, finally squealing with delight when she uncovered the camel. 'Martin, come here.' Without waiting for him to move, a delay that might have proved interminable, she wrapped her arms round her brother, kissing him repeatedly.

'I'm tempted to do the same,' said Wendy to his amused parents, 'but the poor lad's embarrassed enough without me starting an' all.'

'It was a lovely thought,' Leah told her scarlet-faced brother. 'Thank you, Martin.'

'Yes,' said Sylvia, 'it was a lovely gesture, Martin.'

Martin didn't fully understand about gestures. He'd only wanted to stop his sister feeling unhappy and crying at night, and he thought he might have succeeded in that. It was just a pity it had to be so embarrassing. Meanwhile, Nina was having a wonderful time. She'd already found a dog biscuit inside the wrapping paper, and now she was busily shredding the paper itself. It was a special moment, and one that would continue to give pleasure to the whole family for some time to come.

That night, Leah slept with Charlie the Camel and Nina for company. They seemed to exert between them a special kind of enchantment, because she opened her eyes in the morning after nine hours' uninterrupted sleep, after which she felt much better equipped to face life and its challenges.

6

VILIFIED

Three weeks later, a letter arrived from the Royal Ballet School, informing Leah's parents that they had received Mr Finchley's report and that, much to their regret, they were unable to hold Leah's place open indefinitely. Consequently, her scholarship was terminated and she was no longer a pupil of the school.

She surprised them both by accepting the news more calmly than they had anticipated. The fact was that in the time that had elapsed since her visit to Keighley she had been able to prepare herself for what must have seemed inevitable.

'I think I've probably run out of tears as well,' she confided. 'That must help.'

'It's distinctly possible,' her mother told her, 'but no one's blaming you.'

'At the risk of sounding conventional....'

'Who, you, Dad?'

'If I may be allowed to continue, it's time to be positive and look ahead.'

'What can you see, Dad? I don't see much of a future for me.'

'I know, darling, but we have to look at the immediate future. You can't go back to school. I know you're more mobile now, but when they operate on your knee, it'll make it impossible, and as we've no idea when that will be, we have to make other arrangements. What "A" levels were you taking?'

'English Literature, History, French and German.'

He looked at her in surprise. 'No one ever opts for German. I know I did, but it was my father's decision. Why did you choose to do it?'

'In case the balloon goes up again. Someone's got to take her place in the after cockpit, facing aft and keeping an eye out for trouble.'

'Heaven forbid.' He couldn't help smiling. Mickey-taking was a sure sign that Leah was recovering.

'No, seriously, I just like languages, and someone has to love German, in spite of its funny ways.'

Smiling at a schoolboy memory, he said, 'I'm reminded of a joke about an exam question. "Write all you know about nineteenth-century German literature. Time allowed: five minutes".'

'There's quite a lot of twentieth century literature, now, Dad, the bits they didn't burn, and I'm not talking about *Mein Kampf*, either.'

'I'm sure you're right. At all events, I can probably give you some help with German, and possibly English Literature and French as well. As far as History is concerned.... Which period were you studying?'

'The English Civil Wars and the Commonwealth and Protectorate.'

He nodded. 'I'll speak to Miles Stapleton.'

'Who?'

'He's the Rector of St Jude's.'

'Why, Dad? I don't want to get married.'

'I should hope not. No, I seem to remember that he read Modern History at Cambridge, as well as Theology, and you never know. He may be able to help.' As one memory led to another, he said, 'He's no slouch as a batsman, either, as I recall. He was a Cambridge Blue, and he captained the Challengers when we played the local club in a charity match.'

'Oh, I'll let him teach me History, but I draw the line at cricket.'

'What a day that was,' said her mother, missing the immediate message. 'Your dad impressed everyone with both the bat and the ball, and Thea brought the house down in a completely different way.'

'Go on, I'll buy it.'

'I'll put some coffee on while you tell her, Freddy,' said her mother.

'Right, Dad, let's hear it.'

'We hadn't had her very long. I think it was about a year before you were born.'

'Everything happened before I was born. It seems to me I missed a lot of excitement.'

41

'Anyway, I'd been trying to train her to retrieve,' he said, smiling already at the memory.

'But she was a terrier, Dad.' The explanation was obvious to her, but not, apparently, to her obtuse parent.

'That's what she kept telling me. "Fetch," I'd say. "Fetch it yourself," she'd tell me. "I'm a terrier, not a retriever. Anyway, you threw it. Don't expect me to bring it back." She would chase after the ball readily enough, but then she'd sit behind it, waiting for me to join her. Well, on the day of the cricket match, I was fielding at leg slip—'

Leah rolled her eyes and adopted a theatrical expression of boredom.

'Think of the right-handed batsman in the middle of the clock face, and I was close behind him, but at eight o' clock.'

'Right, I'm awake again. Carry on.'

Ignoring her irreverent response, he continued. 'The ball came flying past me,' he said, 'and it went to the boundary. Two fielders set off after it, but Thea got there before them. She sat guard over the ball and defied all attempts on their part to pick it up. Your mum and I had to retrieve both Thea and the ball before the match could go on.'

'Brilliant. She was a lovely dog.'

At the sound of the last word, Nina stood up and wagged her tail.

'So are you, Nina,' Leah assured her, and you don't need to take part in a cricket match to prove it. You've already made your mark.'

* * *

Enquiries revealed that the Northern Universities Joint Matriculation Board listed the Civil War and its Aftermath in its Modern History syllabus, so the next step was to arrange, if possible, some tuition.

Freddy caught the Reverend Stapleton in his study. Being something of a perfectionist, the rector was agonising over his next sermon, as he later explained and, when his phone rang, he welcomed the interruption.

'Saint Jude's Rectory. Miles Stapleton speaking.'

'Rector, it's Freddy Hinchcliffe. I don't know if you'll remember me.' Not being a regular attender at St Jude's, or anywhere else, for that matter, he now felt a little awkward about contacting the Rector and asking for his help.

'Of course I remember you, Freddy. Right-arm fast-medium and a useful late-order batsman, as I recall. Also a prolific writer and director of excellent pantomimes and musical plays.'

'You amaze me, Reverend.'

'Surely not. Everyone knows you and, anyway, call me "Miles". How can I help you?'

Freddy took a large breath. 'Until late last year, my daughter Leah was a scholar at the Royal Ballet School,' he began.

'Yes, I remember hearing about her. You must be very proud of her.'

'We are, Miles, although her future as a ballerina is now… let's say less than… in the balance. She was hit by a car in November, and she spent six weeks in hospital with multiple fractures.'

'My dear chap, how devastating. You know, I had no idea.'

'That was probably our fault, Miles. The thing is, she wants to continue with her "A" level studies at home, and one of her subjects is History. To be precise, she was studying the English Civil Wars and the—'

'The Commonwealth and Protectorate, a fascinating period and one of extreme importance. You know, I was fortunate some years ago in finding a First Edition of John Evelyn's Diary.'

Suddenly, things were coming together. 'Miles, the reason for this phone call is to ask you if you would consider tutoring Leah privately.'

There was a pause, during which Freddy wondered if he'd asked too much of a busy man, but then he heard the Rector say, 'My dear fellow, I should be delighted. In fact, I'm looking forward to it already.'

'I'm more grateful than you can possibly imagine, Miles. If you'd care to name a fee, I'll be happy to—'

'I won't hear of it, Freddy. I should be a poor sort of cleric if I were to make a charge for helping Leah in her difficulty, and I should be obliged if you didn't mention it again.'

* * *

Freddy and Leah were making a list of the textbooks she'd used in her studies so far, when Sylvia answered the phone in the kitchen. When she came into the room, she was obviously concerned.

'What's the matter, SP? I haven't forgotten an appointment, have I?'

'Nothing so ordinary. That was Martin's school. He's in trouble, and they want one of us to go and collect him.'

'*Collect* him? Is he injured?'

'Not as far as I know.' With an air of hopelessness, she said, 'They're suspending him. For how long, I don't know, but it sounds serious.'

'As usual, it sounds ridiculous. I'll go, SP, if you don't mind helping Leah make her shopping list.'

'Don't be too hard on him, Freddy.'

'He'll be innocent until proven guilty,' he promised.

'You've got an appointment with a cockatoo this afternoon,' she reminded him.

'I'll be back before then.' He kissed her and Leah, and went out to the car. It wasn't the first time he'd been called into school because of an incident involving Martin, and such occurrences were usually connected with his son's inability to communicate in moments of stress.

As he drove towards Northallerton, he wondered who was dealing with the problem. He hadn't asked Sylvia who'd made the call; she was already flustered and, knowing her as he did, he was disinclined to upset her with unnecessary questions. He did know that he disliked Oakes, the headmaster, whom he found self-important, dictatorial and too ready to sit in judgement. He could only hope that Martin had done nothing to worsen his case, because he could expect little understanding from such a man.

Eventually, he pulled in beside the school and parked. There was a movement afoot to have double yellow lines painted along the front of the school, but so far, nothing had happened. He locked the car and made for the outer office, where the headmaster's secretary was based. The door was open, and he found her behind her desk.

'Good morning,' he said. 'My name is Hinchcliffe and I've been asked to collect my son. I also intend to find out what this is all about.'

'One moment, please, Mr Hinchcliffe.' She pressed a button on a kind of console, and a voice said, 'Yes?'

'Mr Hinchcliffe is here, Mr Oakes.'

'Very well. Send him in and ask Mr Evans to bring Martin Hinchcliffe to me.'

'Very good, Mr Oakes.' Turning to Freddy, she said, 'He'll see you now, Mr Hinchcliffe.'

'How very accommodating of him.' Freddy turned the handle and entered the Headmaster's office.

'Good morning, Mr Hinchcliffe.'

'Is it? I've yet to be convinced. What's been happening, Mr Oakes?'

'Take a seat, Mr Hinchcliffe. I have to tell you that your son carried out a vicious and unprovoked assault on two boys, leaving them bruised and shaken. This isn't the first time it's happened, either, but we'll hear more when Mr Evans arrives with Martin.'

'I don't believe his action could have been unprovoked. He's not capable of it.'

Oakes shrugged. 'Those are the facts, Mr Hinchcliffe, and that is why he is being suspended for a week. Had it been an ordinary case of bullying, I should simply have caned him, but in this instance I believe an opportunity to reflect on his behaviour may help him to mend his ways.'

The intercom buzzed, and the secretary announced that Mr Evans had arrived with Martin.

'Send them in, Mrs Lockhart.'

Freddy wondered if a week away from school might help Mr Oakes reflect on his deplorable manners. He doubted it.

'Ah,' said Mr Oakes as they entered the office, 'what can you tell us, Mr Evans?' In an aside to Freddy, he said somewhat belatedly, 'Mr Evans is my deputy.'

'Frederick Hinchcliffe,' said Freddy, offering his hand. He felt that someone should set an example.

'How do you do, Mr Hinchcliffe? I've spoken to Martin, but he's told me nothing. Alan Jackson and Keith Whitworth, on the other hand, tell me, for what it's worth, that they did nothing to provoke or upset Martin, and that he attacked them for no reason. Alan has a bruised cheek and a black eye, and Keith has a burst lip.'

Freddy asked, 'What really happened, Martin?' Martin stared at his feet, as if he'd not heard the question, and Freddy knew better than to insist. Instead, he said, 'Still waters, Mr Oakes, run very deep. Martin is obviously finding it difficult to talk about the incident, but I intend to find out the truth.'

'I don't know about finding it difficult, Mr Hinchcliffe. During the war, we called it "dumb insolence".'

45

'Yes, ignorance abounded, as I remember only too well. Just out of interest, how did you spend the war?'

'I held a commission in the Army Education Corps,' said Oakes importantly.

'What an exciting war you must have had.'

Oakes bridled visibly, but kept his feelings to himself. 'The fact remains,' he said, 'that your son is suspended forthwith, and he will only be readmitted in seven days' time when he makes a frank apology to his unfortunate victims and to me for his unpleasant and unacceptable behaviour in my school.'

'I don't know if it has any bearing on the case,' said Mr Evans, who had remained so far largely silent, 'but both Jackson and Whitworth have a well-documented reputation for bullying.'

'I can't see that it has any bearing, Mr Evans. The case is clear, and I must ask Mr Hinchcliffe to remove his son from the school premises.'

'Come on, Martin,' said Freddy, 'we're doing no good here.' As they left, he detected a look of shamefaced embarrassment from Mr Evans. It seemed that he, too, had been less than impressed with his superior's handling of the matter.

Martin remained silent on the way home, and Freddy made no attempt to engage him in conversation. When they arrived home, Martin went straight to his room. 'He's not going to say anything,' said Freddy, 'but I'll lay a pound to a pinch of anything he was provoked.'

'Who were these alleged victims?' asked Leah.

'Two lads from this village, as it happens.' He searched his memory for their names and said, finally, 'Alan Jackson and Keith....'

'Whitworth,' said Leah. 'I remember those two, and they're both horrible.'

'Anyway, Martin will only talk when he's ready. You know what he's like.'

'Let me try talking to him,' said Leah, going to the stairs, which she could now negotiate, albeit with the assistance of the banister rail.

'All right, but be careful.'

She returned after a few minutes, but without success. 'He just sits there, looking at his feet,' she said. 'It's obviously important, to affect him like this. I wish we could get through to him.'

Sylvia got up and went to the kitchen.

'I think she's going to phone your grandad,' said Freddy, 'but I don't know what he can do.' Walter's history of problem-solving was a by-word in the Hinchcliffe household, but he would never use his capacity as a school governor to exert influence on behalf of a family member.

Sylvia returned to say, 'My dad has a meeting with a client this afternoon, but he'll come as soon as he's free.'

* * *

Good as his word, Walter arrived shortly after four, and Freddy explained the problem to him while Martin remained steadfastly in his room.

'The problem is that wretched headmaster,' said Sylvia. 'He won't give Martin a chance.'

'I've told you, SP, your dad can't use his influence as a governor for the benefit of a family member.'

'I bet the horrible man doesn't even know Martin's related to a governor.'

'Even so.' Freddy was about to say more, when the doorbell rang. As he was on his feet, he went to answer it and was surprised to find Wendy on the doorstep. She looked unusually serious.

'Freddy,' she said, 'can I talk to you?'

'Of course you can, love, but it's a bit awkward just now. We've got Martin and Leah's grandad here. There's been some trouble at school.'

'I know. That's what I've come to talk to you about.'

It was completely unexpected, but if Wendy could shed some light on the matter, her visit was no less welcome. 'Come on in, Wendy.' He took her through into the sitting room, where Walter recognised her immediately, even without her costume and make-up.

'Hello, Jack,' he said, 'you gave an excellent performance in the pantomime. Well done.'

'Thank you, but I've come to… to stick up for Martin 'cause he won't help himself, an' I think it's rotten, what they've done to him.'

'That's very noble of you, my dear. Would you like to tell me what it's all about? There's no need to be shy.'

Freddy smiled to himself. No one who knew Wendy could call her

47

even remotely shy, but she was thoroughly decent, and that was what really mattered. He sat down with Sylvia and Leah, eager to hear what Wendy had to say.

When she'd finished, Walter said, 'I'm very grateful to you for telling me all that, Wendy. You're a loyal friend to Martin, and that's the best kind of friend there is.'

'I only wanted to do what was right.'

'And you did. Thank you very much, Wendy, and don't worry. Everything will be all right.'

'Will Old… I mean Mr Oakes… let Martin come back to school?'

'He will if he knows what's good for him.'

When Wendy had gone, Freddy said, 'Well, now I have something to tell that ridiculous headmaster. If he has any sense of fairness at all, he must surely realise where he's gone wrong.'

'No, leave it to me, Freddy.'

'But what can you do, Walter? You're related to Martin….'

'I am,' he agreed, 'but I know someone who's not, and who has rather more influence than I have.'

7

HARSH WORDS AND FIRST LETTERS

The Reverend Miles Stapleton, MA, BTh. (Cantab) was a frequent visitor to Yoredale High School, conscientious as he was in his role as Chairman of the Governors and, because he was a popular figure, several pupils returned his friendly greetings as he made his way up the stairs to the headmaster's office.

He stopped inside the open doorway to exchange pleasantries with Mrs Lockhart, who told him with something akin to satisfaction that Mr Oakes was expecting him.

'I believe he is, Mrs Lockhart.'

She pushed the button on her console and announced, 'The Chairman of Governors is here, Mr Oakes.'

'Right.' His response, like his very nature, lacked warmth but, after a few seconds, the door to the inner office opened, and Oakes greeted the Chairman.

Once in the office, Miles said, 'I think you should ask Wendy Albright to join us, Headmaster. She, after all, witnessed the incident and knows the truth about the matter we are about to discuss.'

'If you insist, Reverend Stapleton.'

'Oh, I do, Headmaster.'

Oakes spoke to his secretary, telling her to locate Wendy Albright and summon her to his office.

'You know, Headmaster,' said Miles when the door was closed, 'for one who spent only a few wartime years in the Army, you have a most disturbing, not to say disconcerting, military manner.'

'Have I?' Oakes sounded genuinely surprised.

'You certainly have. You know, an occasional "please", "thank you" or "would you be so kind?" would oil the wheels so much more effectively than the kind of peremptory order that has become your stock-in-trade.' Smiling disarmingly, he said, 'I offer the advice purely in the spirit of helpfulness, you understand.'

'I'm obliged to you, Reverend Stapleton,' said Oakes coldly.

The intercom buzzed, and Mrs Lockhart said, 'Wendy Albright is here, Mr Oakes.'

'Right.' Seeing Miles raise an eyebrow, he added, 'Thank you, Mrs Lockhart. Will you please send her in?' He was rewarded by a nod of cautious approval from his mentor.

The door opened, and Wendy stood in the doorway, surprised at first to see Miles. 'Hello, Rector,' she said uncertainly.

'Good morning, my dear. Don't worry, you're not in any kind of trouble. In fact, we're hoping you'll be able to help us.'

'The Reverend Stapleton is here in his capacity as Chairman of the Governors,' said the headmaster. 'Come inside and close the door behind you.'

'But Wendy and I are old friends,' said Miles, 'so let's not be formal. I'd like you to tell us, Wendy, what you told Mr Charlesworth yesterday afternoon.'

'Mr Charlesworth?' After a second's thought, Wendy made the connection. 'Do you mean Martin's grandad? Right, well, Keith Whitworth and Alan Jackson were tormenting Martin. They're a pair of bullies, them two, an' they were really making him mad, talking about Leah and what they wanted to... how much they... fancied her.'

'Leah Hinchcliffe is Martin's sister,' explained Miles for the headmaster's benefit. 'Until recently, when she suffered a tragic accident, she was a scholar at the Royal Ballet School, but I digress. Forgive me for interrupting you, Wendy. Please go on.'

'That's all right, Rector. They were talking... you know, the way rough lads do about girls. Some lads have got minds like... well, you know, Rector. Then they started on about me. They reckoned we'd done things... you know, Martin and me, an' that's rubbish, 'cause I've never even gone out with him, an' he's not like that, an' I'm not either. Well, Martin couldn't take any more of it. He told them to stop and....' She lowered her voice to say, 'He told them to buzz off, except... it had two g's in it. Well, they started pushing him against the wall and punching him, an' that's when he lost his temper and laid 'em both out. He didn't beat 'em up or anything like that. In fact, he only hit 'em once or twice.'

'So you actually saw them assault him?'

'I saw 'em hit him. That's right, Rector, but there was nowt... I mean nothing... I could do, an' then I heard Martin had been suspended. I tried telling Mr Oakes, but he said he was too busy to see me, so when I got off the bus I went round to Martin's an' told Freddy and Mrs Hinchcliffe about it. Martin's grandad was there, too.'

'So he was, and he spoke to me about it. Thank you, Wendy. As I expected, you've been more than helpful.'

'That's all right, Rector. I only wanted to tell the truth, 'cause you could grow old waiting for Martin to speak up for himself.'

'I'm glad you did, and I look forward to seeing you, as usual, on Sunday morning.'

'Okay, Rector.' She looked uncertainly at the headmaster, who said, 'That will be all, Wendy.' At a sharp look from Miles, he changed the dismissal to, 'Thank you, Wendy. You may return to your lesson.'

'Well,' said Miles when Wendy had left the office, 'so much for the unprovoked assault of which those boys accused Martin. Salacious remarks about his sister, foul and unfounded accusations against Wendy and him, and finally, physical assault, all of which amounted to provocation beyond normal human forbearance. Those two, it seems, are strangers to the truth and to decency as well, and yet, for some obscure reason, you accepted their word readily enough.'

'But Hinchcliffe made no attempt to put his side of the argument. As I explained to his father, the only reaction I got from him was one of sheer, dumb insolence.'

'Absolute nonsense.' Miles continued in spite of the headmaster's shocked reaction. 'It's obvious to me that the unfortunate youth suffers from a malady that renders him mute in time of crisis, and that he was clearly unable, through no fault of his own, to plead his case. Thank goodness for Wendy Albright, a girl who would no sooner utter a falsehood than steal from the poor box. I know her well, Headmaster. I buried her unfortunate father; I guided her through confirmation and I welcomed her into the choir at St Jude's. I would accept her word gladly, rather than that of the two ruffians whose mendacious account you found so credible.'

51

Clearly rattled, the headmaster tried to martial his defence. 'I think you're being unnecessarily harsh, Reverend Stapleton. The situation was far from straightforward.'

'It seems straightforward enough to me. Wouldn't you describe your action as harsh when you accepted the uncorroborated word of two foul-mouthed bullies and suspended an innocent boy on the strength of it? I think you need to re-examine your values, Headmaster, radically and as a matter of some priority. Even before that, though, you need to reinstate Martin Hinchcliffe and, whilst an apology from those two scoundrels wouldn't be worth a gossip's breath, one from you might at least help to mask the unpleasant taste of injustice.'

* * *

'Dad, remind me, please. What's the French alexandrine?'

Freddy paused on his way to the studio to answer his daughter's question. 'It was a meter used in French poetry and drama. You're familiar with Shakespeare and iambic pentameter, aren't you?'

'Yes, I know it's a meter. I'm just not sure of the form it takes.'

'French alexandrine is the same kind of thing, except that it's dodecasyllabic.'

She laughed. 'Anyone can say that.'

'It has twelve syllables,' he explained patiently. 'What are you reading?'

'Racine's *Phèdre*. I can't help thinking that Dumas would be more entertaining.'

He wrinkled his nose and considered the possibility. 'What do you have in mind by Dumas?'

'*La Dame aux Camélias*.'

'No,' he said categorically, 'it's completely unsuitable.'

'In what way?'

'It's not right for a girl of your age.'

She sighed heavily. 'Why not?'

'Your mum will explain it to you.'

It seemed an odd thing to say. Leah wasn't aware that her mother had studied French literature. 'Does she know the story?'

'I don't know. If she doesn't, I'll tell her about it, and she'll explain why it's not suitable.'

Suddenly it made sense. 'Is it something you find embarrassing to talk about?'

'Yes.' Previous arguments with Leah had taught him that there was nothing to be gained by hedging.

'I thought so.' Leah read on, eventually finding a synopsis of the novel as well as the cause of her father's embarrassment. Parents could be feeble sometimes, and she still felt that Dumas would have been preferable to Racine, even though elements of *The Lady of the Camellias* were admittedly less than wholesome. However, her mind wasn't entirely closed to other possibilities and, in any case, time would tell. Her thoughts were interrupted when the telephone rang. With no one else about, she went through to the kitchen to answer it.

'Hinchcliffe Photo Services.'

A voice asked, 'Am I speaking to Mrs Hinchcliffe?'

'No, this is Leah Hinchcliffe, her daughter. Who's calling?'

'Oakes, Headmaster of Yoredale High School. I should like to speak to either Mr or Mrs Hinchcliffe.'

Leah was almost tempted to ask, 'What does Brian say?' However, she went to the studio and said, 'Dad, the Headmaster of Yoredale High School wants to speak to you or Mum.'

'Thanks, Leah.' He picked up the extension in the studio, leaving Leah to return to her studies. After a minute or so her mum came downstairs to ask, 'Who was that on the phone, Leah?'

'Martin's headmaster. He wanted to speak to one of you, but if you ask me, I'd say what he really needs is a lesson in manners.'

'From what I've heard, it wouldn't surprise me.'

'That,' said Leah's father, coming into the room, 'was Martin's headmaster. According to him, there's been "an unfortunate misunderstanding", and Martin can return to school tomorrow. I asked him whose misunderstanding it was, and he had the grace, if I can use the word in his case, to own up and apologise for it. He takes the line that the two false accusers have probably suffered enough already. I suppose it's hard to disagree with that. Anyway, I'll go upstairs and give Martin the good news.'

'It certainly is good news,' said Leah's mother.

'It's just one excitement after another,' said Leah.

'Yes, the Reverend Stapleton's coming to dinner this evening. He won't accept any payment for tutoring you, so it's the least we can do.'

'Just him? Isn't he married?'

'He was. He's a widower, so he'll welcome an occasional act of hospitality, and it'll also give you an opportunity to get to know him before he begins teaching you.' Remembering something else, she said, 'Another excitement is that Bailey and Elaine are bringing Janice at the weekend, so you'll be able to give Janice her first reading lesson.'

* * *

Miles Stapleton proved to be an entertaining guest. Leah found him completely engaging, and Martin managed to overcome his natural difficulty sufficiently to thank him for his intervention in the matter of his suspension, although Miles made the point that his thanks were largely due to Wendy and her timely initiative. It would be interesting to see how he coped with the task of thanking her.

Miles was particularly impressed by Leah's plan to teach Janice to read, pointing out that he had agreed, in the first place, to become a school governor because he believed that everyone should be given a chance to learn.

* * *

When the time came, however, Janice had to be convinced. 'Why,' she demanded, 'have I got to read words?'

'You don't have to,' Leah told her, 'but I enjoy reading so much that I thought you'd want to.'

That gave her cause for thought. She asked, 'Does Martin like reading?'

'Yes, he does.' It was true. He spent most of his free time reading, usually about science in its various forms.

'And Auntie Sylvia and Uncle Freddy?'

'They read all the time,' Leah assured her.

'All right, then.' It seemed that reading was an acceptable pastime. Considering Janice's brief concentration span, Leah had chosen a book that taught only one vowel and a few consonants at a time. Pictures for reinforcement appeared in the back of the book, and Leah had to be very firm about the rules. There was to be strictly no cheating by looking at the pictures. Having accepted that, Janice learned 'bad', 'cab' and 'dab', and was delighted when Leah turned up pictures of a mother scolding a child, a London taxi and someone dabbing a dirty mark with a cloth. That, however, was the limit of her concentration, so they spent the next ten minutes knitting. When they returned to reading, Leah was reminded of Janice's inability to retain new facts without repeated reminders. Still, they both had time on their hands, and Leah was confident that perseverance would ensure success. Her labours earned Elaine's gratitude and admiration. 'You're so patient with her, Leah,' she said. 'I think you have a flair for teaching. It's something you might consider as a career.'

'Why not, Elaine? I'm denied the one career I wanted, so I'm open to suggestions. I have to be.'

8

CONSENSUS

A mid 'A' level studies and her self-appointed obligation to help Janice achieve a realistic level of literacy, Leah received a letter offering her an appointment at St John's Hospital, this time with a Mr Livesey. Memories of her last appointment, with Mr Finchley, had left her less than optimistic, but she took the line that any proposed improvement to her knee would be welcome, and she prepared herself for another series of x-rays and examinations.

With the x-rays done, they were shown into a consulting room, and Leah was surprised from the outset when Mr Livesey introduced himself and shook hands with them all.

'Leah,' he said, 'what a rotten time you've had.' In that moment, all thoughts of Mr Finchley and his superior and distant manner were forgotten. Here was a man who clearly cared about his patient. 'I've been looking at the x-rays of your right knee,' he said, 'and, frankly, it's a mess, but it's not beyond repair.' As Leah's hopes were rekindled he added a cautionary word. 'I'm not saying that you'll dance on the stage at Covent Garden or any other professional venue, if it comes to that – we have to be realistic, and it would be wrong of me to engender false hopes – but, with the procedure I have in mind, followed by conscientious physiotherapy, you should regain some, at least, of the dexterity you enjoyed before the accident.'

'That would be wonderful, Mr Livesey.' Tears of happiness were pricking Leah's eyelids, and she brushed them away self-consciously while her parents also expressed their gratitude.

'I must reiterate my warning,' said Mr Livesey, 'that it's extremely doubtful that you'll ever become a professional dancer, but that's not the only level to which you can aspire, is it? My daughter, who was keen on ballet from a very early age, now derives great satisfaction from teaching dance.'

'Having to forfeit her scholarship and her place at the Royal Ballet School was calamitous at the time,' said her mum, 'but I think that in some strange way, the shock helped Leah come to terms with the situation.'

'I can imagine it would.'

'In view of everything,' said Leah, 'I think I could enjoy teaching dance, too.' It would be infinitely preferable to turning her back on it altogether.

The consultant smiled sympathetically and asked, 'Do you enjoy swimming, Leah?'

'I did. I haven't swum since before the accident.'

'She's actually a strong swimmer,' said her mum. 'I taught her when she was a toddler.'

'Well, I'll tell you when it's safe to get back into the pool after the operation, and you'll find there's no finer or safer strengthening exercise. If you enjoy swimming, Leah, so much the better.'

* * *

Buoyed by the good news, Freddy spent some time on the public phone after leaving the consulting room, and he looked even happier when he rejoined his wife and daughter.

'What have you been up to?' asked Sylvia, reading his expression as unerringly as ever.

'I wondered if Leah might fancy the treat she couldn't face after the last appointment.'

Leah looked at him in surprise and delight. 'I'd forgotten about that,' she said. 'What do you have in mind?'

'We're going to meet a few people and have a celebration. You'll see.'

The secret kept, to Leah's frustration until they arrived home, when Freddy broke the suspense by saying, 'I phoned the County Hotel in Northallerton when we were at the hospital, and reserved a table, and Martin, your grandma, grandad, Bailey, Elaine and Janice are going to join us there, so you'd better change into something glamorous.

Leah needed no further encouragement, and she and her mother went upstairs to change, while Freddy, who always boasted that he could do it in a fraction of the time, took Nina for a walk.

The school bus was just stopping outside the Shearers' Arms, so he waited for Martin to join him.

'Hello, Dad.' As usual, the greeting came with scant expression.

'Hello, Martin. Do you want to join us?'

'Okay.'

'We're having a celebration this evening.'

'Are we?' If Martin was at all curious about the nature of the celebration, he was evidently disinclined to enquire further.

'We took Leah to the hospital, today, to see the specialist, and he thinks he can do a lot with her knee. It's very good news.'

'Yes, it is.' Perhaps feeling that he should enlarge on that observation, he said, 'I find it's awful when Leah gets upset and cries in the night.'

'I know you do, Martin, but it hasn't happened for quite a long time, and you did a lot to help her.'

'Mm.' He sounded less than convinced. It was as if he associated hospital visits with disappointment, and it would take more than one piece of good news to dispel that expectation.

'It really is good news this time, Martin.' Freddy studied his son discreetly, although he knew it was impossible to read his thoughts. There was one matter, however, about which he felt he had to reassure him. 'I know we've spent a lot of time recently with Leah because of her accident and everything else,' he said, 'but you must realise that you're equally as important to us.'

Martin nodded, waiting patiently while Nina relieved herself on the grass verge. 'Grandad made them take me back into school when I'd been suspended.'

'Yes, he did, and that's what I mean. As a family, we're always ready to help both you and Leah.'

Martin nodded again. It was as if he'd always suspected as much, and Freddy left the conversation there for the time being, further meaningful discussion being more than a challenge.

* * *

It was a happy party that gathered that evening at the County Hotel in Northallerton, and possibly the happiest among them was Leah. For as long as she could remember, ballet had been her reason for living. Mr Finchley's prognosis had been the kind of cruel blow no child of her age should have to suffer, but she'd recovered remarkably well from her initial devastation, and her consultation with Mr Livesey had given her hopes a new boost. Resigned to the fact that she would never be a professional dancer, she could nevertheless look forward to the possibility of a career at least connected with ballet. More immediate, however, was the knowledge that the eight people with her at the table were all there because they welcomed her good news and wanted to celebrate it with her, and that knowledge was priceless.

As she listened to fragments of conversation, the talk came round, as it always would, to the year's musical events. Freddy Hinchcliffe and the Dalesmen continued to be in demand for balls and other special occasions, and both of Leah's parents were once again to be involved in rehearsals for Yoredale Players' annual production in June.

'What's it to be this year?' asked Leah's grandad.

'They've finally decided on *My Fair Lady*, and we're casting it next week,' said her dad.

'That should be popular.'

'I hope so. It's taken them long enough to make the decision, and there's a lot of work to be done.'

'At least you don't have to write the show this year,' said Elaine, who had starred in Freddy's debut production seventeen years earlier.

'Thank goodness. After *My Fair Lady*, we have to start work on the pantomime.'

'What's the pantomime, Dad?' asked Leah, purely out of curiosity, because she couldn't see herself taking part in it.

'*Peter Pan.*'

'Wonderful,' said Bailey, who had much in common with that hero.

'When's the pantomime?' demanded Janice, almost knocking Bailey's wine over in her agitation.

'Not until Christmas,' Elaine told her. 'Calm down, Janice.'

'Christmas? I can't wait that long.'

'I'm sorry, darling,' said Bailey. 'We can't make it come any quicker.'

Leah saw Martin stare at them both. Knowing him as she did, she had an idea of what was going through his mind. As far as he was concerned, it stood to reason that time was constant. He knew that, and he expected everyone else to know it as well. Her father put Martin's difficulties down to shyness, but she was sure there was something else as well, something that made him so literal in his thinking that figures of speech were meaningless to him.

'How's the girl who had appendicitis?' asked Elaine.

'Oh, she made a quick recovery. It was just as well, as she's going to university next year, with any luck.'

'Where's unisersary?' asked Janice. 'Can I go?'

'You wouldn't like it there,' said Bailey. 'They don't have pantomimes.'

'Right, I'm not going.'

'That's probably a wise decision, darling. We won't insist on it.'

'Wendy won't be available for *My Fair Lady*,' said Leah's father, 'more's the pity. She'd be an excellent Eliza Doolittle.'

'Why isn't she available?' asked Leah's grandad, who'd taken an avuncular shine to her.

'She'll be taking her CSEs.'

Clearly puzzled, Bailey asked, 'What are CSEs?'

'They're school exams,' Leah told him. 'They're not as hard as "O" levels but they're still something to show for five years at secondary school.' If she were honest, and by and large, she was, she'd been somewhat dismissive of them at first, but learning how much they meant to Wendy had softened her attitude towards both them and those less-academically inclined than herself.

'I admire anyone who can pass exams,' said Bailey.

'You passed human kindness with flying colours, and without even writing your name on the paper,' Leah told him. Her observation earned her smiles of agreement from everyone.

'I've been thinking,' said her dad.

'I thought you were in pain,' said her mum.

'Seriously, while you're at home, Leah, surrounded by books and fired by enthusiasm for your studies, you mustn't forget that all work and no play makes Jill a dull girl.'

'That has a rough-and-ready, homespun sound to it, Dad.'

'What I'm suggesting is that you take an occasional break, actually a regular break, from your studies and accompany rehearsals for *My Fair Lady*.'

'I'm not that good on the piano, Dad.'

'And you never will be if you don't get the practice. Give it some thought.'

'I was thinking of teaching her some cooking and baking,' said her mum.

Leah studied her parents for the usual signs of leg-pulling, but in vain. 'You really mean it, don't you, both of you?'

'That's when you're not weeding, lawn-mowing and car washing,' said her dad. 'Then you're not living completely rent-free.'

'Oh, be fair,' said her mum. 'I think weeding is asking a little too much.'

'All of it's too much when she's been so poorly,' objected Martin with barely observable reproach. 'I'll mow the lawns and wash both cars for her.'

'Oh, Martin,' said Leah, patting his hand, 'you get nobler by the minute.'

'What do you mean?'

'I mean you do things for the best of reasons, and I'm grateful to you.'

'That's all right.'

'Martin's an example to us all,' said Bailey seriously. 'He sees a job that needs to be done, and he gets on with it. Things have fallen apart since he went home, haven't they, Janice.'

'Yes, my dolls' house has fallen down.'

'I'll come over and mend it,' said Martin.

Janice greeted his offer with her usual shout of, 'I love you, Martin!'

'Not so loud, Janice,' said Elaine. 'If everybody hears you, they'll all want Martin to go to their houses and mend things.' She shook her head minutely at Martin to show that she didn't mean it.

Leah's dad had been quiet for some time, but he said seriously, 'I agree with Bailey, you know. In this life, there are talkers, ignorers and doers, and Martin is a doer, which is by far the best thing to be.'

Martin looked at him uncertainly; at least, Leah thought his look was uncertain, because no one could be sure with Martin. She only knew that he was considerate, well-meaning and ungrudging, which was as well, because, with another operation in prospect, she was going to need all her family's support.

9

March

The Next Stage

Within a surprisingly short time, Leah was called to St John's Hospital for her knee operation. She took with her photographs, taken by her dad, of Charlie the Camel and Nina, because, for reasons of hygiene, neither was allowed on the ward. She also took the good wishes of her family and friends.

Although she'd been denied breakfast, she wasn't at all hungry, being naturally nervous about the operation and, shortly after what would have been lunch, she was weighed and sent for a bath, after which she changed into a gown similar to those she remembered from St Thomas's.

Mr Livesey came to reassure her, and then a doctor who introduced himself as the anaesthetist, spoke to her while a porter helped her on to a trolley.

He asked her, 'Have you had general anaesthetic before?'

'Yes.'

'How did you feel?'

It seemed an odd question. 'I don't know,' she said, 'I was unconscious.'

'I meant afterwards.'

'Horrible, but not because of the anaesthetic. It was the pain.'

'Ah, I'll be giving you something for pain relief while you're still under anaesthetic.'

'Why?' It was a fair question.

'It's to help control your pain when you come round.'

'I see. Thank you.'

'You're very welcome, Leah. I'm just going to give you a small injection that will take away any worries you may have.'

That sounded too ominous for words, but then she remembered the pre-med from the last time, and before she could comment on it, she began to feel light-headed and peaceful. The porter pushed her trolley off the ward and on to a long corridor, at the end of which the anaesthetist spoke to her again. She had no idea what he was saying, because the next injection was the last thing she remembered.

* * *

Someone was saying, 'Come on, Leah, spit it out.' She wondered what they meant. Spitting was a foul thing to do. Then she heard the same voice say, 'Come on, get rid of that dummy.' Oddly enough, there was something in her mouth, and then some vague memory from her earlier operation returned to her and she let them take out the thing that had been holding down her tongue. The voice said, 'Well done, Leah. Just lie there and have a nice sleep.' She thought it was a strange thing to say, when she was obviously incapable of doing anything else, but the thought dwindled and disappeared as sleep claimed her once more.

The next time she woke up it was morning. A nurse was taking her temperature and pulse. She removed the thermometer and asked, 'Would you like a bedpan or anything?'

'Not yet, thank you.' Even the thought of any kind of movement caused a violent stab of pain. It would be some time before she was able to perform the necessary functions without great discomfort.

After a dose of pain relief, she dozed off again, wishing she could have Charlie the Camel. Nina, she knew, was out of the question.

At visiting time in the afternoon, her parents arrived with Martin, as it was Saturday, and she felt immediately better.

Martin asked her, 'Are you going to cry again?'

'I'll try not to, Martin. Actually, I think I ran out of tears last time.'

He gave her a strange look; at least, it was strange for him. 'You can't do that,' he told her. 'The body keeps the tear glands supplied with water, so no matter how much you cry—'

'I meant that I got the awful feeling of hopelessness out of my system. I'm sorry, I didn't put it very clearly.'

'Oh.'

She imagined the Fourth Year at Yoredale High School hadn't dealt with similes and metaphors in any great depth, and when they did, Martin would struggle.

Turning to her mother, she asked, 'Can you bring me some make-up in, Mum? I forgot to pack it, and I'm sure I look like a zombie.'

'Of course I will, darling. You want to look your best with all these handsome doctors about, don't you?'

'Don't tease, Mum, I'm fragile.'

'Fragile you may be,' said her father, gently taking her hand, 'but I've never seen anyone look less like a zombie. Have you, Martin?'

'No, she doesn't look at all like a zombie. She's just looks... weak and poorly.'

'Thanks, Martin,' said Leah. 'I think I might cry, after all.'

'You won't when I tell you that lots of people have sent their love,' said her mother. 'Grandma and Grandad are coming. I haven't the slightest doubt Bailey, Elaine and Janice will be here, and Wendy and Reverend Stapleton are going to try and visit you as well.'

'Oh, that's lovely.' She couldn't help looking at Martin, who was possibly wondering how those people could send their love, and whether it took an ordinary postage stamp. Despite his problems, though, he'd given her welcome support when she needed it, and she would never forget that. She took his hand and squeezed it, causing him to look away in embarrassment. To cover it, she asked, 'Did you manage to cast *My Fair Lady* all right, Dad?'

'We managed to cast it,' he told her, 'but how "all right" remains to be seen. Both Lorna Jenkins and Wendy Albright are swatting for exams, which means there's no young female talent to call on. Not surprisingly, though, Emily Dent auditioned for Eliza Doolittle, and as she was the only candidate, we had to give her the role.'

'But she's too old for it. She must be at least forty.'

'Ancient,' said her mum, reminded of her forty-four years.

'You know what I mean, Mum,' said Leah, realising she might have been a little insensitive. 'Eliza Doolittle's barely twenty.' She treated them to a line from the show. "I washed me face an' 'ands afore I come, I did." '

Her father smiled at her effort. 'You could have acted the part, Leah,' he said.

'I couldn't sing it, though.'

'You can't be good at everything,' said her mother, patting her hand in consolation.

Visits helped Leah pass her time in hospital. Some, mainly from her parents and grandparents, were cosy and reassuring, whilst others were entertaining, and there were times when her spirits needed a lift. The pain in her knee was slow to recede, and she was feeling very disconsolate by visiting time on Wednesday evening, so the surprise was all the better when the Reverend Stapleton arrived with Wendy.

'It's lovely of you both to come,' she said, and she meant every word.

'Not at all,' said her tutor. 'It's my duty as well as my absolute pleasure. As for my young friend,' he said, inclining his head towards Wendy, 'I'll let her speak for herself.'

'I just thought I'd come and try to cheer you up,' said Wendy in her usual modest and down-to-earth way.

'Oh, you've done that already.' Leah was almost tearful in her appreciation of them both.

'My mum's sent you these,' said Wendy, handing her a Co-op carrier. It felt quite heavy, and Leah opened it to find various items of fruit.

'Oh, that's kind of her. I'll come and see her when I come home, but will you thank her for me, please?'

''Course I will, but we all have to do what we can.'

'My offering is hardly as appealing,' said the reverend. 'I've brought you some reading.' He placed a book on her bedside table and said, 'I've bookmarked the appropriate sections.'

'Thank you, Rector. I'll read them thoroughly.'

'Good girl.'

'The Rector's been helping me with my CSEs,' said Wendy. 'I was strugglin' a bit with the English comprehension, but he sorted me out last Thursday, after choir practice.'

Leah wasn't at all surprised. It seemed to her that she and the rector were a matching pair.

'I don't know if I should mention this in front of the Rector,' said Wendy, but do you know Stephen Wilkins, Leah?'

'I remember him, yes.' She recalled a tall, shy lad, maybe a year older than her.

'He's really keen to go out with you when you're up and about.'

The rector was smiling. 'I don't know why you hesitated to tell her that, Wendy,' he said. 'It all sounds innocent enough to me.'

'Well, Stephen Wilkins is not all that bad, unlike some.'

'Thanks for telling me, Wendy,' said Leah. 'I'll bear that in mind.'

Perhaps to change the subject to one that was completely safe, the rector asked, 'Are you both going to be involved in *My Fair Lady*?'

'I'll only be playing the piano for rehearsals,' said Leah.

' "Only" doesn't do justice to a highly necessary job, Leah.'

'I can't be in it,' said Wendy wistfully, 'not while I'm getting ready for exams, and I don't know about the pantomime. Lorna's going to be at university, so there'll be no shortage of parts for girls. I just hope they don't cast me as Wendy.'

'It could be confusing,' said the rector, 'for the audience as well as the cast.'

'It's not just that, Reverend. I'm too tall for Wendy. She's supposed to be about twelve, an' I left that behind a while back.' It was true. Wendy was near enough five-foot-eight and still growing.

'I think you were born to play Peter Pan,' said Leah, 'especially after you were so brilliant in *Jack and the Beanstalk*. Surely they'll be able to find a little girl to play Wendy.'

'Thanks, Leah. I hope so.'

'For what my opinion is worth,' said Miles, 'you should have no competition, Wendy. You're… sixteen, aren't you?'

'Fifteen until next month, Reverend.'

'Well, I think that for a girl of your age you have a tremendous talent.'

'Thanks, Reverend.' She was clearly affected by the compliment.

'I think so too,' said Leah. 'When's your birthday?'

'The fourteenth of April.'

Leah made a mental note of it, and the rector also made an entry in his diary.

It was a special visit by two people whose presence, it seemed to

Leah, would only ever lift the spirits of anyone fortunate enough to know them.

On the following day, her parents came in the afternoon, leaving the evening free for the Bailey family.

After the initial greetings, Janice came straight to the point, asking, 'Will you be able to do ballet dancing again, Leah?'

'Not immediately, Janice, and it's not certain I'll ever be able to go back to it. Not properly, anyway.'

'After all this?' Janice's voice could be heard all over the ward. 'If it were me, I'd have something to say about it!' It was another grown-up expression that had joined the favourites in her repertoire.

'Hush, darling,' said Bailey. 'All these patients have got their families visiting, and they need to hear themselves think.'

Janice calmed down, leaving Leah to wonder how Martin might have responded to the concept of patients hearing themselves think. She wasn't alone with her thoughts for long, however, as Bailey was as entertaining as ever, and Elaine's sympathetic company was equally therapeutic.

* * *

In time, Leah was ready to begin physiotherapy, and little by little, she became conscious of increased facility in her knee.

On one of his rounds, Mr Livesey said, 'You're making excellent progress, Leah.'

'Thank you, Mr Livesey. I'm very grateful to you for everything.'

'Not at all, my dear, but you mustn't forget my original *caveat*. There's no guarantee you'll ever dance on the professional stage. I know it would be too wonderful to be true, and it probably is. Even so, you're going to have considerably more movement in your knee. I expect you're waiting to hear when you can go home.'

'I am, rather.'

'Is tomorrow soon enough?'

'Oh, yes. Thank you.'

'I'll see you again in about six weeks' time. Meanwhile, you'll have continued physio, and when you're given the go ahead, you'll be able to start swimming, but not before.'

'I'll remember,' she promised. 'Thank you again.'

* * *

Once again, Bailey arrived with her parents and, inevitably and in consideration for her 'delicate state' as he called it, a Rover saloon. She'd noticed that the windows were slightly open and, when Bailey opened the back door for her, Nina greeted her excitedly.

When they were on the road, with Nina between her feet, Leah asked, 'Do your bosses really let you carry dogs in their cars, Bailey?'

'By the time I've had this car valeted, they won't know anyone's been in it,' he said, 'including our goodselves. Now, just enjoy your homecoming and let me worry about everything else.'

'You're wonderful, Bailey.'

Although he was facing the windscreen, his smile was still visible when he said, 'So are you, dearest goddaughter mine, and that's why today is so special.'

Considering the company she was enjoying, which included Nina's, she was inclined to agree that it was a special day indeed. All she had to do, now was to follow advice and see how much she could achieve after her operation.

10

NOT THE TYPE

It was a spring and summer of birthdays. First, there was Wendy's in April, which Leah remembered and marked appropriately, to Wendy's genuine surprise. Secondly, there was Martin's in early May, when it seemed that his greatest pleasure was to receive the books he wanted on the subject of computing. Finally, at the end of May, there was Leah's seventeenth birthday, when she was presented with, among other delights, a series of driving lessons with a professional instructor, her dad and grandad having decided that driving instruction was best left to those who made it their business. Her knee was now healed, and driving and swimming were added to her normal activities, but she surprised her mum, when returning from the swimming pool in Northallerton, by voicing her uncertainty about driving.

'It's all so complicated,' she said.

'Do you really think so?'

'Yes, Dad and Bailey make it sound like the hardest thing imaginable.'

'I suppose they do. Just a minute.' Her mum signalled left and pulled into a housing estate, where she stopped the car.

'What have we stopped for, Mum?'

'I want to show you something. You see, when I was training to be a telegraphist during the war, our instructor reduced everything to the simplest and most basic elements. He was instructing a crowd of clueless females, you see, and he didn't want to put too much information into our pretty little heads all at once.'

'That's too patronising for words.'

'Ah, but it did the trick. By the time he'd trained us, none of us was at all apprehensive about operating wireless sets and learning practical procedure, because he'd made it all seem so simple. Anything's difficult if you over-complicate it, and everything's easier when you keep it simple.'

'Right.' Leah wasn't at all sure where this was leading.

'This,' she said, 'is called the clutch. All it does when you push it down or, "out", as it's called, is separate the engine from the wheels. As long as the brake is on, you can do anything you like, and the car won't move.' She revved the engine to demonstrate. 'Now, I'm going to ease off the handbrake, and just watch what happens when I let the clutch "in".' She looked in the mirror, signalled right, selected first gear and let in the clutch.

'It's moving.'

'That's right. That wasn't so complicated, was it?' She stopped the car and parked again.

Leah was encouraged, but she still had reservations. 'What did you do with this knob-thing?'

'That's the gear lever. I used the clutch to separate the engine from the wheels, and then I pushed the lever into first gear, That's for setting off. When you start going faster, you can change into second, third and fourth gears, but let's do one job at a time, and one gear at a time.'

'It's easier than I thought. Who taught you to drive, Mum?'

'To begin with, your dad, and he nearly had a nervous breakdown. He's not cut out for a life of excitement. He puts it down to being an air-gunner, facing aft and keeping his back to everything that was happening. Anyway, I went to a proper driving instructor after that, and then both your dad and I could relax.'

'I think there's a lot to be said for doing it the way your instructor did in the war, Mum.'

'You can't beat it, love.' Adopting a rough, gruff voice, she said, 'One: set your transmitter to deliver one watt, like this. All right, girlies? See how I did that? Easy, innit? Two: set the knob on your right to the middle. That's straight up, if you don't know what the middle is. Three: turn the left hand knob until the needle in the winnder dips dahn. Four: that was so much fun, do it again. In fact, fiddle abaht wiv it an' do it until the needle in the winnder always does it in the same place. Nah they can 'ear you in Australia. I bet they're 'avin' a right old laugh, them Aussies.'

Leah was laughing, more at her mum's impression of a petty officer instructor than at what she said. 'That's unbelievable.'

'You should have heard the drill instructors. I'll tell you about that another time.'

'Was it always like that?'

'Most of the time. When I was drafted to Dover, there was a lovely man on our watch called Leading Telegraphist 'Will' Hay. His name was actually Ronald, but we called him 'Will' after an actor and comedian you won't have heard of, so don't worry. Will had a soft spot for me, and he always made sure I was all right.'

'Oh, Mum.' It was time for Leah to tease. 'Did he fancy you?'

'I don't think so, although he did catch me under the mistletoe on Christmas Day 1943, or so he said. When I looked up, there was no mistletoe there at all.'

Leah shook her head in mock-disapproval. 'If my dad had only known.'

'I'd only just started writing to your dad. He'd be surprised to get a letter dated Christmas Day.'

'Poor old Dad. What a rotten time he must have had.'

'That's what I kept thinking. Anyway, listen, Leah. On our way back, we'll call at the DIY shop and get a pair of "L" plates. I want to set your mind at rest as soon as possible.'

'All right, Mum, but keep it simple.'

* * *

At other times, Leah studied, or accompanied rehearsals for *My Fair Lady*. She'd been apprehensive about it, but she was all right most of the time. When Henry Higgins had to sing, 'Let a Woman in Your Life' or Eliza sang, 'I could have danced All Night', her dad took over from her, as the music was too fussy for her to cope with.

Meanwhile, she had a few driving lessons from her mum, so that when she started with the driving school, she was reasonably confident, especially when she realised that the instructor went about his job in a similar way to her mum's old instructors in the war.

It was during this time that Stephen Wilkins plucked up the nerve to ask her out. He did it on a second visit ostensibly to enquire after her health, a gesture her mum called 'sweet', but one which set her dad worrying.

'What are you worried about, Dad?' asked Leah. 'We're going to the pictures. No more than that.'

Before he could answer her, her mum said, 'He's worried because he remembers what he was like when he was eighteen, and he's afraid today's lads are just as bad.'

'Oh, for goodness' sake,' said her dad, visibly embarrassed. 'I just hope he's going to behave himself.'

'I've been out with lads before, Dad, in London.'

'Have you?' His alarm was immediate and tangible. 'I didn't know about that.'

'It's just as well, isn't it, Mum? He's not cut out for a life of excitement, spending all that time in the after cockpit with his back to everything that was going on.'

'That's quite enough from you, young lady. I've every right to be anxious. You're only... seventeen.'

'But sensible and responsible,' said her mum. 'Besides, it's taken Stephen so long to ask her out, I'd be surprised if a naughty thought has ever crossed his mind.'

'I don't know what you're talking about,' said Leah. 'We're just going to the cinema.'

'What are you going to see?' demanded her dad.

'*Far From the Madding Crowd*,' she told him.

'Oh well, at least it's decent.'

'Listen to him,' said her mother. 'Dermot the hermit. Let the poor girl have a night out, for goodness' sake. You wouldn't make a fuss it was Martin.'

'No, but I'd be surprised. Anyway, Martin's a lad.'

'And that makes all the difference. Go and get changed, Leah. I'll fend off Lord Longford, here.'

* * *

73

Leah came downstairs to find her mother by herself.

'Your dad's in his darkroom,' she said. 'I've persuaded him that both you and Stephen are as innocent as new-born babies, and he's gone quiet, which usually means he's thinking over what I've said before coming round to my way of thinking.'

'Thanks, Mum.'

'You're welcome.' Cocking an ear to the window as she heard Stephen draw up in his mother's car, she said, 'Off you go and enjoy yourselves, and behave yourselves as well.'

'Mum!'

* * *

Leah found Stephen quiet. He seemed shy at first, but she coaxed him into conversation on the way to the cinema. It seemed that, like Martin, he was keen on the technical side of things. It wasn't a promising sign, but she was prepared to give him a fair chance. As she'd told her father repeatedly, they were only going to the cinema.

When the lights came down in the Lyric Cinema, Leah settled down to watch what for her was an enchanting story. After a while, she was conscious that Stephen was moving his arm behind her seat, and she wondered why lads did that. They seemed to think that if they made their moves gradually enough, the girl wouldn't notice. She felt his hand on her shoulder, and then his arm followed it. Well, that was all right until he moved closer. He was obviously going to kiss her, so she whispered, 'I want to watch the film. Do you mind?'

'What?'

'I want to watch the film. Have you read this novel?'

'No.'

He was probably too caught up with watts and horsepower to find time for reading. 'Well,' she said, 'watch the film instead.'

It was superbly made, with some brilliant performances, and with Stephen's grudging cooperation, she managed to see it all the way through.

'That was marvellous,' she said on the way out.

'Good.'

'Didn't you enjoy it?'

'It was all right.'

Conversation was hard work on the way back, and when they reached the lane leading to Leah's house, she said, 'Thanks for this evening. I really enjoyed the film.' She inclined her cheek for the polite peck she'd expected, but before she knew it, he was kissing her full on the lips, and she could smell the chewing gum he'd got rid of earlier. It was quite unpleasant, but she decided to give it a few minutes before getting out of the car. She didn't want to be completely unsociable. That was until his right hand moved purposefully to the neckline of her dress.

'No,' she said firmly, 'you can leave them where they are.'

'Oh.' Her rebuff seemed to have thrown him. 'Don't you like it, then?'

'No, I'd rather you didn't.'

Her response seemed to surprise him. 'I thought you wouldn't mind.... I mean, you haven't got that much, and....'

'I don't believe this.' She found the door handle. 'Thank you for this evening, Stephen. Let's not do it again.'

'Don't you want to go out with me again?'

'I just said not.' She opened the door and got out. 'Good night, Stephen.'

She never heard his reply, but he took off, spinning his wheels on the unmade road. Considering his driving had been quite responsible until then, she put it down to frustration or anger. It didn't really matter which of those two it was, because she was still resentful about his attitude and his remark about her being flat-chested.

When she got in, her mum asked, 'How did it go?' Her dad simply waited to hear.

'It's a wonderful film. I can really recommend it.'

'What about Stephen?' asked her mum, by far the more intuitive of her parents.

'He wasn't keen. I think he'd have been happier doing something else.' It was truer than they knew.

'Are you going to see him again?'

'No, he's not my type.' That was true as well.

A few days later, she got into conversation with Wendy, who naturally asked her about the date, so Leah told her what had happened.

'The dirty bugger,' said Wendy. 'He waited until the second night to try it on with me. He starts out all shy and quiet, but then he lets his hands loose. I put it down to him not being a ready talker.' She considered that explanation and found it incomplete. 'That,' she said, 'and he's a mucky-minded sod.' She grimaced at the memory. 'He's got cold, clammy hands, an' all, like a wet, chammy leather.'

'Why didn't you warn me?'

'I didn't think he'd try it on with you, you being educated an' that.'

'I don't see how that would make a difference.' Now that she'd confided in Wendy, she decided to be totally honest. 'He actually thought I'd welcome it.'

'What?'

'Oh yes, he thought that, being flat-chested, I'd probably be grateful for the attention.' Reflecting, she said, 'I don't know what he thought he was going to play with, the patronising... sod.' Leah didn't make a practice of swearing, but she thought Wendy's word was appropriate and quite useful.

'Oh, well.' Wendy was inclined to look ahead. 'There's plenty more fish in the sea,' she said.

'Yes, but they can keep the octopuses.' As well as that, lads would come and go, but she had more important things to occupy her time.

11

SQUARE-BASHING AND SAFETY PINS

etween driving lessons with Mr Dawson, the instructor, Leah's mum took her out for driving experience, and that experience was invaluable, giving her time to practise her various manoeuvres under the simplest and most patient guidance she could have.

She'd just completed a piece of reverse parking to her mum's complete satisfaction, and the memory of an earlier conversation prompted her to say, 'You were going to tell me about some people you called... I think you said, "drill instructors" in the war.'

'Oh, yes. Switch off the engine.' She waited until the engine was off, and Leah had pulled on the handbrake.

'Ready, Mum.'

'Right. Everyone had to have regular squad drill. That's marching, turning and whatnot.'

It was a world that meant little to Leah. 'If you were a telegraphist,' she asked, 'why did you have to do that?'

'Search me, but the rule was the same for everyone, and we were usually drilled by a male petty officer.'

'What's a petty officer, Mum? I know Dad was one, but I never did work out what it meant.'

'It's like a sergeant in the Army or the Air Force, really. They were terrifying people – except your dad, of course, and he wouldn't scare a nervous wreck.'

'Okay, I just needed to know.' She was also keen to hear the story.

'One day,' her mum went on, 'we were being drilled by a petty officer called Barton. He was very condescending, and he said things like, "I know it's 'ard for you gels to step hinto a man's world an' do all of what we 'as to do, but you'll 'ave to do your best." Well, there was one girl, Elsie Crabtree, who was adept at winding him round her little finger. She played the brainless blonde to perfection, although she was a very bright girl who went on to become an officer, and he'd just had a silly conversation with her, during which she convinced him that she actually believed she had two left feet. Anyway, he set us off marching again and ordered us to do an about-turn.'

'What on earth's that?'

'It just means that you turn a hundred-and-eighty degrees and face the way you came from. There are two ways of doing it.' She demonstrated with her hands. 'When you're stationary, you just sort of swizzle round with your right foot and then bring the left foot round to join it. Then there's the about turn on the march, which is what PO Barton ordered us to do. You have to turn round, stamping three times, and then march off in the opposite direction.'

Leah was laughing already. 'It sounds crazy to me.'

'We thought it was crazy, too, but we daren't say so.'

'Go on, Mum.'

'Right. We did it as well as we could, but it wasn't good enough for Petty Officer Barton.' She adopted her gruff petty officer voice again and said, "Dear, oh dear, oh flippin' dear. My little boy of three could do it better than what you lot can. There's just one gel who has any idea at all of how to do it. What's your name, my dear?" Well, the girl was called Iris Dean, and she was another who could manipulate men without even trying. He said, "Now, Wren Dean, don't be shy." That was a laugh, calling Iris shy. "I want you to show these gels how you do it." So, Iris explained, complete with actions, how she used her right foot to make a letter "L" heel to heel with her left, almost like first position in ballet, and then she used her left foot to form the cross of the letter "T".' Her mum demonstrated with her hands. 'Then, she moved her right foot to make a "V" and moved off again with her left. The only trouble was, with each movement, she lifted her feet high, like a soldier. Petty Officer Barton was very impressed except for the high stepping and stamping. He asked Iris, ''Oo told you to do it like that?" Iris said, "My brother, PO." "Oh," he said, "an' what, may I hask, does your bruvver do that makes 'im so clever at drill?" This was where we all had to work hard at not laughing, because Iris said, "He's a lieutenant in the Grenadier Guards." Well, a mere petty officer wasn't going to argue with a guardsman about a thing like squad drill, and an officer's word was law, but he said, "In the Royal Navy, we don't bounce our feet like pongos do" – he meant soldiers – "in fact, such a practice could prove 'armful to the female hanatomy." Iris asked him which part of the female anatomy it could harm, and all she could get out of him was, "The parts what *moves* hindependently." He was very embarrassed.'

'No.' Leah was convulsed, again more by her mum's portrayal of the two characters than by the story.

'That's right, and then Iris asked him, "But don't men have moving parts, too?" By this time, we were all helpless.'

'That was priceless, that her brother was a guardsman.'

'Ah, but he wasn't.'

'Wasn't he?'

'No,' said her mum, still laughing twenty-five years later, 'he was only twelve, and he was a boy scout.'

It was a while before Leah was able to drive off.

* * *

That evening, she sat at the piano in Easingthorpe Primary School, where Yoredale Players held their rehearsals.

' "The Ascot Gavotte", please,' said her dad. 'We'll concentrate on the chorus for now, so will you give us two bars in, please, Leah?'

They managed four bars before he had to stop them. 'It's a gavotte,' he reminded them, 'a very stately dance from the seventeenth and eighteenth centuries, and it needs to be very precise and staccato.'

'Nay,' said one of the chorus, 'it's no use swearin' at us in Foreign, Freddy.'

' "Staccato" means detached and clipped,' he explained. 'Will you demonstrate on the piano, Leah?'

Leah played from the chorus entry, emphasising the staccato until her dad said, 'That's enough, Leah.'

It was the cue for another chorus member to make his views known. 'I beg your pardon, Freddy,' he said, smiling at Leah.

'Sorry, I'm not with you.'

'I think you've forgotten something.'

Leah prompted her parent. 'What does Brian say?'

'All right. Thank you, Leah.'

'This young lady,' said the chorus member, 'has come here out of the goodness of her heart – 'cause let's face it, nobody's goin' to pay her – an' she's doin' a grand job, so we think the least you can do is treat her with respect. Don't you worry, Leah, love, we won't let your dad bully you.'

'I quite agree,' said her dad. 'Now, can we move on?' Receiving a reproving look, he added, 'Please.'

They rehearsed the 'Ascot Gavotte' and several other numbers, happily without interruption, at least from Leah's dad's point of view. At the end of the rehearsal, the chorus member who had queried the meaning of 'staccato' asked, 'Why does the "Ascot Gavotte" have to be sung short and clipped, Freddy? It sounds soppy.'

'It's a soppy kind of number. The gavotte was a dance performed by society people in wigs and frills, and another reason is that if you sing it without the staccato, it sounds *gauche*.' He added, 'That's Foreign for "clumsy".'

When they went out to the car, Leah said, 'When you were explaining about staccato, you reminded me of a story Mum told me this morning, about a petty officer who took them for squad drill during the war.'

'I imagine this is going to reflect badly on me.'

'No, Dad, honestly. It was the people answering back who reminded me of it.'

He unlocked the passenger door for her and opened it. 'Was it the story about the girl who said her brother was an officer in the Guards?'

'Yes.' He'd obviously heard it.

'I used to like to watch Wrens being drilled,' he said, letting himself into the car.

'That's pervy, Dad.'

'It was about as pervy as things got in those days. No, it was because when they became good at it, they were a treat to watch. Maybe it was the way their skirts swung when they moved, or maybe it was just that we weren't used to seeing them do it, but they seemed to do it with tremendous flair. Matelots tended to shuffle along in an untidy heap, but the Wrens did it with pride.'

'Happy days, Dad?'

'Some of them, at least until nineteen-forty-two.'

'I'm sorry, Dad. I wasn't thinking when I said that.'

'Don't be sorry, darling. If I hadn't been taken prisoner, I'd never have met your mum, and then you'd have been born to completely different parents, maybe ones that never said, "Please", and "Thank you", and never even thought of telling you *riské* stories from the parade ground.'

'Yes, I've a lot to be thankful for.'

* * *

Later in the week, Leah was carrying out a three-point turn in the quietest street they could find. As she turned the wheel to full lock, she said to her mum, 'Not that it'll ever be a problem for me, but I wonder how women with big boobs manage to do this.'

'That's not the nicest word you could have chosen, Leah, but I've wondered about that, too.'

'They should be retractable, like ballpens, or detachable, and then they could hire them out to people like me, the poor and needy.' She completed the manoeuvre. 'Or maybe I should say, the thin and weedy.'

'If we're going to have a silly conversation, Leah, you'd better pull into the side, here.'

'If I could hire a splendid pair of bosoms for special occasions,' said Leah, drawing up beside the kerb, 'it would be such a novelty, I'd probably treat them very gently and carefully and make sure I returned them in one piece.' Correcting herself, she said, 'Well, two pieces.'

'You think of the strangest things, Leah, and you could always invest in a padded bra.'

'No.' Leah switched off the engine. 'At least I have the satisfaction of knowing that what little I've got is my own.'

'Why have you switched off the engine?'

'I'm waiting for one of your war stories. Driving lessons have become like bedtime when I was little, but with the war thrown in.'

Her mum had to smile. 'I have to admit, you've reminded me of someone I knew on Malta in nineteen forty-five.'

'When your eardrum was perforated?'

'That's right. The woman I remember had the kind of bust that would have caused problems for most women, but she lived with it quite happily. Her name was Daisy Watson, and she was a PO Wren, a secretary in the Paymaster Branch, and she produced shows.'

'What kind of shows?'

'Variety, I suppose. The idea was to entertain service personnel between visits from ENSA.'

'Who?'

'The Entertainment National Service Association. They did what they could to keep our chaps' spirits up, and there were some good people among them. The standing joke, although not a good one, that ENSA stood for "Every Night Something Awful" wasn't universally true.'

'I'm sure it wasn't, but tell me about the Daisy woman.'

'All right.' She mustered her thoughts. 'I'd just arrived on Malta, and one of the first people I met was Dorothy.'

'I thought you met in Dover.'

'We did, but she was drafted to Malta, and then so was I. Anyway, Dorothy told me about the show, thinking I might contribute something to the dance element, and she introduced me to this statuesque woman Daisy. Now, Daisy was hard on the nerves. She was full of new initiatives, and not the most patient of people. As far as she was concerned, there was never any time like the present, and when energy and enthusiasm were needed, Daisy was your woman. She would deliver her newest ideas with the kind of fervour no one could resist, and all the time she would jump up and down with excitement. I used to wince when I thought of those magnificent bosoms crashing up and down inside an ill-fitting Admiralty "brassiere, size forty-two, 'E' cup, Wrens for the use of".'

'Suddenly, I don't feel quite so awkward,' said Leah, laughing.

'I was quite busy with my own duties, and I was also nursemaiding an awkward, unpopular Wren, but I took on choreography and dance supervision simply because what they were doing was so deplorable.' She stopped again to assemble her thoughts. 'Then, one day, Daisy told me she wanted something big. Now, Daisy knew all about "big", and she was halfway to the moon with enthusiasm. All the time she was telling me about it, she was jumping up and down, and those splendid bosoms of hers were trying their hardest to force an exit.'

'She sounds wonderful.'

'Oh, Leah, she was hard work. She'd talk 'til the cows came home, but she wasn't a great listener. As we used to say in the service, she was switched permanently to "Transmit". She wanted to use the old, corny songs that had been around at the beginning of the war, and they would have been a disaster, but I persuaded her eventually to settle for a song that was popular then. It was called, "Tomorrow is a Lovely Day", and my plan was to have it played while the years were being plucked from a calendar. We knew the war was nearly over, at least in Europe; it was only a matter of time, and while the years were being torn off, the chorus would rotate, like two wheels in a clock, with a dancer pirouetting on a dais in the middle of each *en pointes*. As the final year was torn off, the last chorus would begin.'

'Oh, Mum.' Twenty-three years later, Leah was caught up in the excitement. 'That must have been wonderful.'

'It worked well,' said her mum modestly. 'I knew that, because Daisy was backstage in her shirtsleeves, and she got so excited, she burst several buttons, her bra gave up the unequal struggle, and her huge frontage tumbled out.'

'Poor woman.'

'Not Daisy. She just hauled them back in and cadged three safety pins for her shirt.'

'Brilliant.'

'Then I went outside to do something even more important.'

'What was that?'

'Your dad and I had agreed, three or four months earlier, that everything we said in our letters was delayed by about a month, because that's how long our letters took to be delivered. Well, your dad suggested we did something together, for a change. We would both make a wish on the new moon in March. We would wish that the war could be over and that we could be together. I'd no idea when I stood there, looking at the moon, that he was already on the Long March, as they're calling it now, and that he was lying in a barn somewhere in Germany, wishing on the same moon.' Hearing a heavy sob, she turned and held out her arms to Leah. 'Don't cry, darling,' she said. 'We got together in the end.' Then, ever one to brighten the landscape, she said, 'And that was a copybook three-point turn you just did.'

12

JUNE

GRACEFUL TO DISGRACEFUL

Sylvia watched Leah transfer the cake mixture to a lined tin, making sure it filled all the available space, and gave her approval.

'Have I to put it in the oven now?' asked Leah.

'No, it's not up to temperature yet. Wait for the light to go out.'

'Right.' Leah had done some baking at school, but once again, she'd found an infinitely better teacher in her mother.

'Do you want to sit down? You've been on your feet long enough.'

'Maybe I'd better, although it's improving all the time.' She pulled out one of the dining chairs and sat down.

'It's all that swimming and driving. It's doing you a power of good.'

Leah eyed her suspiciously. 'You've got that look,' she said.

'What look is that?'

'The look that says you're thinking up something else for me to do.'

'The very idea.' Sylvia smiled to herself as the oven light went out, and she opened the door to put the cake in. 'You know your dad has a gig later this month, don't you?'

'Yes, I've heard that the Dalesmen are in demand. Where is it this time?'

'It's in Bradford, and it's the Federation of Dyers' and Finishers' Annual Ball, a truly grand event and, quite appropriately, they're holding it at the Event Suite in Forster Square.'

'Wonderful. I wonder if they'll all have blue hands and green faces, like Edward Lear's Jumblies.'

'You'll find out soon enough, because they've given your dad two complimentary tickets. Not surprisingly, Martin's said he doesn't want to go, so that leaves you and me.' She took a seat opposite Leah at the table. 'When you've rested your knee, would you like to brush up your Ballroom and a bit of gentle Latin?' Looking at the clock, she said, 'Your dad shouldn't be long. You can go through your steps with him while I cast the eagle eye and offer advice.'

Leah laughed good-naturedly. 'I'll never be bored as long as I live here,' she said, 'but you know that when you mention dancing I'll never hang back.' In a belated double-take, she asked, 'What do you mean by "*gentle* Latin"?'

'The rhumba, basically. I don't want you to overdo things with your knee.'

'I've started practising *pliés*. The physio said it was okay as long as I started gently.'

'Be careful, Leah.'

'Oh, I shall. If it comes to that, Ballroom and Latin are going to come as a big shock to muscles that have only just started getting used to ballet again.'

'They're very different from ballet, I know, but they shouldn't cause a problem.'

The front door opened and closed, and then the inner door opened to allow Nina into the room, excited and full of affection.

Leah asked, 'What have you been doing to her, Dad? She can't get away from you fast enough.'

'You know what a cruel master I am, Leah.' He bent to kiss both his wife and her.

'I'll put the kettle on,' said Leah's mother, 'but I was just saying to Leah that she would benefit from some Ballroom and Latin practice before the big event. We were just waiting for you to come home.'

'How reassuring it is,' he said, 'to have my evening mapped out for me.' Taking Leah's hand, he said, 'It's a good idea, but let's do it properly, and "properly" doesn't stand a chance on a carpeted floor. Come to the band rehearsal, both of you, and we'll have the benefit of the school hall.' The hall at Easingthorpe Village School was quite small, but its parqueted floor offered, as he said, a much better surface for dancing. And so it was decided.

* * *

Leah was surprised, when she entered the school hall, to be greeted with applause, as she'd been the previous December at the pantomime rehearsal.

'We're just pleased to see you on your feet again, love,' said Reg Clough.

'I've brought Leah for some physiotherapy,' her father told them, 'and Sylvia's come to keep an eye on things in case I'm too rough with her.'

'Don't you worry, love,' said Reg. 'We won't let him ill-treat you.' It was almost a re-run of the chorus rehearsal for *My Fair Lady*, and the friendly banter alone made the journey worthwhile.

'Let's start with "By The Sleepy Lagoon",' said Freddy. When the parts had been passed around, he said, 'I'll start you off, and then it'll be time for Leah's therapy.' He counted them in and turned to Leah. 'May I have the pleasure?'

'Feel free.'

'I hope you won't say that to just anyone,' he said, taking her in hold. Then, more seriously, he said, 'Let me know when it gets too much for you.'

'I'm tougher than you think, Dad.' She followed his lead into Eric Coates's dreamy waltz. Her father danced an excellent waltz and foxtrot, although she wasn't all that sure about his quickstep and rhumba. Still, no one was perfect, and it was wonderful to be back on the dance floor, anyway. They danced to the end of the number, when Leah looked inquiringly at her mother, who simply nodded approvingly.

'That was good,' said her father to the band, who were generously applauding them both. 'Let's try a foxtrot. I have "Stay as Sweet as You Are" down on the programme, so let's try that.' When the parts were out, he counted them in and took Leah in hold.

It was one of Leah's favourite foxtrots, and she followed her parent like a shadow throughout the number. At the end, she briefly acknowledged the band's applause and said, 'Thanks, Dad. I'd like to rest my knee for a bit, if you don't mind.'

'Of course.' He returned to the band to continue practising the programme for the Dyers' and Finishers' Association Ball while Leah joined her mum.

'Go on, Mum,' she said, 'let's hear the worst. You're going to tell me I was awful, aren't you?'

'You weren't awful at all. You're tending to go forward on your toe rather than your heel, but that's not surprising after years of ballet.' She gave her a squeeze and said, 'It's just good to see you on your feet and dancing again.'

It was soon Leah's turn to watch her mum, as the band started to run through 'Embraceable You', which was one of her favourite foxtrots, and one that she and her dad always danced together. It was also a lesson, because, whilst Leah had enjoyed the benefit of five years' professional ballet tuition, her mum was the Hinchcliffe family's undisputed mistress of Ballroom dancing. Leah watched with total admiration as her parents demonstrated grace and musicality, seemingly without effort.

At the end of the practice, her dad addressed the band, saying, 'You're playing well. I didn't think there'd be a problem, but it's always good to guard against complacency by doing a run-through.'

'You just fancied having a bit of a dance, Freddy,' said Arthur Bell on trumpet.

'I can't fool you lot, can I?'

A chorus of laughter confirmed their agreement.

'The next practice will be different.'

Reg asked, 'Are you going to sing for us an' all, Freddy? We could do with a laugh.'

'No, but someone else will. I'm bringing a young chap who'd like to have a go. I've heard him sing with piano accompaniment, but I want to hear him with the band before I accept him.

* * *

Leah learned that the aspiring vocalist's name was Robert Parry, and that he was about to graduate from the University of Birmingham.

'What's he been studying, Dad?' Leah asked the question out of passing interest.

'English, I believe. You can talk to him about it at next month's band practice.'

Leah thought she probably would ask him out of politeness. Meanwhile, she had something else on her mind, and breakfast time was as good a time as any to air the topic. 'I think I should get a job,' she said.

Her mum asked, 'Do you think you're fit to work?'

Her dad said, 'There's no problem about money.'

'I'm grateful for that, Dad, and yes, Mum, I think I'll be all right as long as I don't have to spend too long on my feet.'

'That narrows it down,' said her father. 'I suppose you could be a test pilot in a furniture factory.'

'Ha, ha, ha. Thank you for that suggestion, Dad. As a matter of fact, I think I've found the ideal job.'

Both parents waited expectantly. Martin showed no interest in the conversation, intent as he was in pursuing the last cornflake, which was stuck to the side of his bowl, although he would be more likely to see it as being held against a smooth surface by ambient air pressure.

'Wendy has a job lined up at the supermarket for when she leaves school,' said Leah, 'and she says they're looking to recruit more young people.'

'Why young people, particularly?' asked her mum.

'Because they're cheaper than adults,' said her dad. 'Are you talking about the Saver Stores Supermarket, Leah?'

'Yes.'

He nodded, as if his suspicion were confirmed.

'If it's all right with you both, I'll make enquiries.'

'You'll need references.'

'What do you mean by references, Dad?'

'Two people who'll write about you in glowing terms.' They'll have to assure Saver Stores that you don't use foul language and pick your nose. That sort of thing.'

'Dad!'

'You should be used to him by this time, Leah,' said her mum. 'It comes of being an air-gunner, facing aft and—'

88

'Everything going on behind his back, I know. I'll ask the Reverend Stapleton and the Royal Ballet School. Hopefully, they may just remember me if they try hard enough.'

'Don't be bitter, darling. It wasn't their fault.'

* * *

Assured of references from Miles Stapleton and the Academic Principal of the Royal Ballet School, Leah walked the short distance to the supermarket and came to the Enquiries Desk.

A motherly assistant asked, 'What can I do you for, love?'

'I'm looking for a job.'

'Are you, now? Just a minute.' She tapped on the door behind her and spoke to someone inside. After a few seconds, she said, 'The Manager can see you now, love. Do you want to come through?'

'Yes, please.' It was turning out to be easier than she'd expected. She walked into the office and found the manager behind a battered desk. He wore black-rimmed glasses that had evidently suffered some damage, because one leg was stuck to its frame with sticking plaster. His dark hair was liberally plastered down apart from an unruly cone that projected from his crown. His lips appeared to be permanently wet, and Leah found that feature more alienating than any other.

'Hello,' he said.

'Good morning.'

'I'm Mr Shaw, Branch Manager. I understand you're lookin' for a job.'

'That's right.'

'How old are you?'

'Seventeen.'

'Sit yerself down.' He pointed to a plastic chair and took a form from his desk drawer. 'As it happens, there is a vacancy. Have you got a pen?'

'Yes.' Leah took her pen from her bag.

'It's a while since I've seen one of them,' he remarked.

'A fountain pen?' They'd always been a normal feature in Leah's life.

'Yeah. What colour's your ink?'

'Blue.'

He opened his drawer again and said, 'You'd best use one of these.' He handed her a ballpoint. 'The company like their forms to be filled in with black ink,' he explained. 'Where are you working now?'

'I'm not.'

'School-leaver, are you?'

'Not really.'

Before she could explain, he asked, 'Well, what have you been doin' with yerself?'

'I was at the Royal Ballet School, but I was knocked down by a car, and I've spent a lot of time in hospital.'

'There's no need to be bloody sarcastic,' he told her sharply, 'an' I've a right to ask.'

Leah showed him the name and address of the Academic Principal. 'I really was at the Royal Ballet School,' she said as firmly as she could, bearing in mind the circumstances, 'and I spent very nearly two months in hospital.'

'Oh, right.' He handed the note back to her. 'What was it like down there,' he asked with a sly smile, 'livin' with a crowd of poofters?'

'They're not, not all of them, and I'd still be there if it weren't for that lunatic driver.' She disliked the man very much, and she had to make an effort to be more polite than he was.

'Oh well, fill that form in. Write everything in block capitals, an' let me have it.'

She filled in her name, address and date of birth. When she came to 'Present Employment', she wrote what she'd told the manager, hoping he'd leave the subject alone. Finally, she filled in details of her two referees, signed the form, and passed it across the desk to him.

'Have you done already?' He sounded surprised.

'Yes.'

'Right, well, if the company takes you on, they'll pay you nine pound five and six a week *pro rata*, which means, as you'll be on twenty-five hours a week, you'll come out with five pound fifteen and six before tax and National Insurance. You'll learn how to work the tills, and you'll have to do some shelving.'

'What's that?'

'Puttin' stuff on shelves. What do you think?'

'I didn't know. I've never worked in a supermarket.'

'Right. Stand up a minute.'

She couldn't imagine why he wanted her to stand, but she did as he asked.

He looked her up and down, taking rather longer than he needed to say, 'You're not very tall, are you?'

'Not really.' Considering the upper height limit set by the Royal Ballet, it was hardly surprising, but she kept that observation diplomatically to herself.

'Still, I suppose you'll be able to reach t' top shelves wi' a step-stool.'

'I'll do my best.'

Attempting another smile, he said, 'An' you'll look nice on t' checkout.'

'Thank you.' She couldn't imagine why he bothered to say that. It just seemed to be his creepy way.

'It'll be up to t' company to approve your application, but I can't see a problem, meself. Anyroad, they'll let you know by letter.' He stood up, and she took that as the cue for her to do likewise.

'Thank you, Mr Shaw.'

'That's all right, love. I think you'll be all right.' He put one hand on the door handle to open it, and placed his other arm round her shoulders. 'Take care of yerself, an' we'll no doubt see you soon.' As he opened the door, his hand left her shoulder and gave her bottom an enthusiastic squeeze. She wasn't sure which she liked less, that or the arm-round thing, but she hoped it was an isolated instance.

'Goodbye, Mr Shaw.'

''Bye, love.'

13

THE MALE OF THE SPECIES

With the benefit of an indulgent mother skilled at choosing the moment when her husband was 'facing aft', Leah went to the ball in a new, apple-green evening dress. Having been to several of the band's gigs, she was used to extravagant surroundings and wasn't at all daunted by the marble pillars and intricate plaster mouldings of the Victorian function room. The band was playing softly, but without assistance from Leah's dad, because he was at the bar, getting drinks for his family.

'In the early days,' her mum told her, 'Bailey used to come to gigs as the band's manager. He never actually did anything, of course. It was just a way of getting a ticket.'

'Good old Bailey.'

'Then Elaine came along, and she sang with the band until she was expecting Janice, and she could no longer get into her evening dress.'

'I'd like to have heard her.' Leah had heard many times about things that had taken place before she was born, and she felt sometimes that she'd missed all the best moments.

'That all came to an end. Caring for Janice is a full-time job.'

'Yes, they're both brilliant.' Because it had only just occurred to her, she asked, 'Do you think that people like Janice are usually born to parents who can cope?'

'Sometimes. There are parents who adjust and learn to cope, but there are also those who can't and never will.'

'What happens to the children then?'

'They're brought up in institutions. If they're lucky, they're cared for by the best of people, but it's not always the case.'

Leah thought of Janice and the loving homelife she enjoyed with Bailey and Elaine. 'That's awful, Mum.'

'Agreed, but here's your dad, so don't look miserable.'

Leah took the orange juice from the tray and smiled happily. 'Thanks, Dad.'

'Thanks, darling.' Her mum took the gin and tonic that would last her half the evening. She was a modest drinker.

'The place is filling up nicely,' said her dad, looking around the ballroom. 'It should be a good night.' He took a sip from his glass and said, 'I'm going to start things off, as usual, then I'll come down and dance with my lovely wife and, unless my glamorous daughter has been whisked away by an acceptable youth, I'll dance with her.'

'How will you know he's acceptable, Dad?'

'I'm laying it on the line now, Leah. If you take up with a wrong 'un, there'll be trouble.' He looked at his watch and then stood up to go. 'See you soon, folks.'

The band burst into its recently-adopted signature number 'I Got Rhythm', indicating that the evening's fun was about to begin. It's predecessor 'Zip-a-Dee-Doo-Dah' had been deemed inappropriate in the light of recent legislation and the new, socially-inclusive mood. The Gershwin number wasn't a bad substitute, however, and the band had soon adjusted to the change, even if Harold Wilson remained unpopular with some of them.

When the shortened number reached its end, Leah's father came to the microphone to say, 'Good evening, ladies and gentlemen, and welcome to the Forster Square Event Suite for this annual celebration. Let's begin with a waltz by that master of melody, Eric Coates. Let's dance to "By the Sleepy Lagoon".'

'Hello. Would you like to dance?' The voice came from Leah's left, and she turned to see that she was being addressed by a young man of twenty or so, with dark, wavy hair. To say he was so young, he seemed very self-assured.

'Yes. Thank you.' She followed him on to the floor, where he started badly by leading with the wrong foot. She was adept at following, however, so that he wouldn't be aware of his gaffe.

'I don't recall seeing you around,' he said, pumping her arm for no obvious reason. He really was a hopeless dancer.

'I'm not a dyer or finisher,' she explained. 'I'm here because my dad's the bandleader.'

'Oh.' He seemed amused. 'She was only the bandleader's daughter—'

'I've heard it.'

'I haven't finished making it up, yet.'

'Someone got there before you.' She added for good measure, 'In fact, more than one person. You're about the fourth I've heard, and there must be lots more.'

'Oh, I was on the point of creating a masterpiece.' He was almost serious.

'Never mind. What do you do by day?'

'I'm a trainee dyehouse manager.'

'Well,' she said as comfortingly as she could, 'maybe you're better at that than you are at making up jokes.'

'I'm usually quite good at it, really.'

Leah wanted the number to end, but she knew it was only halfway through. Sometimes a few minutes seemed to last forever.

'What do you do?'

'Not much. I was at ballet school until last year.' She'd just received an offer of a job at the supermarket, but she wasn't going to tell him that. 'I'm doing my "A" levels,' she told him, 'at home.'

'Oh, I didn't bother with those things.' Then, as if he'd just thought of it, which he probably had, he said, 'You dance like a ballerina.'

'I hope not.'

'Why not?'

'The techniques are completely different.'

'Oh.'

It seemed he was unable to follow that, so they danced to the end of the number in silence.

'Thank you,' said Leah, applauding the band.

'Maybe you'll dance with me again,' he said hopefully.

'They say you should never rule anything out. Thank you.' She rejoined her mother, who gave her a disapproving look.

'You were a bit off-hand with him, weren't you?'

'You had to be there to see the problem, Mum. He made a pathetic job of trying to make up a dubious joke about the bandleader's daughter, even though he told me he was good at making up jokes; he made a fatuous remark about dancing like a ballerina, and to cap it all, he couldn't dance to save his life.'

'I'll grant you the first two offences, but you shouldn't put a man down because of his lack of dancing ability.'

'Why not, Mum?' Dancing meant everything to Leah. It was an accomplishment to be approached with nothing but total commitment, and half-heartedness was a crime.

'You have to remember, it's not everyone's reason for living. Many people do it simply for enjoyment, and there are lots who've never learned how to do it properly, because, sadly, it's no longer fashionable.' Looking around the ballroom, she said, 'It wouldn't surprise me if most of the younger end here tonight would rather be jerking around to the latest cacophonous row by the Rolling Stones.'

'I still don't see why a man being hopeless on the dance floor should call for diplomacy.'

'No, well, you see, even when it means less to someone than it means to you, it's still a very personal thing, and to criticise a man, particularly, for that is like criticising his…. Oh, dear.' She seemed unable to find the words, which was most unusual for her.

'What's it like, Mum?'

'You'll understand when you're older.'

'Ah.' Realisation made its belated appearance. 'You're talking about things that go "hump" in the night, aren't you?'

'Really, Leah.'

'Don't be embarrassed, Mum. Everybody does it.' Countering her mother's shocked expression, she said, 'Except me, that is, and the way things stand, it's unlikely I ever will.'

'What are you saying, Leah?'

'Just that it's a pity I wasn't born otherwise inclined, that's all.'

'For goodness' sake, Leah.' Her mum put her glass down and pushed it away from her, as if it were the cause of her consternation. 'What on earth put that thought into your head?'

'Only that the male population has done nothing so far to impress me.' Seeing that her father was about to join them, she added, 'There are a few obvious exceptions, of course.'

'I should hope so.' Jack, the pianist, was announcing 'Embraceable

95

You', and Leah's mum got up in response to her husband's unspoken invitation. The look she gave Leah suggested that her daughter might find a more acceptable topic on her return.

An immaculately-groomed man, maybe in his thirties or possibly older, came up to her to say, 'Are you all alone?'

'Just for now,' she assured him.

'Would you like to dance?'

'Yes. Thank you.' She let him take her hand and lead her on to the floor.

'You're with the band, aren't you?'

'Yes.' In the light of recent experience, his gentle manner assured her that his enquiry was genuine.

'And an excellent band it is, too. I'm Roger Danby, by the way. You won't have heard of me, but it's only right that I should tell you.' He smiled as he said it, and that made their conversation less formal.

'I'm Leah Hinchcliffe.'

'And I'm delighted to meet you. I imagine the bandleader is your father.'

'That's right.'

'He's doing a superb job, and it's quite fitting that his daughter is such an excellent dancer.'

'Thank you. You're not bad yourself.'

He laughed. 'I do my best.'

'Are you a dyer or a finisher?' Dyeing spoke for itself, but she hadn't the first idea what a finisher was or did. It just seemed good manners to take an interest.

Laughing again, he said, 'I have to admit to being both. My firm's called Jacob Danby Limited, Dyers and Finishers.'

'So you're the boss.'

'Yes, and I'm also the host tonight, as Chairman of the Association, but I have to say that the highlight of this evening for me has been the privilege of dancing with a delightful young lady who is also a lovely, natural dancer.'

'It's very kind of you to say so, Mr Danby.' The music drew to a close, and he took her back to her table. 'Thank you, Leah.'

'I enjoyed dancing with you. Thank you, Mr Danby.'

When her parents returned to the table, her mum asked, 'Who was that you were dancing with, Leah?'

'The Chairman of the Association and boss of Jacob Danby Ltd. You know, I may just revise my opinion of men, at least, up to a point.'

'Oh, yes?' Her mum was still visibly impressed by his credentials.

'Yes, I really prefer older men.'

'In that case,' said her dad, 'will you grant this ancient relic the pleasure of the next foxtrot?' Jack was at the microphone to announce, 'Stay as Sweet as You Are'.

'If you think you can stand the pace, Dad.' She got up to join him in her favourite foxtrot.

After a while, he said, 'Don't give up on the male population just yet, Leah. You're only seventeen and, believe it or not, there are some decent specimens among us.'

'Somebody's been talking.'

'Naturally.'

Leah was still trying to come to terms with the conundrum. 'Mr Danby was nice,' she said. 'He didn't try to impress me.'

'He doesn't need to. Have you seen the gorgeous woman in the light-green gown?'

'The redhead?'

'I thought you might have spotted her. She's Mrs Danby.'

'I wonder why he danced with me.'

'He was being an attentive host. I imagine he just wanted to make sure everyone was having a good time.' As the music reached its end, he applauded the band and said, 'I'd better get back up top. I'll be down again later.'

Leah knew he would. He always came down to the floor to dance 'All the Things You Are' with her mum. It meant an awful lot to them.

14

THE VILE AND THE VULNERABLE

Leah was relieved to learn that she and Wendy were to start work at the supermarket on the same day. With Mr Shaw's familiar behaviour still fresh in her mind, she felt that they'd be able to give each other moral support. She wasn't at all sure what form it would take or how they would go about it, but it had an encouraging ring.

They were given uniform tabards and name badges and, with an hour to go before opening and with Mr Shaw hovering in the background, two assistants, Annie and Sonia, showed them how to operate the tills.

Watching Leah, Mr Shaw said, 'You've got "O" level Maths, haven't you, love?'

'Only just.' At first, she thought he was joking. Reckoning up money didn't call for anything more than simple arithmetic, but she remembered from her interview that he usually signalled an attempt at humour with a crooked leer, so the likelihood was that he was serious.

'You should be okay at counting cash, then.'

'I hope so.'

'You haven't, have you?' He directed this question at Wendy.

'Haven't what?'

'Got "O" level Maths. That's if I remember rightly.'

'I haven't got "O" level anything. Not yet, anyway.' The CSE results weren't due for another month. Only then would Wendy know if she'd managed a Grade One CSE in any of her subjects.

'Will you be okay, counting money?'

'I should hope so. When you're as hard up as we are, you have to keep track of it.'

'All right, there's no need to get clever.' He left them so that he could answer the ringing phone, and Sonia said to Wendy, 'Well said, love. We 'ave to keep 'im in 'is place.'

'Another thing to remember,' said Annie, 'is not to let the bugger get you on your own. His hands don't exactly wander – they take a direct route, like homing pigeons.' She nodded to underline her warning. 'Right, let's ring a few more things through, an' then you'll both be ready for the rush.' Leah could see from her desk that the carpark was almost empty, so she imagined Annie was being droll. She hoped she wasn't entirely serious about Mr Shaw, as well, but her one experience with him had already cast doubt on that. She resolved to be extra careful when he was around.

* * *

At five minutes to opening time, Mr Shaw came out of his office to speak to Sonia and Annie. 'You two go on t' checkout,' he told them. These new lasses need more trainin' before they can be let loose on that.'

Annie asked, 'What are you goin' to give 'em to do?'

'We've just had a delivery of sugar and flour. They can help us shelve it.'

'Aye, well, mind you keep your grubby 'ands to yourself.'

'Mind your own business, you, an' get on that checkout. Right, you lasses, follow me.'

Warily, but still eager to please, they went with him to the covered delivery area, where a quantity of groceries was stacked. Wendy asked, 'How are we going to get that lot to the shelves?'

'Get a trolley apiece and take it a load at a time, and don't take all day about it.'

They brought two trolleys from the entrance and set about loading them with goods. After three loads, their hands ached from picking up two-pound bags of sugar and flour, and it was inevitable that one of them would drop something.

'Why do they have to keep flour on the top shelf?' asked Wendy, picking up the next bag, which slipped from her hand, bursting when it hit the floor. 'Oh, heck! I'll go and find a brush and shovel.'

While she was gone, Mr Shaw came and saw the mess. 'What's all this?' he demanded.

'Wendy's gone to find a sweeping brush and a shovel,' Leah told him. 'Oh, aye?'

Wendy returned with a long-handled soft sweeping brush, a hand shovel and a refuse bin. Leah took the shovel from her and, between them, they set about clearing the mess. Mr Shaw watched impatiently. 'Make sure you get it all out from under the rack,' he told her, circling her waist with his arm, ostensibly to lend encouragement.

'That's what I am doing,' she told him, sweeping flour on to Leah's shovel.

'Right underneath,' he said, accentuating the message by running his hand down to her bottom and stroking it.

With a meaningful look at Leah, Wendy straightened up and swung the brush handle backwards and upwards. There was a howl of anguish from Mr Shaw, who was now doubled up and clutching his private parts. 'Oh, I'm sorry, Mr Shaw,' she said. 'I didn't realise you were standing so close.'

His audible distress brought staff and customers to see what was happening. Meanwhile, thespian that she was, Wendy made the most of the scene. 'That were really clumsy of me. Are you all right, Mr Shaw? I'm not being nosey. It's just that your face has gone all red and your eyes are watering.'

Leah turned away, not trusting herself to maintain a sympathetic countenance, but the members of staff who'd been alerted to the incident were less discreet. One of them said, 'That's what happens when you get too close to female employees, Mr Shaw. It's worth bearing in mind for later.'

Another said, 'Instead of keeping your 'and in, you're better keepin' 'em both to yourself.' Both women were laughing unrestrainedly.

'It's not... bloody... funny!'

Neither could agree, but Wendy's stock was now high with the rest of the staff, because word went around with remarkable speed.

* * *

100

It seemed to Leah that there were slow learners and there were hopeless cases, and she suspected that Mr Shaw fell into the second category, because she became the next object of his unwanted attention.

Annie was about to go for lunch, and she was handing over the till to Leah. Mr Shaw hovered close by, ready to perform whatever function was needed to set up the till for its new operator, his recent misfortune apparently forgotten.

'Right, Mr Shaw,' said Annie, 'do your stuff.'

Opening the wicket door, he inserted his key into the till and pulled out the cash drawer. At the same time, he rested his spare hand on Leah's knee, squeezing it.

'I recently had an operation on that knee, as well as both legs,' she told him, angrily removing his hand.

'You dirty bugger,' said Annie, 'you still haven't learned, have you?'

'Mind your own business, you, and get off for your lunch,' he told her. Turning then to Leah, he said, 'A bright lass like you could do well in this firm. You just need to be more cooperative.'

'And that's a word we don't use in this supermarket,' said Annie, but I bet the Co-op staff get treated with more respect than we do here.'

Still angry, Leah said, 'My godfather was Royal Artillery Heavyweight Champion, and if he gets to know about you and your tricks, he won't be very pleased.'

'Oh aye, an' I'm James Bond's stunt double.'

Tears were pricking her eyelids, but she was desperate not to let him see them. 'Just keep your hands off me,' she said.

'You need to mind your manners, young lady.'

'Tell him,' said Annie. 'Tell that godfather o' yours, Leah, an' I'll sell tickets. It'll be a full house.'

'Off you go an' get your lunch.' He returned to his office, leaving Leah to calm down while she served her customers.

After all the unpleasantness, it was good to see a friendly face, especially when it was the face of someone she liked. She hadn't seen Bruce since Christmas, and he was her favourite cousin.

'Hello, Bruce.'

'Hi, Leah. I just thought I'd drop in and see how you're getting on.' He wore a T shirt and shorts, and stood in his usual attitude, with his arms folded across his chest.

'This is Wendy,' she said, inclining her head towards the till behind her, where Wendy had relieved Sonia. 'Wendy, this is Bruce, my cousin.'

'Hi, Wendy.'

'Hi, Bruce.'

'Have we to call you "Doctor" now?' asked Leah hopefully.

'No, we're still waiting for the exam results. It won't be long, though.'

'Bruce is a medical student, Wendy.'

'Lovely.'

'How's it going?' asked Bruce.

'All right, really,' said Leah.

'It'd be better,' said Wendy, who was never less than forthright, 'if the manager could keep his hands to himself.'

Before Bruce could react, Mr Shaw arrived at Leah's till. 'What's all this?' he demanded. 'You're not paid to pass the time of day with individual customers.'

Still angry from the earlier episode, she said, 'This is my cousin, and he's not impressed with your nasty habit.'

'No,' said Bruce, normally so gentle and mildly-spoken, 'I'm not. You'd better keep your sweaty hands off Leah and her friend. Do you hear me?'

'All right.' The startled manager backed away, white-faced. 'I didn't mean nothing by it.'

'Pull the other one. Keep your hands to yourself. Right?'

'Yeah, okay. There's no need to get shirty.'

'If I hear you've been at it again, you'll be in serious trouble.'

'All right, all right.' He slunk away to his office, no doubt to ponder the unfairness of life.

Meanwhile, Leah was tearful in her relief. She'd never thought of Bruce as being at all scary, but now she realised what had terrified Mr Shaw. Printed on his T shirt below his folded arms were the words, *Karate Squad*. Now she didn't know whether to laugh or to cry.

'Have a tissue,' said Bruce, taking a pack from the pocket of his shorts. As he did so, he revealed the extent of the lettering on his T shirt. Above *Karate Squad* was the name *Mothercare*.

Before long, both girls were helpless with laughter. Eventually, Leah recovered sufficiently to say, 'You'd better go before he finds out the truth, Bruce.'

Wendy asked, 'What's that Japanese fighting-thing they do with funny masks and long sticks?'

'I'm not sure,' said Bruce. 'I think it's Kendo.'

'Well, that's what I did to him this morning. He's had quite a day of it, all told.'

Again, both girls gave in to laughter.

'I'd better go,' said Bruce, leaning forward to kiss Leah on the cheek.

'What about me?' asked Wendy.

'I was coming to you.' He kissed her as well. 'Nice meeting you, Wendy. 'Bye, both.'

'Oh, said Wendy when he'd gone, 'he can come to my bedside anytime he likes.'

The story soon circulated, so that, at the first sign of unwanted attention from Mr Shaw, all any of the female staff had to say was, '*Hasso!*' It was a salutary and necessary reminder.

* * *

As well as being excellent preparation for 'A' level History, Leah's lessons with Miles Stapleton served as a cushion against the occasional unpleasantness of everyday life. His company was so unworldly, it could not do otherwise, and Leah was thankful for it.

One evening shortly after the 'Karate episode' as it had come to be known, when Leah felt she'd gained particular insight into Cromwell's influence, the Rector asked, 'Why don't you come along to St Jude's some time, Leah? Wendy is a regular attender, so you wouldn't be alone. You could come to Matins or Evensong, just to find out if it appeals to you.'

'Yes, I could.' She felt awkward about accepting the Rector's help with her studies whilst apparently ignoring his official efforts.

'You were baptised at St Jude's, as I recall. You could consider confirmation classes.'

'How do you know I was baptised, Rector?' She felt sometimes that people knew more about her than she knew herself.

He laughed amiably. 'I remember holding you in my arms and performing your baptism myself.'

'I'd no idea.' In a way, it was quite embarrassing.

'You were very young, although you made your feelings known.'

'Was I difficult?'

'No, I managed to calm you down.'

She closed her eyes awkwardly. 'I'll speak to Wendy and decide what to do,' she said.

'Yes, I gather you're both working at the supermarket now.' It was clear from his tone that the fact caused him some anxiety.

'We both started this week. I'm only there part-time.'

He nodded thoughtfully. 'I have to say that it has the reputation of being less than safe as a workplace for… women and girls.'

Leah thought for a moment that he was going to use an old-fashioned term, such as 'the fair sex'. That would have been amusing, though probably not for him.

'The problem arose,' she said, trying not to be too explicit, 'but it was solved.' She told him about Bruce's timely visit, but left out the earlier incident involving Wendy and her brush handle, in case it offended him.

'Oh, full marks to your cousin,' he said. Then, reverting to the previous subject, he said, 'I'm thinking about your knee, Leah. If you come to church, don't feel that you have to kneel. The Lord can hear you just as easily when you're seated.'

She was grateful for that assurance.

* * *

A little while later, Leah's father returned from a practice with the Dalesmen and reported that the young singer Robert Parry would not be joining them. 'He's not a bad singer,' he said regretfully, 'but his range is all wrong, and he's not at ease with the published keys.'

'What are they?' asked Leah.

'The keys that bands traditionally play in. More often than not, they're B flat, E flat and A flat, the most convenient keys for brass and woodwind instruments.'

Leah was more interested in the singer himself. 'What was he like?' she asked.

'Quite friendly, but a bit full of himself, if you know what I mean.'

Leah did know what he meant. She'd met such people, and she was less than impressed so far with the male of the species.

15

A SWIM AND A STORY

Leah and Wendy were taking their mid-morning break, when Leah said, 'There's something I don't understand.'

'Join the club, Leah. There's lots of things I don't understand.'

'You knew how to stop old Shaw in his tracks with that brush handle. It would never have occurred to me.'

Wendy appeared to consider the matter, but only for a moment. 'It's all about experience,' she said. 'You've had a good education and got "O" levels an' all that, an' you can do brilliant things on the stage, but I've learned how to survive, an' that's where you're laggin' behind.'

'Am I?'

'Yes, you see, I knew how to take his mind right off naughtiness an' make it look, at the same time, like an accident. You learn these things when you have to contend with lads who keep their brains in their breeches. I expect the lads you knew at ballet school weren't right interested in lasses.'

'Quite a lot of them weren't,' she had to admit.

'Anyway,' said Wendy, remembering the start of their conversation, 'you said there was something you didn't understand.'

'Yes, as far as I could see, you hit old Shaw quite gently, but he made an awful fuss.' The memory of it provoked her to laughter, and Wendy joined in readily.

'It was *where* I hit him,' she explained when they'd stopped laughing. 'Them bits and pieces are more sensitive than what you'd think. They're a fella's weakness.'

'His Achilles' heel?'

'It's funny name for it, but okay, if you say so.' She seemed to tire of the subject, because she asked abruptly, 'What have you got lined up for tomorrow?'

'Not much. My mum and I are going swimming in the morning. I have to swim regularly as part of my physio. Apart from that, though, I'm back here for the afternoon.' Recalling a previous conversation, she said, 'It's your day off, isn't it?'

'Yes.' She took her empty coffee mug to the sink and said casually, 'I quite like swimming. I'd probably like it more if I were better at it, but I seem to work hard an' not get very far.'

It struck Leah as odd, given Wendy's athletic physique, but the answer seemed obvious. 'Come with us, Wendy. I can give you a few tips.'

'Will you?' As ever, Wendy, whom Leah's father had dubbed 'Kindness on Legs', was taken aback at being offered help.

'It's no trouble.'

'I bet your mum's brilliant at swimming.'

'We're both pretty good,' said Leah in a rare show of self-assuredness. 'You won't be short of advice.'

* * *

'You drive, Leah,' said her mother, passing her the keys. 'You need as much practice as you can get before your test.'

'When's that, Mrs Hinchcliffe?' Wendy had joined them promptly, living just across the road. Curiously, she always addressed Leah's mother formally whilst addressing her father as 'Freddy'.

'It's in just over a week's time. Can you manage in the back, Wendy? I'd let you ride in the front, but I have to sit beside Leah, as I'm the qualified driver.'

'I got into the giant's oven at Christmas,' Wendy reminded her. 'I think, if anything, the back seat of your car's a bit bigger.' She inserted herself into the Mini and arranged herself on the back seat. 'It's one of the disadvantages of being tall,' she said. 'It comes in handy when you have to reach things off the top shelf, but it catches you out at times like this.'

Mention of the top shelf seemed to trigger something in Sylvia's memory, because she said, 'I've heard things about that supermarket. I hope you girls are all right there.'

'It's all taken care of, Mum.' Leah still laughed at the memory. 'Bruce popped in and laid the law down. There won't be a problem.'

'*Bruce* did?'

'Yes, old Shaw was shaking in his shoes.'

'Well, I never.' She looked to the rear as Leah started the car and pulled out. 'As long as you're both safe.'

'There was one dodgy moment, but Wendy dealt with it. I suppose you could say she *handled* it.' By this time, both girls were laughing, so it was evident that neither of them felt at all threatened.

They continued on their way and, when they reached the swimming pool, Wendy said, 'I'm no expert, Leah, but I think you're a crackin' driver.'

'She's made a lot of progress,' Leah's mother told her, leading them into the building. 'Put your money away, Wendy, it's my treat.'

'Thanks, Mrs Hinchcliffe. That's really kind of you.'

'Not really. I might as well pay for all of us while I've got my purse out.' She paid for them all, and they went through to change.

First out and into the pool was Leah.

'You were quick off the mark,' said Wendy when Leah swam to the poolside where she was standing.

'I don't like to hang around in a swimsuit,' Leah confessed. 'These scars are taking too long to fade. I'm not sure they ever will.'

'Give them time,' said her mother, turning then to Wendy to say, 'Right, Wendy, show us what you can do, and then we'll tell you how to do it better.'

Wendy took the steps down into the shallow end, self-consciously launching herself forward into a busy, disorganised front crawl, which she maintained for half a length before reaching for the side. 'That's as far as I ever get,' she said, coughing and panting.

'You're working too hard,' Leah told her. 'Slow down your leg action and breathe more regularly. Try every three strokes.'

'You're making it too complicated, Leah,' her mother told her. 'Listen, Wendy. Can you do the breaststroke?'

'Sort of.'

'I'll go down the pool with you, and we'll sort out your breathing.

In, as you pull your arms back, and out, as you go forward with them. Let's go.' She swam beside Wendy, prompting her all the time until her breathing was regular and rhythmic. Together, they did a length and a half. 'There,' she said, 'you're not out of breath now, are you?'

'No.'

'Good girl. Let's do another length together.'

When they reached the shallow end, Wendy said, 'I never realised it was so easy.'

'Who taught you?'

Almost as if it were her fault, Wendy said, 'I went to swimming lessons with the school. They just got us swimming so that we could do a breadth, and then it all stopped.'

'That's a shame, because you could be a strong swimmer, with those long arms and legs. Come on, let's go back up to the deep end.' She swam beside Wendy, adjusting her pace to stay with her.

They reached the deep end in time to see Leah dive from the side, gracefully knifing into the water.

'Oh,' said Wendy, 'that was fantastic.'

'It's all that ballet training,' Sylvia told her.

'But who taught her to swim?'

'I did. Freddy lent a hand as well, but he's what I'd call an adequate swimmer. He's not bad, but he's not brilliant, either. We started taking Leah to the pool, though, when she was a toddler, and we did the same with Martin. He's quite good, not that he'd ever tell you that. Actually, he's not likely to tell you very much, he's so shy.'

'Yes, he's lovely.'

It wasn't the response Sylvia was expecting, but it was no less welcome, although she had no time to remark on it, because at that moment Leah surfaced beside them.

'All done?' she asked.

'We've mastered the breaststroke,' Sylvia told her. 'Wendy's rather taken with your diving.'

'Are you?' Leah swam to the steps and climbed out. 'We can do a bit of that, if you like.'

'I'll never be able to dive like you.'

'Be positive,' said Leah.

'I've never really done any diving.'

'Well, now's the time to start.'

Sylvia swam two lengths of front crawl, leaving Wendy to Leah's patient tutelage. Talk of Leah's early experiences in the pool had become an unwelcome reminder of her balletic ambitions. Perhaps it also served as a cautionary lesson about the dangers of investing too heavily in her daughter's aspirations.

* * *

Dried and dressed, they returned to the car. Leah took the driving seat again, but she seemed reluctant to drive away immediately.

'What's the matter, darling?' asked Sylvia. 'Have you forgotten how to drive?'

'Hardly. I'm just wondering if you're going to treat Wendy and me to another story.' For Wendy's benefit, she explained, 'Whenever we come out driving, my mum tells me a story about her time in the Wrens. It's completely exotic and unreal.'

'It was real enough for us, Leah,' said Sylvia, wondering what to tell them, although being in the pool carpark served as a convenient prompt. 'Actually, being in the pool just now reminded me of swimming in St Paul's Bay.'

'Where's that?' asked Wendy.

'Malta, where I was based in nineteen forty-five. We always went to St Paul's Bay to swim, mainly because the boys hadn't discovered it, and we could change on the beach without being under their gaze.'

Wendy rolled her eyes, knowing the problem, or one that was very similar to it.

'It was on the eighth of May. I know that, because we had a huge celebration, that evening, to mark VE Day.' In answer to Wendy's questioning look, she explained, 'It stood for "Victory in Europe Day". It was all terribly exciting for most of us, but not for me. I'd had a telegram from my mother, telling me that Freddy was alive and well, and that he was staying with them in Leyburn. It was wonderful news, because I'd heard nothing from him since February. I tried to get a draft home, but that was where the story suffered a hitch. There were too many of us with husbands and sweethearts coming home from Europe, so VE Day was a damp squib for me.'

'Oh.' Wendy was clearly sharing her misery.

'Well, with the morning's swim behind us, we all returned to barracks to get ready for the Victory Dance, but two things happened that night to make it even worse for me. One was hearing 'All the Things You Are'. It was our favourite song, the one we were looking forward to dancing to when we eventually met, and Freddy was more than a thousand miles away. The other thing was that something that had started as an irritation in my right ear was becoming painful. In fact, it was so awful that I reported sick the next morning. The doctor took one look at my ear and had me admitted to hospital. A tiny creature in St Paul's Bay had swum into my ear and caused an infection.'

'Couldn't they give you antibiotics?'

'No, penicillin was very new and reserved for wounded servicemen. Instead, they gave me a powder that was so thick I had to drink gallons of water with it, just to get it through my kidneys. That kept me on the move, I can tell you. I spent as much time in the heads as I did on the ward.'

'What are the heads?'

'The loo,' Leah translated, having met the word in the normal course of events at home.

'Eventually, the pain receded, and I began to feel normal again. Then a doctor came to examine me, and he found that my eardrum was perforated by the infection. I was as deaf as a post in my right ear, and I still am.' Wendy's mouth hung open with wonder and, thus encouraged, Sylvia continued. 'I thought nothing of it. Being young and optimistic, I took the line that I still had my left ear, so what was the problem? However, my divisional officer sent for me and explained that I couldn't carry on as a telegraphist with only one ear working. I would have to be discharged on medical grounds.'

'So you got to meet Freddy at your mum and dad's house?' The story was very real to Wendy, although Leah knew the basic facts.

'No, Wendy, I couldn't even speak to him on the phone. My train was delayed – that was quite common in wartime, what with doodlebugs and V Twos – and I reached home after he'd been drafted to an air station in Hampshire. I was sent to Whitehall Wireless Station in London until someone found enough sheets of carbon paper to type my discharge notice, while Freddy instructed air-gunners at Worthy

Down. Eventually, though, he got a leave pass and a rail warrant to London, and I managed to get some time off.' Sniffs from either side made her search her bag to find tissues for them both. 'Freddy and I met in the afternoon in Trafalgar Square, for the first time, and then again the next evening at the Savoy Hotel.' Seeing Wendy's eyes open wide, she explained, 'No, it wasn't a naughty get-together. We had a drink in the American Bar and then went to a French restaurant for dinner. After that, we went on to a night-club, where we danced to… guess what?'

' "All the Things You Are"?'

'Spot on, and in a short time, I was discharged. It was longer for Freddy, but we came back to Leyburn, to begin with. We got our own place later, the house where we live now.' Looking at them both, she said, 'It's as well we've all got our swimsuits with us. This car's going to be full of tears in a minute.'

16

A TESTING TIME

It was the day of Leah's driving test. Mr Dawson was going to give her a lesson immediately before it to get her 'on her toes', a familiar enough concept for a ballet student, but she had the whole of the morning to suffer the kind of nervousness she thought she'd left behind her, along with her *pointe* shoes. There was a distraction, however, during the course of the morning, when her mum returned from a walk with Nina.

'I'm sure she's limping on that forepaw,' she said, 'and now she's licking it. I'd better get a magnifying glass from the darkroom.' Both of Leah's parents had found it necessary of late to wear glasses for close work. Her dad had taken it particularly to heart, having previously had what he called, 'air-gunners' eyesight'.

'Don't worry about that, Mum,' said Leah, realising that any reference to the frailty of old age might be ill-considered at that moment. 'Let me have a look.' To avoid kneeling, she lifted Nina on to the sofa. 'Which paw is it?'

'The... off-side one.' Her mum still struggled with 'left' and 'right' although, curiously, near-side and off-side presented no difficulty.

'Give me your paw, Nina,' she said. 'You can have it back in a minute.' Crouching low, she examined the heavily-licked paw. 'There's a hole between two of her toe-things,' she said.

'Claws, darling.' It sounded strange, coming from her mum, who usually spoke about dogs as if they were human.

'All right, Mum, but there's a hole between two of them.'

112

'What's the matter?' asked her dad, coming out of the darkroom.

'Nina's got a hole between two of her claws,' Leah told him. 'She won't leave it alone.'

'I'll get a magnifying glass.' He went to the darkroom whilst Leah rolled her eyes.

'He just wants to be sure,' said her mum, equally impatient, but defensive as usual.

He returned with a large magnifying glass. As he approached Nina, she stiffened, no doubt at the sight of her master, greatly enlarged by the lens, and barked in alarm. Leah tried to control her laughter, but had to give way.

'What's the matter with her?' asked her dad.

'She's just seen the biggest air-gunner that ever was, staring at her through his sights,' she said, still shaking. 'It must have been a terrifying experience. Will you take my word for it that there's a hole between the middle two claws on her right paw?'

'All right. She'd better go to the vet, but I've got a session with a kestrel at ten-thirty.'

'I'll take her,' said Leah's mum. 'Leah can come for the ride. It'll take her mind off her test.'

It was a good idea. In any case, Leah was anxious about Nina's paw, and she would hear the diagnosis all the sooner by accompanying her mum to the vet's surgery, so having made a conveniently early appointment, they set off together.

'Young Mr Helliwell's a different kind of vet from his father,' said her mum as she drove there. 'The old man didn't usually have much time for small animals. He only looked after your grandad's dogs because he was a client. After that, of course, he took Thea on to his books.'

'Grandad has a way of getting favours out of people,' observed Leah.

'He has a network all of his own,' agreed her mum, although not without pride.

They parked outside the surgery, where Leah slipped the check chain over Nina's head and coaxed her inside with some difficulty.

'It's not one of her favourite places,' said her mum, 'but she'll just have to be grown-up about it and realise that life can't always be fun and frolics.'

Leah wondered, as she often did, about her mother's anthropomorphic approach to dog ownership, but her musing was cut short when the receptionist asked them to take a seat between an angry-looking Persian cat that glowered at Nina through the bars of its basket, and a corgi that bared a set of discoloured teeth at her. Hoisting Nina on to her knee, Leah said quietly, but so that her mum could hear her, 'Aren't you glad, now, that we brush your toothy-pegs every night before bye-byes?'

A woman carrying a budgie in its cage left the consulting room and went to the desk to pay her bill. Meanwhile, Mr Helliwell came to the door to summon the ill-natured corgi and its mistress.

In time, the corgi was booked in for dental work, and the Persian cat left with a mysterious prescription. Leah really didn't want to know the details. In any case, the cat didn't encourage sympathy.

'Nina,' called Mr Helliwell, 'would you like to come through?' Seeing the two generations, he said, 'Leah, how nice to see you. How's your knee bearing up?'

'It's getting better all the time, thank you, Mr Helliwell. I'd let you examine it, but I'm not carried away with those dog biscuits you hand out afterwards.'

'Leah will have her little joke,' said her mum. 'It's Nina who's in the wars. There's something the matter with her front off-side paw.'

'There's a hole,' Leah explained, being the one who'd found it, 'between the middle two claws.'

'Ah,' said Mr Helliwell, who needed no magnifying glass. 'My money is on an arrowhead seed.' He examined it more closely. 'I can't see it at this stage, so I think I'll have to locate it and remove it under anaesthetic.'

'Be brave, Nina,' said Leah. 'I've had it twice, recently, and it's not as bad as some people make it out to be.' As she spoke, she crossed her fingers behind Nina's back.

'She had the spaying operation,' her mum reminded her.

'Yes,' said Mr Helliwell, 'she knows the routine. I can do it tomorrow. Make sure she gets no dinner tonight and nothing in the morning, and bring her in at eight-fifteen.' He gave Nina a dog biscuit, which she devoured enthusiastically.

They thanked the vet and returned to the car. After her earlier light-

114

heartedness, Leah was now feeling apprehensive. Her mum was quick to notice her change of mood.

'She'll be fine, Leah. It sounds like a very minor operation.'

'I hope so.'

'You know, it was Mr Helliwell's father who found Thea for us. Your dad was determined to get an Aberdeen terrier, and the nearest breeder was miles away, in Newcastle, I believe. It was a consideration in those days, with petrol rationing.'

'How did he find her?' Leah knew her mum was trying to distract her from worrying about Nina's operation, and simply knowing that gave her some comfort.

'Thea belonged to an old man with a weak heart, who couldn't look after her any longer. As well as that, he'd just moved in with his daughter and her husband, a horrible man who resented having to share his home with either of them.'

'How can anybody be so horrible?'

'Such people exist,' her mother assured her. 'I'll never forget that poor old man. He was so upset at having to let Thea go. It was only the second time I'd seen a man cry, and it was awful.'

Leah couldn't help asking, 'The second time?'

'Yes, the first was during the war, when I was based in Dover. I'd just delivered something to the Wrens in the Ferry Port Signal Station, when an RAF air-sea rescue launch came in. They'd picked up a German airman, and they left him on the jetty until an ambulance came. I had to pass him on my way back to the WT Office. His shoulder was bandaged and his arm was in a sling. He was in awful pain, and the funny thing was that I felt sorry for him. The Germans were holding your dad prisoner and they'd killed the boyfriend I had before him, but in spite of those things, I couldn't help feeling sorry for the poor man.'

'I didn't know you'd had another boyfriend, Mum.'

'I was only human, Leah, although it was the most innocent thing.' Now remembering the events clearly, she said, 'It was writing to your dad that helped me get over losing James.' She tore her thoughts away from that and went on with her story. 'When the German airman saw me, he asked me for a cigarette. I smoked in those days – I suppose everyone did – and I lit one for him and gave it to him. He said, "*Danke schön, gnädige Fräulein*", and a tear rolled down his cheek.'

'Oh, that's really sweet, Mum. I mean, smoking's foul, but it was a kind thing to do.'

'It stopped me smoking, as well.'

'How did it do that?'

Laughing at the memory, she said, 'A horrible RAF flight sergeant saw me talking to the German, and he was really vicious about it. If I remember rightly, he called me a stupid bitch.'

'Surely not.' Leah was clearly horrified. 'I wouldn't have stood for that.'

Her mother laughed. 'It was different in those days, Leah. You just said, "Yes, sir, no, sir, three bags full, sir", and got on with your duties. As a matter of fact, a really nice RAF officer, the skipper of the launch, sent him about his duties. We had a nice chat, and then the ambulance came to take the prisoner away. Still, it gave me a chance to practise my German, and it made me stop smoking. I just couldn't bear the idea of having black teeth like the flight sergeant had who shouted at me.'

'Do you know something, Mum?' Leah had been thinking about it. 'You know how they say that we're all put on earth for a purpose? Well, I reckon yours is to make people feel better.'

Her mum gave her a broad smile. 'Do you really think so, darling? Your dad said something like that, more than once. In fact, he even wrote a song about it.'

* * *

After an uneventful lesson, Mr Dawson directed Leah to the Test Centre and left her for a moment while he reported her arrival to the examiners. After a few minutes, a large man with a bushy moustache and thick-rimmed glasses opened the car door and got in. He carried a clipboard. 'Leah Hinchcliffe?' he asked.

'Yes.'

'Can you read the number plate on the Mini across there?' He pointed with his pen towards the end of the carpark, where two cars stood, conveniently parked.

'Yes.'

'Well, do so, please.'

'All right. RYG 365C.'

'Good. I actually meant the one that's nearer, but that's fine.' He ticked a box and said, 'I want you to join the main road outside and turn left when you can.'

That sounded easy enough, so Leah started the car, checked her driving mirror and drove off.

The examiner asked her to perform all the tasks she'd practised with Mr Dawson and her mother, including reverse parking, which went better than it ever had, and then he directed her back to the Test Centre.

'I want you to pull up outside the entrance, and then I'm going to ask you some questions about the Highway Code.'

'Right.' She thought it best to sound keen.

'What is the sequence of the traffic lights?'

She hadn't been expecting that one, but she concentrated and said, 'Red, red and amber, green, amber, red.'

'Good. When should you never overtake?'

'Where the road narrows, on a hump-back bridge, when there's something coming the other way… oh, heck… when to do so causes other vehicles to swerve or lose speed, when it means crossing a double white line… oh, bugger.' Now she was embarrassed. She'd no idea why she'd said that. It was a word her dad sometimes used when he thought no one could hear him. 'When it means exceeding the speed limit… oh, crumbs.'

'That's all right. What is a slip road?'

'I don't know. I think it's how you get off a motorway.'

'In that case, what is an approach road?'

'Oh, heck. I think it's one that takes you on to a motorway.' Miserably, she explained, 'I didn't bone up on motorways. I couldn't see the point when learner drivers aren't allowed on them anyway. I suppose that was daft, really.'

He signed something on his clipboard. 'You can forget your nerves, now,' he said.

'It wasn't just that.' Convinced that she'd failed because of the motorway questions, she saw no reason for holding back. 'Our dog has a problem, and she's having an operation tomorrow. I'm tensed up about that. I don't suppose it helped.'

'Well,' he said, passing her a pink note, 'when she comes round from the anaesthetic, you'll be able to tell her that you passed your driving test. Well done.'

* * *

The cosy glow of success was dimmed somewhat by the forthcoming visit to the vet, although Leah's parents tried their hardest to allay her fears. Her own recent experiences, however, had coloured her attitude towards operations generally, and Nina's enforced fast was an added irritation, especially when the patient dropped a less than subtle hint by carrying her empty food bowl into the sitting room.

Characteristically, Martin was unfazed. As he saw it, it was a common and straightforward operation, and animals were subjected to general anaesthesia all the time. It was unfortunate that Nina was hungry, and it was only his father's intervention that prevented him explaining to Leah the danger of feeding an animal before an operation.

Leah had to work at the supermarket the next morning, which was a welcome distraction, but she insisted on going to the surgery with her mum to collect Nina in the afternoon.

'As I suspected,' said Mr Helliwell, 'it was an arrowhead seed, but we got it out, and she'll be as right as rain. Bring her back in a week, and we'll have a look at it and re-dress it.'

They thanked him and led the limping patient to the reception desk. Her limp wasn't caused by pain or discomfort, but simply by the well-padded and securely-tied dressing.

Sylvia attended to the bill, and they took Nina out to the car.

'Will you stop at the supermarket on the way home?' she asked.

'What are you short of, Mum?'

'Sandwich bags.'

That was unexpected. 'Are we going on a picnic?'

'No, they're to keep Nina's dressing clean and dry when she goes out for walks.' As well as making people feel better, she was reassuringly practical. Even so, it would be nice for her to take a rest for a week and enjoy Yoredale Players' production of *My Fair Lady*. After that, the next excitement was Bailey's birthday.

17

FORWARD PLANNING AND DEEP THOUGHTS

Bailey's birthday celebration had to take place at the County Hotel in Northallerton because nowhere else in the neighbourhood was appropriate to his larger-than-life persona. It was also capable of accommodating his guests, who included, as well as the Hinchcliffe family, Walter and Jessie, whom Bailey counted among his friends. His association with Walter had begun before Leah was born, when a jealous party had tried to separate Elaine and him, and Walter's advice as a Justice of the Peace had been crucial in countering that threat.

'Bailey didn't know his date of birth until he applied to join the Territorials,' Freddy told his family on the way. 'He'd always invented a convenient date until then, but they insisted on documentary evidence, so he had to apply to Somerset House for a copy of his birth certificate.'

'Oh, heck,' said Leah. 'Did it cause problems?'

'No, he was eighteen, old enough to join up. Basically, it told him nothing he didn't already know. The fact that he'd never had a father was old news, and he didn't care, anyway. He was always a pragmatic soul.'

Martin asked, 'What does that mean, Dad?'

'Pragmatic? It means that he's practical rather than idealistic.'

'And a free spirit,' added Sylvia.

Possibly suspecting that his hero might attract some criticism, however gentle, Martin said firmly, 'He's very kind.'

'He is,' agreed Freddy, 'to a fault.'

'What was he like when you met him?' asked Leah. 'It was such a long time ago, and people change, don't they?'

'It was only twenty-five years ago, although I suppose that seems a long time to you. He was flamboyant even then, but never in a way that caused anyone to take exception.'

'He always says you saved his life on the Long March,' Sylvia reminded him. With Leah driving, she occupied the back seat with Martin.

'It wasn't just me. There was another chap, an American called Randy, would you believe? In his case, it was short for "Andrew", and he turned out to be a good hand. You see, Bailey had been there since nineteen-forty, and four years on cabbage water and black bread is no preparation for a long trek, even in favourable weather. All Randy and I did was keep Bailey moving. We never let him give up, because that would have been the end for him. I persuaded a German guard to give him extra rations, but that was all.'

Martin asked, 'How did you do that, Dad?'

'I just spoke German better than most of the other prisoners.'

Sylvia turned to Martin and put a finger to her lips to dissuade him from pursuing the question further.

'When we get to the big roundabout,' said Leah, 'you will tell me which way to go, Dad, won't you?'

'You know the way to the County Hotel, surely.'

'I know it basically, but I hate that roundabout.'

'I'll tell you which way to go, Leah,' said her mother. 'Your dad's brilliant at directions, but only until he gets lost.'

'Oh, ha, ha, ha.'

'Be honest, darling. Finding your way isn't your best thing.'

'Well, it's not surprising.'

'No,' said Leah, 'it's not. It probably comes of being an air-gunner, facing aft and seeing everything in hindsight. You never knew where you were until after you'd been there.'

'Now Leah,' said her mother, 'don't tease your dad.'

'No,' he said, 'that's your mum's preserve.'

'When it's safe,' said her mum, 'move to the crown of the road.'

'Thanks, Mum.' Leah completed the manoeuvre and drove up to the roundabout.

'When you can, take the middle lane. Let this Land Rover on your near side come through, and begin to move over to the lane he was in, then the outside one, and then take the exit.'

'Thanks, Mum.'

'The County Hotel's about half a mile on your left.'

'Got it.'

'It's a short half-mile,' said her dad.

'I said, "*About* half a mile". I wasn't being exact. There it is, Leah, with the blue, neon sign. The entrance to the carpark is just before it.'

'Thanks, Mum.'

'I don't know what's so difficult about remembering that,' said Martin.

'Well,' said his mum, 'as soon as you get your licence, you can do the driving.'

'No problem.'

Leah pulled into the carpark and reversed into a convenient space.

'Well done, darling,' said her mum.

'That was my best bit of reverse parking since my driving test,' she announced.

'I don't see what's so diff—'

'That's enough, Martin,' said his mum. Let's go in and be sociable.'

They made their way to the main entrance, where they were directed to the lounge. There they found Bailey, Elaine and Janice. Walter and Jessie were still to arrive. Bailey welcomed everyone in his usual, ebullient way.

'Hello, folks. Come and join us. Tell me what you're all drinking.' He and Freddy went to the bar to get the drinks. As usual, Janice wanted to help, but Bailey persuaded her that her responsibility was to keep watch for Walter and Jessie, who would be arriving very shortly.

Their arrival occurred within minutes, and it took most of Elaine's considerable skill to prevent Janice from informing everyone in the hotel of the fact.

With everyone gathered, Bailey took them to their table, seating them according to his plan. 'You know, folks,' he said as he joined them, 'After the excitement of *My Fair Lady*, which really takes some following, I find it a little quiet in this place nowadays. Don't you, Freddy?'

'It's certainly subdued,' agreed Freddy, 'particularly after *My Fair Lady*.'

All but Sylvia and Elaine looked at them curiously, so Bailey

121

expanded on his observation. 'Freddy, Sylvia, Elaine and I remember the Grand Opening of this Hotel in nineteen-fifty, which featured the Dalesmen. It was a grand night, as I recall.'

'It would be,' said Leah. 'Like everything else that caused excitement, it happened before I was born.'

'Now, you know that's not the case, Leah,' he said. 'There was great excitement when you were born, and there's been plenty since then.'

The waiter came to attend to their order, so the argument ended there, at least for the time being.

'Have you something in mind, Bailey?' asked Walter innocently. 'Something that might liven things up at the County Hotel?'

'Well, you know, I've thought from time to time that what the place really needs is a regular event, such as a dinner and dance.'

'All right,' said Freddy, 'I can take a hint. I'll write to the management and put it to them.'

'You may just find,' said Elaine, inclining her head knowingly towards her husband, 'that the management will be in touch with you.'

'It was a chance conversation that took place when I made this booking,' said Bailey. 'All I did was make the suggestion.'

'And, like so many of your suggestions, Bailey,' said Freddy, 'it was a good one. Thank you for that.'

'My dear old soul, it was my pleasure. It'll be like old times.' With a quick look in Leah's direction, he added, 'Plus a few more that have taken place since Leah was born.'

'You're priceless, Bailey,' said Leah.

'Was I borned after Leah was?' demanded Janice.

'Yes, you were,' Bailey assured her. 'You were another excitement in Leah's lifetime.'

'I'm beginning to feel guilty, now,' said Leah.

'You mustn't, dearest one. Not tonight, anyway.'

'Was Martin another excitement in Leah's icetime?'

'Yes, Janice, as well as in her lifetime.'

'Somebody, change the subject, please,' begged Leah.

'Yes,' said Walter obligingly, 'how are your studies progressing, Leah?'

'I'm fairly confident, Grandad. 'I've another year, yet, before the exams.'

'As a matter of fact,' said Freddy, 'I'm glad you brought that up, Walter. I've helped out so far with English, German and French, but I am working rather to my limit, unlike Miles Stapleton.'

'Where does he come into it, Freddy?' asked Jessie, who had been trying to follow the conversation.

'He's been tutoring Leah in History, Jessie.'

'And he's brilliant,' said Leah.

Walter emerged, apparently from deep cogitation to say, 'I've heard good reports of the local technical college. I don't know about the subjects Leah's interested in, but it's a thought.'

It must have sounded to Leah like a step into an abyss, because she asked, 'Would I have to go full-time?'

Freddy was quick to reassure her. 'I shouldn't think so for one minute,' he said.

'Our apprentices go there on a part-time basis, day and evening,' said Bailey. 'That's motor engineering, of course, but I don't see why it shouldn't apply to Leah as well.'

'There's also the girls' grammar school,' Sylvia reminded her.

Leah groaned. 'I don't want to go there,' she said. 'It's for kids.'

'You know,' said Bailey, intervening before anyone had a chance to challenge her, 'Leah's probably right. She's been living in a grown-up world since the accident, and I think she's probably outgrown a great many girls of her own age, at least in terms of maturity.'

'What are you talking about?' demanded Janice. 'Leah is a grown-up. She teached me to do reading and knitting.'

'Yes, she is, darling,' said Bailey. 'Well said.' Turning to Martin, he said, 'You're very mature as well, Martin.'

'Right.' Martin seemed unsure.

'What does Brian say, Martin?' asked Freddy.

'Thank you, Bailey.'

'Anytime, old chap.' He broke off to taste the wine, directing the waiter towards Freddy and Walter, who'd ordered their own. 'That's excellent,' he said. 'Thank you.'

Leah looked at her watch and, suddenly fearful, she said, 'Nina's been on her own quite a long time.'

'She'll be all right,' Sylvia told her. 'I arranged for Bruce to call in and give her a walk.'

'And I asked him to do the same for Adams,' said Walter. 'It looks like being a lucrative evening for him, one way and another. I must say, it's good that he hasn't taken his parents' lead and turned his back on the world of pets. He's the second Doctor Reynolds now, you know.'

'As well as a member of the Mothercare Karate Squad,' said Leah, trying not to laugh.

'What was that, Leah?' asked Jessie.

'It was just something it said on his T shirt, Grandma. We had a laugh about it at the time.'

'As long as you weren't belittling his achievement.'

'I wouldn't do that. I'm very fond of him, and I think he's going to be an excellent doctor.' She added, 'So does Wendy.'

'Who is Wendy?'

'She played Jack Trott in the pantomime,' Walter reminded her, 'a very nice girl indeed.'

'Well, I think Bruce will have little time to spare for girls in the coming months.'

'Just as long as he can find time for dogs,' said Sylvia.

'What was that, Sylvia?'

'I said, it's good of him to look in on the dogs.'

'Yes, it is.'

'Well, souls,' said Bailey, 'here it is.' He was referring to the first course, which was just arriving.

* * *

On the way home, Leah said, 'I won't have to go to the grammar school, will I?'

'No,' said her father. 'Your mum was only floating it as an idea. I must say I agree with Bailey about that. You probably are more mature than most seventeen-year-olds.'

'Agreed,' said Sylvia, 'it was only an idea. I think the other idea, the technical college, is more promising.'

'Why are they called technical colleges when they teach things like English and the other things Leah's doing?' asked Martin. 'They're not technical subjects.'

'They were set up originally to teach apprentices their trades,' said Freddy, 'and they branched out into other subjects.'

'If it comes to that,' said Leah, 'how did grammar schools get their name? They teach lots more besides grammar.'

'What a brain-teaser for a late night,' said Sylvia. 'Do you know the answer, Freddy?'

'Funnily enough, I do. The first grammar schools were created so that children of humble origin could be taught Latin grammar. I think it must have been considered more important that Latin prose or verse.'

'Thank goodness that's all in the past,' said Leah.

'*Quod praeteritum est, factum est.* What's past is done,' agreed her parent.

'Honestly, Freddy,' said Sylvia, 'that's far too deep a thought, so late at night.'

'I can't help it, SP. It comes of being an air-gunner, facing aft and thinking deep, solitary thoughts.'

'How could we have known that?' asked Leah.

18

A MODEL CITIZEN

In her determination to strengthen her knee, Leah was a regular visitor to the public swimming pool, and with Wendy as her companion. It pleased Leah to be able to help Wendy in what seemed to be one of the few activities in which she lacked her usual, easy confidence, and her pupil was naturally grateful for her tuition.

They were returning from the pool when she asked, 'How old were you when your mum taught you to swim?'

Leah had to think about that. Swimming had been a part of her life for as long as she could remember. 'I think I must have been about two, but I really can't remember the first time.'

'I think that's amazing. I mean, you couldn't have been walking all that long.'

'A year or so, I suppose, but it's just as I told you this morning, swimming is a natural thing to do.'

'Yes, I was really chuffed when I found I could float. I'd always thought I had to swim as soon as I got into the water, or I'd drown.'

It was difficult for Leah to comment, knowing Wendy's background as she did. Even if her mother had been able to teach her to swim, all her efforts had gone into supporting them both financially, and time was therefore precious.

As it happened, she had no need to say anything, because just then, it became clear that an incident of some kind had occurred ahead of them. She slowed down and saw, between two parked vehicles, someone lying in the road.

'There's been an accident,' said Wendy, somewhat unnecessarily. Leah was already out of the car.

Someone, presumably the driver involved, was protesting his innocence. 'She just stepped out,' he said. 'I'd no warning.'

Someone else said, 'Aye, well, you can sort that out later, but this woman needs help.'

Leah asked, 'Has anybody phoned for an ambulance?' The bystanders looked from one to another, but no one answered. 'Does anybody know where the nearest phone box is?'

'There's one just round t' corner,' said one of them.

'Good,' said Leah, kneeling beside the casualty, an elderly woman. 'Will you go and dial nine-nine-nine?'

'All right.' The woman hurried off on her errand, while another said, 'Would she be more comfortable with something under her head, a coat or something?'

'No,' said Leah, 'she mustn't be moved until the ambulance arrives. The old woman was whimpering softly. 'She's in shock. Wendy, will you get the rug out of the car, please?' Lowering her head, she asked, 'Can you hear me?'

'Yes.' It was little more than a whimper.

'What's your name?'

'Edna... Parker.'

One of the onlookers said, 'If she's in shock, she needs hot, sweet tea.'

'No, she doesn't,' said Leah, taking the car rug from Wendy and using it to cover the injured woman.

'The ambulance is on its way,' reported the woman who'd gone to make the call. 'Police an' all, apparently.'

'Oh, hell.' The driver was almost hysterical.

'Wendy,' said Leah, 'will you have a word with the driver and try to calm him down?'

'Okay.' Wendy pushed her way through to the man and spoke to him. Leah heard her say, 'Now, listen. Everything's going to be all right, so just be patient and wait for the police. You can tell your story to them.'

Leah bent over the old woman and said, 'Mrs Parker, listen to me. You're going to be all right. The ambulance is on its way, and you'll be fine, but you mustn't go to sleep. Tell me where you live.'

Before she could answer, one of the small crowd that had gathered asked, 'Who does this lass think she is, givin' orders? What the old girl needs most of all is hot tea with loads of sugar.'

'I'll tell you who she is,' said Wendy, leaving the driver for a moment, 'she's somebody who knows what she's doing. It's not long since she was in an accident like this, so she's best placed to deal with it.'

'Come on, Mrs Parker,' said Leah, 'talk to me. Tell me where you live.'

'Thirty-four, Chestnut Grove.... What's your name, love?'

'It's Leah. You're doing well, Mrs Parker. Keep it up. Have you been shopping?'

'Yes, I... think so.' Her shopping bag lay with various items in the road.

'Right, so you live in Chestnut Grove and you've just been shopping. Have you any family? Come on, keep talking to me.'

'Leave her alone,' said one of the women nearby. 'She's not in a fit state to answer questions.'

'She must stay conscious,' said Leah. 'Come on, Mrs Parker, tell me about your family.'

'My daughter....' She seemed to lose the thread.

'Yes, tell me about your daughter.'

'She lives in... Northallerton.'

'Leave the poor old woman alone,' insisted the busybody. 'Can't you see she's in a poor way, an' what do you know about it, anyway? You're not old enough to be out of school.'

'She knows what she's doing,' said Wendy, 'an' you're old enough to know better.'

'You cheeky young minx.' Her attack was interrupted by the urgent clamour of a police car siren followed by another, and Leah felt relieved, although she would be happier still when the ambulance arrived.

A policeman came to the place where the old woman lay and asked, 'What's happened here, love?' He had two silver badges on his shoulder, and Leah imagined he must be an inspector or something important.

'This woman's been hit by a car,' Leah told him. 'She's going into shock, and I'm trying to keep her conscious and make sure nobody moves her. These people keep wanting to give her tea and things.'

'You're quite right, love.' Standing up, he said, 'I'd like anybody who saw the accident to stay behind. Also, who made the nine-nine-nine call?'

'I did,' said the woman.

'I'll need your name and address, too. Where's the involved driver?'

'He's here,' said Wendy. 'It wasn't his fault.'

'Well, we'll sort that out in a minute.'

'It isn't the only thing that needs sorting out,' said one of the crowd. 'I don't know who Little Miss Bossy-Boots thinks she is, givin' orders. We were only tryin' to help.'

'She was quite right,' said the inspector. 'It would have done the injured person no good at all to be moved or given food or drink. Now, we'd like to see the driver of the involved car, anybody who saw the accident, the person who made the nine-nine-nine call, and I have to ask everybody else to leave the scene, please.' Recognising an omission, he said hurriedly, 'Except for this young lady, who seems to have done an excellent—' he broke off at the sound of an ambulance siren. Crouching again beside the casualty, he asked, 'Will you give me your name and address, love?'

The only response was a whimper, so Leah said, 'She really is going into shock, but I can do that. She's Edna Parker, and her address is thirty-four, Chestnut Grove. I imagine that's nearby. She has a daughter who lives in Northallerton, but I didn't get her name and address.'

'Do you know her?'

'No, I only found that out when I was trying to get her to talk to me, to keep her conscious.' She looked around anxiously and saw that the ambulance staff were about to join them.

One of them asked, 'Is there just the one injured person?'

'Yes,' said the inspector. 'This young lady tells me that Mrs Parker's in shock. She's made an excellent job of looking after her and persuading others not to move her or give her food or drink.'

'Well done,' said the ambulance man. 'You can relax now and leave her to us.'

'Thank you.' Leah unwound herself carefully and raised herself on her good leg.

The policeman asked, 'Are you all right, love?'

'Yes, thanks. I was in the same position as Mrs Parker last year. I've had two operations since then.'

'Oh well, no wonder you know the drill.'

'It wasn't that. I learned first-aid at ballet school. Dancers are always injuring themselves, so it's important.'

'Whose rug is this?' asked one of the ambulance men.

'It's my mum's,' said Leah. 'It's her car I'm driving.'

'The Mini behind the involved vehicle?' asked the inspector.

'Yes.'

'Okay, I'll tell the officers who are controlling traffic to let you out. What's your name?'

'Leah Hinchcliffe.'

'Well done, Leah,' he said, shaking her hand. 'You're a model citizen.'

'Thank you.' She took her leave of him and re-joined Wendy in the car. She backed away from the involved car and waited to be beckoned forward.

'I wonder where the driver's got to,' said Wendy, noticing his absence.

'I expect they'll have taken him somewhere.'

As the officer signalled to her, and she moved forward, she saw the driver seated beside another officer in a police car. 'I hope he's not in trouble,' she said. 'It's bad enough just being involved in an accident, without having to go to court as well.'

On the way home, Wendy said, 'You were really good back there, Leah.'

'Was I?'

'Yes, taking charge and giving everybody jobs to do.'

' "Little Miss Bossy-Boots"?'

'That woman didn't know what she was talking about. I thought you were....'

Leah was in suspense. 'What did you think I was, Wendy?'

'It'll come to me in a minute. Don't worry, it's good.'

Leah laughed. 'I never thought it would be anything else.'

They were almost home when Wendy remembered the word. 'Magnificent! That's what you were.'

'It's good of you to say so, Wendy.'

* * *

Leah was back on shift at the supermarket that afternoon, which was something of an anticlimax for her, but she didn't mind that. She did wonder, from time to time, how Mrs Parker was faring, and if the driver had managed to persuade the police of his innocence, but she was relieved now the incident was over, at least, as far as she was concerned. Meanwhile, the shoppers arriving at her till provided a ready distraction from all other considerations.

The line of shoppers had actually dwindled by the end of her shift, until one man, who appeared to have been hanging back until everyone else was gone, finally addressed her. He wore a clerical collar with an everyday suit, and his expression was one of consternation. He carried only a tube of toothpaste and a box of teabags. Leah checked them out. 'That's five shillings and threepence,' she said.

The cleric counted two half-crowns and a one shilling piece out of a folding purse and handed them to her. 'That's six shillings,' he told her, presumably unsure whether or not she was capable of counting the money unaided.

'Thank you, Reverend. That's ninepence change.'

'Thank you, but don't call me "Reverend". I'm a pastor.'

'I'm sorry... Pastor. I didn't realise that.' She couldn't imagine anyone less like the amiable Reverend Miles Stapleton, and she fancied a pastor must be a stern and unforgiving equivalent.

'I want to speak to somebody in authority,' he told her in a tone that didn't bode well for that person, when he finally spoke to him.

'I think you'll find Mr Shaw in his office, Pastor.'

'The manager? Huh! I've already spoken to him, and I got no sense out of him at all.'

That didn't surprise Leah at all, but she had little more to offer. 'I'm afraid Mr Shaw is the most senior person in the store, Pastor.'

'In that case, who can I speak to at head office?'

'I'm afraid I've no idea. I don't know anyone at head office.' Her application had gone to the Personnel Manager, but that didn't seem appropriate in this case. 'Perhaps if you could tell me what you want to discuss, I might be able to help.' She doubted it, but she was at least trying to be helpful. Unfortunately, her suggestion seemed to unsettle him even more.

'I don't think I can discuss it with a... female, especially a young female such as yourself.'

'That's your privilege, Pastor.' She'd heard her father say that to difficult customers, and it sounded right for the occasion.

After a further moment's indecision, he said, 'I don't suppose you've read any of the books on sale in here.'

'No, they're not the kind of thing I read, as a rule.' They were the kind of books people called 'airport reads', mainly blockbusters by female American authors, and Leah had quite enough to read in preparation for 'A' levels.

'I'm relieved to hear it. They shouldn't be available to girls of your age.' He reflected on that judgement and decided to amend it. 'They shouldn't even be in print!'

Leah wouldn't normally consider reading forbidden literature; her conversation with her father about *The Lady of the Camellias* had been largely in fun, but the pastor's remonstrations were beginning to whet her appetite. Maybe she would try one of them, if only for the sake of curiosity.

'They are lewd and enticing,' he told her angrily, as if it were her fault.

'I suppose there's one thing you could do, Pastor.' She was surprised he hadn't thought of it already.

'What's that?'

'You could warn your congregation about it on Sunday, tell them about the dangers and that sort of thing.'

He stared at her for a moment, inspired and charged up. 'Yes, I shall! I'll preach about it! Thank you for that suggestion. You've been a lot more helpful than that so-called manager.'

Again, Leah was less than surprised, but shoppers were beginning to form a queue behind the offended pastor. One of them, who'd been waiting with ill-concealed impatience, said, 'When you've quite finished, some of us would like to get served. We don't all get manna from Heaven, you know. The likes of us have to take it off the shelves and pay for it.'

* * *

Leah told the story at dinner, to her mother's amusement. Her father was similarly amused, but a little concerned that his daughter had been engaged in conversation about matters of which she had no knowledge. Eventually, though, he said, 'It sounds as if you dealt with the situation very capably, Leah. In fact, I'd say you were downright diplomatic.'

It wasn't the first compliment Leah had received that day, as she went on to tell both parents. 'It's not surprising, you know. According to one policeman, I'm a model citizen.'

19

WISE COUNSEL

Twelve months had elapsed since Leah learned of her 'O' level results, and much had happened since then, but she still remembered the excitement and the feeling of achievement that followed it. Consequently, she was concerned when Wendy turned up at the supermarket looking unlike her usual, cheerful self.

'Whassup, Wendy?' To her father's annoyance, Leah had adopted much of the vernacular, which she used occasionally, when it suited her.

'I got my CSE's today.'

'Yes?'

'Five grade twos and a grade three.' She delivered the news as if it were a confession.

'That's good, isn't it?'

'Not good enough.' She waited for Mr Shaw to set up her till and Leah's. When he'd gone, she said, 'I was hoping for an 'O' level or two. I suppose it was just too much to hope for.'

'It's not the end of the world,' Leah told her. 'There must be lots of people who couldn't manage a grade three or a grade four.' She knew very little about the CSE, but it stood to reason that there'd be many who were less able than Wendy.

'I know, but it's still not what I wanted. The Rector will be disappointed, too, after all the help he gave me with the English.'

'Oh no, he won't.' Leah hadn't known him as long as Wendy, but she was quite certain of that.

'Are you two going to talk all day?' demanded Mr Shaw.

'Just find us some customers,' Leah told him, 'and we'll serve them.'

'Aye, well, see that you do.' He always insisted on having the last word, but Leah was learning quickly how best to handle him. Even so, she was about to learn more, and from an unexpected quarter.

During the course of the morning, her mother called in for a few things, as she preferred to do her main shopping at the larger supermarket in Northallerton, and naturally went straight to Leah's till. Wendy was serving a customer at the time, but she waved in recognition.

'Mum,' asked Leah as she checked out her purchases, 'could Wendy come to dinner this week?'

'She can come tonight, if she likes. We're having fish pie, and there's plenty to go round.'

'Thanks. Will you ask her, and then she won't think I'm taking pity on her?'

'Of course I will.' She bent her head to ask, 'What's the problem?'

Keeping her voice low, Leah explained, 'She's unhappy about her CSE grades.'

'Don't worry, we'll soon have her smiling again.'

'That's what I thought, Mum.' As Leah served her next customer, she heard her mother ask, 'Would you like to come and have dinner with us tonight, Wendy?'

'Oh yes, please. The only thing is my mum needs to know.'

'I'll tell her. Don't you worry.'

'What's the hold-up, Wendy? You've got customers waiting.' Mr Shaw surprised no one, being his obnoxious self.

'I'm a customer, and she was helping me,' said Leah's mother. 'What's the matter with you, man? These girls are working as hard as ever they can, and you still can't leave them alone.'

'All right, Missis. No offence.'

'You'd do well to see to it that you don't offend your customers *or* your assistants. Right?'

'All right, Missis.'

With a final nod, she left him admonished and subdued. Only the two girls knew her identity, and the secret was theirs to enjoy.

* * *

'You should have heard her, Dad,' said Leah that evening. 'She really put old Shaw in his place.'

'Poor man,' said Freddy. 'I know how it feels to be given a bottle by Leading Wren Charlesworth. He must have been terrified.'

'Don't listen to him,' said Sylvia. 'He makes it up as he goes along.'

'Well, you certainly cheered me up,' said Wendy. 'That's two members of your family who've told him off, Bruce and you, Mrs Hinchcliffe.'

'Oh,' said Freddy, who knew nothing of the earlier incident, 'how did Bruce come into it?'

'He just told old Shaw to stop picking on us,' said Leah. 'That scared him to death, too.'

'Bruce, eh? He's a lovely lad, but I can't see him scaring anybody.'

'Old Shaw was scared,' said Wendy, laughing.

'Who's for seconds?' asked Sylvia, picking up the dish that contained the fish pie.

'I couldn't eat another morsel, Mrs Hinchcliffe. It's ever so good, but....'

'Martin, you're a growing lad. You'll have some more, won't you?'

'No, thanks.'

'He doesn't need brain food, Mrs Hinchcliffe. He's brainy enough.'

'It's not true that fish develops the brain,' said Martin. 'It's a....'

'Fallacy,' suggested his father.

Everyone else was waiting to hear if Martin said anything else, because it was the first full sentence he'd spoken since they sat down. Leah suspected that he was in awe of Wendy, but she was wise enough not to voice that thought.

'If I'd known that a while back,' said Wendy, 'I wouldn't have eaten so many sardines before my exams. I should have realised it was an old wives' tale when they didn't work.'

'Wendy's disappointed with her CSE results,' said Leah. 'I've told her they're nothing to get upset about, but she won't have it.'

'What did you get, Wendy?' asked Freddy.

She shrugged, and said, 'Five grade twos and a grade three.'

'I think that's pretty good,' said Sylvia, watching her husband help himself to the rest of the fish pie. She'd long been aware of his appetite as an ex-prisoner-of-war, and she knew she had to live with it.

'Thanks, Mrs Hinchcliffe, but it's not good enough. I worked myself silly trying to get one or two grade ones, just so that I could hold my head up and say I'd got them by my own efforts, but it wasn't to be.'

'You were only a whisker away from getting five of them,' said Sylvia. 'I think you've achieved a lot.'

'But, they're only grade twos, when all's said and done. I suppose that makes me a second-class kind of person.'

Leah motioned to Martin to keep quiet. He'd been about to say something, and his record in diplomacy wasn't one that evoked confidence. She'd actually suggested having Wendy over, knowing her mother's remarkable ability to cheer up the downhearted, but it was her father, surprisingly, who did what was needed on this occasion.

'You know, Wendy,' he said, 'I've known a few first-class people. I'm talking about people who can be admired without hesitation, people who always leave the best impression and who leave others the better for having known them, and I can honestly say that you are one of those people. You're a first-class person, Wendy.'

'Do you really think so?'

'Everyone around this table thinks so.' Heads, including Martin's, nodded in agreement.

'Listen to him, Wendy,' said Sylvia. 'Freddy is a son of Kingston-upon-Hull, where the baring of souls is as rare as daffodils in December, so if he says it, you know he means it, and you know it means a lot to him, as it does to all of us.'

'Oh.' Wendy dabbed her eyes with her napkin. 'That's the nicest thing anybody's ever said to me.'

Freddy reached across the table to take her hand. 'Don't ever forget it,' he said.

'It's my turn to say something nice,' said Sylvia. 'Who'd like some ice cream?'

* * *

A few days later, there was a test of a different kind when Yoredale Players held the auditions for the annual pantomime. As Freddy had said more than once, there was never any rest for the willing and able, and he and Sylvia were as willing as most, and more able than any.

Their biggest task was in casting the children's parts, and that had to be done separately from the adult parts, simply because it was so time-consuming. In fairness, most of the children were no trouble at all; the problem came instead from their parents, some of whom saw the Yoredale pantomime as a stepping stone towards a career in show business, television, or even the film industry. Even Sylvia, who habitually carried the torch of fairness to all, recognised that there were geese whose parents were convinced they were swans. At the end of a lengthy and exhausting Sunday, however, Freddy and Sylvia were able to report that the parts of Wendy, John, Michael, the Lost Boys, the Indians and Nana, the dog, were cast, with the girl playing Nana doubling as the Crocodile later in the show. There was a brief period of rest and recovery before the adult auditions that Wednesday.

* * *

The Darling parents had very small parts, and once 'Dame' Smee was cast, the rest of the pirates presented no problem. There was stiff competition for the part of Tiger Lily, but they managed to cast her. Big Chief Dirty Face was a demanding part, in that he needed to have a *basso profundo* voice, so only one candidate stood a chance: the giant from the previous pantomime, who promised to curb his language in mixed and juvenile company. He had also put his name down for Captain Hook, but that part went without realistic competition to Jack Thornton, who had played comic parts in the past.

With Lorna Jenkins now at university, the part of Peter Pan went uncontested to Wendy, who was greatly relieved, because there was now no question of her having to play the part of Wendy Darling, with the inevitable confusion of names and the ridiculous pretence of being considerably younger than she was.

'You had me fooled for a minute,' Freddy told her, 'singing, "You Can Fly". When you sang the children's parts as well as Peter's, I wondered which you were auditioning for.'

'Oh, I couldn't do a child's part now, Freddy.'

'He's only kidding,' said Sylvia. 'You'll get used to his heavy sense of humour before long.'

'Anyway,' said Freddy, 'not a word to the others. I've told you because you're the only one who auditioned for the part, but everyone else will learn the final decision when they get the newsletter.'

One question had been foremost in Wendy's mind. She asked, 'Are we going to fly with wires?'

'I'm afraid not, Wendy. They can do that in professional theatres, but it's much too dangerous here. We'll close the curtains when you're about to fly.'

'Oh, I see.' Another question occurred to her, and she asked, 'Who's playing Tinker Bell?'

'That's a good question. We haven't a Tinker Bell yet, but we're looking.'

'In that case, Freddy, I've got a suggestion.'

'Trot out your suggestion, Wendy.'

'One of my neighbours couldn't audition because she was laid up with a broken ankle. She's only seven, but she's got a lot of ability.'

Sylvia asked, 'How long will she be in a plaster cast?'

'Her mum says it's due to come off in a couple of weeks. She won't be fully mobile for a while, though.'

'If we gave her the part, we'd treat her very gently,' Sylvia assured her.

'I'd keep an eye on her as well, Mrs Hinchcliffe.'

'I don't doubt it, Wendy.'

Those few days proved crucial to Wendy. Having regarded herself as less than successful, she was now the star of the pantomime, chosen this time because of her proven ability, and believing in herself all the more for Freddy's assurance.

20

EDUCATION FOR ALL

Leah was searching the technical college prospectus and making notes as she did so. 'They seem to do everything I want,' she said, 'but they don't say anything much about the courses, except that they follow the Northern Universities syllabus.'

'Well, that's all you need, isn't it?' Her father was practical in most matters.

'What do I do next?' It was new territory for Leah.

'We go there on one of the enrolling nights and you enrol on the courses you want to follow.'

The clash of personal pronouns raised a question immediately. 'Did you say, "*We* go there", Dad? Why do you need to be there?'

'You're an independent soul, aren't you? I suppose there's no reason why you shouldn't do it alone, if you no longer need your aged parent in attendance.'

Reflecting quickly, she said, 'No, you can come. I'm always happier with someone in the after cockpit.'

'Aptly put, Leah. We'll face this one back to back.'

'If such a thing's possible.'

* * *

On Wednesday, the fourth of September, they arrived at Kit Calvert College of Further Education and followed the signs, initially, for the English Department. They sat briefly in the waiting area until they were

140

called by a member of staff, who introduced herself as Mrs Earnshaw. That seemed appropriate to Leah, as the syllabus included *Wuthering Heights*, although she kept that thought to herself. Instead, she said, 'I'd like to enrol for the second year of "A" level English, please.'

'The *second* year?' Mrs Earnshaw seemed taken aback.

'Yes, I started the course at the Royal Ballet School, last year, but I was involved in an accident. I've been studying at home since then.'

'I've helped her as far as I could,' said Freddy, 'but she needs professional tuition now.'

'I see.' Mrs Earnshaw asked her various questions about the set texts and, being satisfied, said, 'Yes, I think we can take you on the second year. That'll be on Thursday mornings.'

They shook hands and went in search of Modern Languages, which they found at the other end of the building. Again, Leah had to explain why she wanted to join the second year and, after some searching questions, she was accepted. That only left History.

After making enquiries, they located the History Department, and were invited to the desk of a young man of bohemian appearance, who introduced himself as 'Kev'.

Once again, Leah said that she wanted to join the second year on the English History syllabus, dealing with the Civil Wars and their aftermath.

'Oh, yes,' said Kev, 'and what has the first year done wrong?'

'Nothing. I started the course last year, at the Royal Ballet School, but then I had an accident and I was laid up in hospital for a while. I've been studying since then with a private tutor.'

'A friend of ours,' said Freddy. 'He was a Cambridge scholar.'

'Oh well,' said Kev, except that it came out like a 'huh', 'I suppose some people are impressed by that kind of thing.'

'As a matter of fact, we both are. The Reverend Stapleton took a double-first in Modern History and Theology.'

'And he's an excellent teacher,' said Leah, now visibly angry.

'Oh well, it takes all sorts.'

'I can't disagree with that,' said Freddy, standing up, 'and I know which sort I prefer. Come along, Leah. The Rector's done you proud in the past. It would be a mistake to change horses now.' He treated Kev to a withering look and guided Leah towards what he thought was the exit.

'Wrong way, Dad. That's the stairs down to the loo. This is the way out.' She pointed to the door marked 'Exit'.

'Right,' he said, 'that's Monday and Tuesday afternoons and Thursday mornings. I think that's quite enough without adding Kev to the week.'

'He was objectionable.'

'Yes, I don't think you and he would have got on at all well.'

'What's funny, Dad?' Freddy was laughing to himself.

'I know just what your grandad's going to say when I tell him.'

'Yes.' Leah adopted a gruff voice and said, 'His kind would benefit from two years in the Army.' After a little thought, she added, 'Or in an after cockpit.'

'An open cockpit, and without a safety harness.'

They were both laughing by the time they reached the car.

* * *

'He was unbelievable, Walter.' Freddy and his father-in-law were enjoying their last month's fishing at Redmire Falls, and Enrolment Night at Kit Calvert College was under discussion. 'At one stage, I thought Leah was going to tell him just what she thought of him. It wouldn't surprise me if something of Leading Wren Charlesworth has come through in the genes.'

'She obviously feels some loyalty to the Rector,' Walter observed.

'Yes, to the extent that she's at church this morning. Of course, her friend Wendy's in the choir.'

'Do you think Leah's heading in that direction? I mean churchgoing, rather than being in the choir.'

'I don't know, Walter, but this is her second time. One thing I do know is that she sees Miles as a kind of mentor, which is appropriate, I suppose.' He looked at his watch and then at his father-in-law. 'Early lunch, do you think, Walter?'

'Why not?' Both men reeled in their lines and retired to the riverbank to find out what their respective wives had packed for them in the way of sandwiches. Their two dogs had been amusing themselves in various ways, but they now turned their attention also to the question of lunch.

'Would you like to try this trout pâté that Sylvia's made, Walter?' asked Freddy.

'Yes, I'll just try the half,' he said, taking half a sandwich from Freddy's box.

'That's all you're going to get.'

'Oh,' said Walter, immediately impressed, 'to think my little girl made this. I must ask her to give her mother the recipe. It really is something special.' Finishing the sandwich, he said, 'I shouldn't say this, Freddy, but Jessie's always leaned a little towards Audrey and her family. I try to redress the balance, of course.'

'I've noticed, Walter.'

'Yes,' he said, offering Freddy a ham and mustard sandwich by way of exchange, 'I often found myself intervening when relations between Jessie and Sylvia were strained. I remember one time when Sylvia was on leave, which didn't happen all that often. Jessie thought she was getting too keen on this PoW she'd never met and, for the best of reasons, she was advising her to be careful.' Shaking his head sorrowfully, he said, 'That might not have been so bad, but she approached the matter in the most authoritarian way, and that's never worked with Sylvia.'

Freddy smiled at the thought. 'No,' he said, 'I don't suppose it would.'

'I brought Sylvia here the next day, and she told me how she felt and what made you so special.'

'She told me about it, Walter, quite recently, as it happened.'

For a moment, Walter sat quite still, watching the River Ure tumble over the rocks. 'I wonder how many problems have been worked out here, on this riverbank, Freddy.'

Freddy laughed. 'I can think of a few,' he said.

'How do you think Leah will take to studying at the technical institute?'

Freddy couldn't help smiling at his father-in-law's old-fashioned language. 'She's looking forward to it, Walter. I've met the people who are going to teach her, and I think she'll be fine.'

'What will she do with her 'A' levels? Has she discussed it with you?'

'Yes, she wants to go somewhere where they teach dance, even though she'll be way ahead of everyone else. She needs a teaching qualification, you see.'

Walter took out his pipe and filled it thoughtfully before saying, 'It's a hell of an adjustment for a child of her age to make, Freddy.'

Freddy had been painfully aware of that for some time. 'I know,' he said. 'Thankfully, Leah is full of surprises.' As one thought led to another, the business of the camel pyjama case returned to him and he said, 'Martin can spring a few, as well.'

* * *

No sooner had she arrived, than Janice produced her reading book, now crumpled, torn in places, and liberally stained with various foods. 'Where's Leah?' she bellowed.

'She's upstairs,' Sylvia told her. 'She'll be down in a minute.'

'Be patient, Janice.' Elaine had told her that many times, knowing it was the hardest thing in the world for her, but she had to keep trying.

Presently, Leah came down and greeted everyone. 'Martin's still in his room,' she said, 'but you know what he's like. He'll come down when he's ready.'

Having demanded Leah's presence, Janice was now searching the room for Nina, unaware that she was at Redmire Falls with Freddy.

'I heard you shout my name, Janice,' said Leah. 'What's the problem?'

'No problem,' said Janice. 'It'll all be the same in a hundred years' time.'

'So you keep saying. What do you want me to do?'

'Learn me to read,' she demanded, waving her book.

'You want me to teach you to read, but what does Brian say?'

Janice rolled her eyes upward. 'Please.'

'All right. Let me find the right page. Here we are. What does this word say?'

'Words don't say anything,' said Martin, joining them. 'They can't talk.'

His observation evidently amused Janice, who repeated it several times.

'All right,' said Leah, 'what is this word, Janice? It begins with a "huh" sound,' she prompted her.

Janice studied the word and shouted, 'Hen!'

'Okay, but what about the wriggly "s" on the end?'

'Hens!'

'Good. What's the next word?'

After some deliberation, Janice said triumphantly, 'Lay!'

'Well done, Janice. What's the last word?'

'Don't know.'

'It's not hard. You could even guess it. You've read, "Hens" and "lay", so what do hens lay?'

'Down!'

Leah had to laugh. 'No, they *lie* down. What do hens lay?'

Janice's face had taken on a familiar look of preoccupation. 'I want the loo – now!' she demanded.

Elaine got up to usher her to the downstairs loo, and Leah said, 'I'll just go and put the kettle on. I'll be back in a minute, folks.'

She returned a few minutes later to find Janice reading again, but with Martin as her unlikely tutor. Elaine was also surprised, but she said nothing.

'Okay,' said Martin. 'That was good. Hens lay eggs, but what do cows give?'

'Muh ih luh....'

'Good, you're doing well. Look at the letter at the end of the word.'

'Kicking kuh!'

'That's right. Now you can read the whole word. What do cows give?'

'They kick.'

'They probably do, but what else do they give. Look at the word again.'

'Muh ih luh kicking kuh. Milk!'

'Well done, Janice.' His praise was echoed by everyone in the room.

Triumphantly, Janice caught Leah's eye and said, 'Martin's been learning me to read an' he's betterer'n you!'

Leah nodded modestly, knowing better than to take offence, but Bailey said, 'Janice, that was very rude and very unkind of you. You'll hurt Leah's feelings, saying that.'

Immediately contrite, Janice threw herself on Leah's mercy. 'I didn't mean it, Leah. You're betterer'n Martin.'

When everything was sorted out, Janice said, 'I need to go again.' It wasn't unusual for her to have urine infections, and Elaine took her again to the downstairs cloakroom.

In her absence, Bailey said, 'You did well, Martin. You know what Janice's problem is, don't you?'

'Yes.' In his usual poker-faced way, Martin explained. 'She has trisomy twenty-one anomaly. Some people call it "Down's syndrome", and it makes it difficult for her to learn.'

'That's right,' said Bailey. 'How did you know about that?'

'I've been reading about it in a book I got by mistake.' No one said anything, being taken completely by surprise, so he continued. 'I thought it was about artificial intelligence when I picked it up, but it was really about superficial intelligence, the basic kind.'

'What is artificial intelligence?' asked Leah.

'It's the ability of computers to make decisions and learn from their mistakes. Alan Turing called it "machine intelligence", but they changed its name after he died.' Still with no appreciable change of expression, he told them, 'There was only a short passage in the book about trisomy twenty-one anomaly, but I read it when I realised it was what Janice has.'

'What have I got?' asked Janice, re-entering the room.

'You've got two clever teachers,' said Bailey, 'and you need to be very nice to both of them.'

Taking her cue, Janice said, 'I love you, Leah and Martin!'

21

INNOCENCE AND ADVERSITY

Christine Wilkinson was tiny, even for seven years, and Freddy and Sylvia learned that she was also an ardent gymnast; in fact, it was during a session at the gym that she'd broken her ankle.

'They took her plaster off, last week,' her mother told them, 'and she's still a bit stiff.'

Freddy's next question took her by surprise, unconnected as it was with gymnastics. 'Would you like to sing something for us, Christine?' he asked.

'All right.' She was a ready performer.

'What are you going to sing?'

Her decision needed hardly a moment's thought. ' "Paul's Little Hen",' she said.

'Right,' said Freddy. He'd never heard of the song; he only wanted to know if Christine could sing a song coherently, and any song would do.

' "Paul's little hen flew away from the farmyard, ran down the hillside and into the dale".' 'Coherently' hardly described her performance, which was not only musical, but accompanied throughout with the actions she'd no doubt learned at school.

'That was lovely,' said Sylvia.

'It was,' agreed Freddy. 'Would you like to be in the pantomime, Christine?'

'*Peter Pan*?'

'That's right. We'd like you to play Tinker Bell, the fairy.'

'Yes!' Christine's enthusiasm was evident, although it was also clear that she lacked a doll like Brian to set her an example in good manners.

'We'll be very careful with her ankle,' Sylvia assured her mother, who was almost as excited as Christine.

'Let's hope she's as careful,' said her mother. 'She's been wound up like a spring all the time she's been in plaster.'

* * *

Leah had also had a successful day at Kit Calvert College, impressing her lecturer with her understanding of the poetry of Schiller. 'He couldn't believe I'd done most of it at home,' she said, 'so, well done, Dad.'

'It's just possible I missed my way,' said her father. 'Maybe I should have been an academic instead of a photographer.'

'You could still do it,' suggested Martin, 'if you matriculated when you were at school. You could even do it as an external student. Miss McCluskey, who takes us for geography, is doing it that way.'

'Maybe,' said Freddy, 'that kind of thing is best left to serious people, such as geography teachers.'

'Not the kind of people who think their deepest thoughts in the after cockpit of an aeroplane?' asked Sylvia innocently.

'Absolutely not. It takes flair to be an air-gunner, and that's not the kind of thing you associate with geography.'

'Didn't you do geography at school, Dad?' asked Leah.

'Not at School Certificate.'

'That's why he struggles with directions,' said Sylvia, adding, 'bless him.'

'When a man loses the respect of his family,' said Freddy, soberly folding his napkin, 'there's nothing else for it but to retire to a quiet place and tie flies.'

'That has a ring to it,' said Leah. 'It's like some of those famous quotations by such as Dorothy Parker and Mrs Patrick Campbell. Also, for what it's worth, Dad, I respect you.'

'We all do,' said Sylvia soothingly.

'Yes,' said Martin, possibly wondering what the fuss was about.

To change the subject as much as to ease her curiosity, Leah asked, 'Did you manage to cast Tinker Bell?'

'Yes,' said Freddy. 'Little Christine Wilkinson's going to do it. I must say she didn't need a lot of persuading.'

'She wouldn't,' said Leah. 'According to Wendy, Christine's only tiny, but she's full of herself.'

Sylvia nodded sagely. 'I've been thinking about the dance numbers, Leah, and I'd appreciate some help, if you're agreeable.'

'Do you mean with the choreography?' It seemed odd, as her mother had always managed on her own.

'Well, we could work on the choreography together, but I was thinking more about teaching the dances. It might be good practice for you as well.'

'As well as playing the piano for rehearsals?' Suddenly, life was becoming more hectic than ever.

'I can spare you at odd times,' Freddy assured her.

'That's big of you, Dad. All right, Mum, I'll lend a hand.'

* * *

Leah found herself lending a hand in a different way, later in the week, when an elderly shopper was found injured and helpless outside the supermarket. The incident occurred at a little after four-thirty, when the rush of mothers with young children had subsided, and Leah was having a quick chat with her cousin Bruce while Mr Shaw's back was turned. Bruce was describing his experiences in the Orthopaedic Department at St John's Hospital in Keighley, when someone called from the entrance, 'Can somebody help? This lady's been hurt.'

With no shoppers currently requiring attention, Leah and Bruce made their way quickly to the entrance, where the woman who'd made the request was supporting an elderly woman in obvious distress. Part of her face was masked in blood, and she was moaning with pain.

'Let's get her into the office,' said Bruce, 'and then I can examine her.' Between them, he and Leah helped the unfortunate woman into Mr Shaw's office.

'What the hell's going on here?' demanded Shaw.

The woman's moans and sobs spoke for themselves, but Leah felt inclined to explain the situation. 'This lady needs to sit down,' she said.

'And you should be on the checkout! Have you left your till unattended?'

'Leah can go back to her till,' Bruce told him, 'when we've got this lady comfortable.'

'Oh, it's you.' Having recognised Bruce from their earlier meeting, Mr Shaw became instantly amenable. 'Sit her down there.' He indicated a wooden chair, and Bruce guided her to it, crouching to examine the woman's facial injury.

'Right,' said Leah, 'if you don't need me, I'll get back to work.'

'Thanks, Leah,' said Bruce. 'I can manage now, but I'll see you before I go.' He gave Mr Shaw a warning look as he spoke, and then turned to the injured woman. 'Now, apart from this nasty bruise on your face, where else does it hurt?'

Leah excused herself and returned to her till, which was as she'd left it. In fact, she saw only two shoppers in the next ten minutes, after which the police arrived, followed by an ambulance.

Bruce left the office and came to the checkout to speak to Leah. 'She needs to go to hospital,' he told her. 'The poor old girl's eighty-one and she has a degree of concussion. Apparently some boys attacked her and tried to take her purse, but another boy came along and stopped them. I don't know how he did it, but I'm glad he did.'

'Good for him,' said Leah. 'It's despicable, picking on an old lady like her.'

'They're taking her away, so she should be all right now.'

Leah followed his gaze and saw the ambulance staff carrying her out on a stretcher. 'Poor old thing,' she said. 'What a horrible thing to happen to her at her age.'

'I don't know what kind of description she was able to give the police,' said Bruce, 'but I hope they catch those thugs.' Suddenly he smiled and said, 'Here comes your boss. I'll hang on here a minute, just to make sure you're all right. It's unfortunate that I'm not wearing my karate T shirt today, but I think he'll behave himself.'

Leah laughed. 'Thanks, Bruce.'

A shopper came to the checkout, so Leah had to attend to her, but she heard Mr Shaw say in an unusually respectful tone, 'Thanks for doing what you did, Doctor. They've taken the old lady to hospital.'

'I know. That was my advice.'

When Bruce was gone, Mr Shaw said, 'I didn't realise your cousin was a doctor.'

'As well as a karate expert? Yes, he either cures 'em or kills 'em. It just depends what day of the week it is.'

* * *

Leah told the story to her parents that evening. 'Bruce was brilliant,' she said. 'He told Mr Shaw to let the lady sit down while he examined her, and then he told him to phone for an ambulance. He was really... in charge of things.'

'I can't imagine it,' said her mum. 'He's normally such a gentle soul.'

'He was really nice with the old lady as well,' said Leah, 'but you'd expect that.'

They had to agree, but that was far as their conversation went, because the doorbell rang, and Leah went to answer it. She opened the door to see a police sergeant and a WPC. The sergeant said, 'Good evening. Is Mr or Mrs Hinchcliffe at home?'

'Yes,' said Leah, wondering what could have happened, 'they're both at home.'

'Do you think we could have a word with them?'

'Yes, come in.' She led them into the sitting room.

The sergeant apologised for disturbing everyone. 'There's nothing to worry about,' he said, 'we'd like to have word with Martin, just to clear something up. Is he at home?'

'Yes.' Freddy went to the stairs, but Leah said, 'I'll speak to him, Dad.'

'Okay, love.' He explained to the police officers, 'I don't know what this is about, but Martin gets very tongue-tied when he's in a stressful situation. Leah's very good with him, though. What's been happening?'

'Is he in trouble?' asked Sylvia, who was naturally concerned.

'No, he's not in trouble, Mrs Hinchcliffe,' said the sergeant. 'There was an incident outside the supermarket today, and we'd like to hear his side of the story, just to wrap everything up. That's all.'

Leah reappeared with Martin behind her. 'Just tell the truth,' she said. Martin stared fixedly at his feet.

'Martin,' said the WPC, 'we'd like you to tell us what happened this afternoon outside the supermarket.'

151

'Go on, Martin,' said Leah. 'There's nothing to worry about.'

'Come and sit with me, Martin,' said Sylvia.

'What happened when you got off the bus?' asked the sergeant.

Now seated beside his mother, but still with his eyes fixed on his feet, Martin said, 'Alan Jackson and Keith Whitworth were beating up an old lady, so I told them to leave her alone.'

'Good lad,' said the sergeant. 'Then what happened?'

'Jackson got something out of her bag – I think it was her purse – so I hit him, and he dropped it, and then Whitworth came at me, so I hit him as well. I only hit them both once… well, maybe twice, but I didn't beat them up or anything like that.'

The sergeant nodded. 'We didn't think you did, Martin, whatever they say. What did they do then?'

'They ran away, and then somebody came to help the old lady, so I got out of the way and came home.'

'He went straight up to his room,' said Sylvia, 'so this is the first we've heard of it.'

'I was in the supermarket when it happened,' said Leah. 'The poor old lady was in an awful state.'

'We know,' said the WPC. 'She's in hospital and she's very shaken, but she'll be all right. Did you actually see the incident?'

'No, the first I knew about it was when someone asked for help with her. My cousin was in the supermarket with me, and we helped her into the manager's office. My cousin's a doctor, and he attended to her.'

'Yes, we've spoken to Dr Reynolds.' It's all right, Martin,' said the sergeant, 'you're not in trouble. In fact, tackling those two makes you the hero of the hour. You prevented the theft of the lady's purse as well as further injury to her person.'

'The two lads have made a complaint against Martin,' explained the WPC. 'They tried to make out that he'd attacked them because of an old grievance. Fortunately, the lady who helped the victim into the supermarket saw the incident, and she's told us everything. We just wanted to hear what Martin had to say.'

Freddy asked, 'Were they the same two that got you into trouble at school, Martin?'

'Yes.'

'It's all right now,' said Sylvia, giving him a squeeze and looking visibly relieved herself.

'What was that about?' asked the sergeant.

'They accused Martin of making an unprovoked assault,' said Freddy. 'They actually got him suspended from school until another pupil managed to make her voice heard. She explained that the two yobs had provoked Martin, and that he'd only hit them in self-defence.'

'Well,' said the sergeant, 'they've been charged, and they'll appear in court, so there's nothing to worry about.' He smiled at Martin and said, 'I don't know where you do your training, but you evidently pack a fair old punch, Martin.'

Martin declined to answer.

'It's all right, Martin,' said Sylvia, much relieved. 'There's nothing to worry about.'

'I think this is one family that did particularly well this afternoon,' said the WPC, smiling, 'Martin, Leah and Dr Reynolds.'

Martin continued to stare at his feet, but Leah crouched beside him to say, 'Well done, Martin. You can relax now.' Turning to the police officers, she said, 'He's very shy.'

'But you're not,' observed the WPC. 'How long have you worked at the supermarket, Leah?'

'Not long. It's only a casual job while I do my "A" levels.'

'Oh? Are you and Martin at the same school?'

'No, I'm a part-time student at Kit Calvert College. I was at the Royal Ballet School until a traffic accident put a stop to it.'

'I'm sorry to hear that.'

'Thanks.' It was very much on Leah's mind, as she was due to have a periodic examination at the hospital in a few days' time.

22

AN APPOINTMENT SANDWICH

Leah would have been happy driving herself to the hospital appointment, but it was necessary for her to be accompanied by a parent, simply because she was not yet twenty-one.

'They're talking about bringing the age of majority down to eighteen,' she pointed out, 'but I don't know exactly when.'

'Well,' said Sylvia, 'that's something to look forward to, isn't it? Meanwhile, you're stuck with me.' She smiled as she said it. 'Anyway, what did Mr Shaw say when you asked him for the day off, Leah?'

'I thought he was going to go into a rant about it, but then I think he remembered Bruce, and he calmed down.'

'I remember, now, about Bruce's T shirt,' said Sylvia.

'Yes, whenever old Shaw looks like misbehaving, all we have to do is say, "*Hasso!*" I think it's Japanese for "*En garde*", or something like that.'

Sylvia chuckled at the thought, and then, more seriously, she asked, 'Did he try anything he shouldn't with you?'

Leah was reluctant to discuss it with her mum, but she had no alternative. 'He didn't do anything awful. He just put his arm round me and stroked… me.'

'That's awful, Leah. You should have told us.'

'Well, he won't try it again.'

'If he does, you must tell me, and you can depend on it that you won't stay in that place a moment longer.'

'All right, Mum, but it's most unlikely.' As a stray thought occurred to her, she said mischievously, 'I don't suppose that kind of thing ever happened when you were my age, did it?'

'Don't you believe it, Leah.'

'Oh?' Leah eyed her mum with teasing curiosity. 'This is something you've never told me.'

'Leah, you're awful.' She appeared to be concentrating on the road ahead, although the traffic was very light. Eventually, she said, 'You youngsters didn't invent these things, you know. They've been happening since time began.'

'Go on, Mum. Tell me a war story.'

Her mum sighed. 'I'll tell you about one girl who came a cropper.'

'"Came a cropper"? What does that mean?'

'She had a most regrettable accident.'

Leah settled more comfortably in her seat and said, 'Go on, Mum. Tell me about it.'

'All right.' Sylvia overtook a lorry as soon as she could. 'Right,' she said, 'now I can concentrate.'

'I love your war stories.'

'I know.' Summoning her thoughts, she began by saying, 'There were three of us in the cabin: Auntie Joyce, Auntie Dorothy and me, and then, when I returned from Christmas leave, I found we had another cabin mate, a girl called Clarissa, who was awful.'

'In what way was she awful, Mum?' Leah liked to know every detail.

'She was superior, snobbish, selfish and inconsiderate. She had a store of things that were impossible to get, including silk stockings, but she refused to consider lending them to her cabin mates. She even persuaded one girl to do her watch so that she could go to a dance, but she made no offer to do one for her, until we put pressure on her. She actually wanted me to knit her a pair of bed socks, but I refused.'

'She must have been awful for you to refuse her, Mum.' Leah shook her head in mock disbelief.

'She was as awful as that, until one day, we learned that she'd applied for officer training. Well, we persuaded her that one of the qualities she needed to demonstrate was generosity of spirit. We told her that we each had to fill in a form saying what she was like as a cabin mate.'

'Surely not.' With the sophistication of her generation, Leah clearly struggled to believe their subterfuge.

'Yes, we persuaded her that if she did a watch for the girl who'd done her the favour, and if she was more generous with the silk stockings, we could probably see our way to giving her a favourable report. Consequently, we each got a pair of Bear Brand's finest stockings, and Clarissa did the decent thing by the girl who'd done a watch for her.'

'Amazing.' Leah was just a little unsure about one detail. 'I can't imagine what it was like, wearing stockings all the time.'

'Tights hadn't been invented. Everyone wore stockings.'

'With those garter things to hold them up?'

'Only in America, darling. They're called "suspenders" over here.' As another memory surfaced, she said, 'We once did some mending for the crew of an American patrol boat, and they rewarded us with nylon stockings. Nylon was a recent invention, and we were overjoyed to be given them, because stockings of any description were almost impossible to find in the shops.'

'No, I just can't imagine it.' Leah gave up the struggle, and asked, 'Was Clarissa a reformed character after that?'

'That would have been too much to expect. She found out about our little game, and things returned to normal until one day, we realised she was missing. On closer inspection, we found that her locker was empty. She'd gone without a word, but we learned from our friendly leading telegraphist that she was on leave, pending official discharge. It appeared that she and one of the junior naval officers had let their enthusiasm run away with them, and she was well and truly pregnant.'

That left Leah in a thoughtful mood. 'I appreciate what you said about her unpleasant ways,' she said, 'but it could have ruined her life, and she was only…. How old was she?'

'About twenty. Some people manage to redeem their lives after an unwanted pregnancy, and knowing Clarissa as I did, I imagine she would find a way of making the baby someone else's problem.'

'Even so, it just shows you can't be too careful.'

'I'm glad you see it that way, and it proves my point that not everyone was blameless in those days. Now,' she said, turning into the hospital grounds, 'let's see if we can find a parking place.'

Parking turned out to be relatively easy, and they walked the short distance to the Orthopaedic Department.

* * *

156

Mr Livesey was as welcoming as before, which was reassuring for Leah. He placed each of her x-rays on a huge screen and studied them before examining her.

'You've been a model patient,' he said finally.

'It's important to me.'

'I know, and you've responded conscientiously with your physio. Have you done a lot of swimming as well?'

'I go to the pool at least twice a week.'

'Leah has a busy schedule,' her mum told him. 'She's studying for "A" levels as well as working part-time in a supermarket.'

At the mention of "A" levels, he asked, 'What will you do next, Leah?'

'I want to get a teaching qualification so that I can teach dance.'

'I see.' He studied the x-rays once more and said, 'I imagine you'll need to audition for a place.'

'I believe so, yes.'

'Right,' he said, making a note for himself, 'I'm going to ask the physio to go through your practice routine with you, just to ensure you're not going to injure yourself. I'm afraid it must be a very gradual return to fitness. You understand that, don't you?'

Leah smiled and said, 'I've been telling myself that ever since the last time I saw you.'

'Good. In that case, I wish you every success in finding the place that best suits your needs.'

* * *

'What a lovely man,' said Leah. 'I feel now that I can start looking at colleges and so on.'

'Yes, we were lucky to get him.'

As they approached the car, Leah asked, 'Can I drive home, Mum?'

'Why not?' She handed her the key and went to the passenger side. 'You need to keep your hand in.'

Leah fastened her belt and started the engine. 'You have some funny expressions,' she said.

'Oh yes? What have I said now?'

'"Keep your hand in". I don't think I've ever heard that before.'

'It's just a phrase we old folks use to mean keeping in practice.'

'It's good. I like it.' She threaded her way out of the carpark, and when she'd joined the main road, she said, 'You must have known lots of strange people, Mum.'

'In the Wrens? Yes, we had girls of every description and persuasion. Happily, they weren't all like Clarissa.'

'Go on, Mum. Tell me another war story.'

'Leah, you're incorrigible.' Even so, she obliged. 'There was a girl I met on passage to Malta. She was one of life's natural victims.' She stopped and corrected herself. 'No, that's not true. Her upbringing had made her a victim.'

'What was her name?'

'Gwendoline. I persuaded her to shorten it to "Gwen", because I thought it might encourage the others to accept her more readily.'

'Did it?'

'No, she still stuck out like a sore finger. You see, she was like a talking encyclopaedia.' After a little more thought, she said, 'She was quite intelligent and well-educated, but unworldly beyond belief, and she had no sense of humour and, consequently, very few friends.' Carrying out a mental count, she said, 'There was Dorothy, a girl called Ruth and there was me. As a leading Wren, I had to take her under my wing.'

'Oh, Mum,' said Leah, patting her mother's hand, 'she could have been in worse hands than yours.'

'Actually, it was Dorothy who saved her in the end.'

'I can believe that.'

'I told you about the entertainment group on Malta, didn't I?'

'The one with the woman who had enormous boobs?'

'Yes.' She frowned briefly at Leah's choice of word, but went on. 'There was a faction of troublemakers and bullies within that group, and they saw Gwen as their personal target. They were taunting her on the bus one morning as it brought the all-night watch back to the place where we lived. I was on a different watch, but Dorothy was there, and by the time she'd finished with them, they wished they were on a different watch, too.'

'Good old Auntie Dorothy.' Leah laughed at the picture her mother had created. 'I wonder if they knew what they were taking on.'

'They found out fairly quickly. Of course, Dorothy wasn't always so confident.'

'Wasn't she?' The observation took Leah completely by surprise. 'I always think of her as being equal to anything.'

'She probably is now, but when she joined us in Dover she was very insecure, and we only found out why when we'd been into Dover to see a film. It was basically because, whilst Dorothy has lots of admirable qualities, by her own admission, she's no oil painting.'

Leah shook her head in wonder. 'That's another new one on me, but I know what you mean. It doesn't matter, though, does it? She found herself a brilliant husband.'

'Yes, she did, and you're absolutely right, Leah. It doesn't matter what someone looks like. At least, it shouldn't, but it made her feel inadequate, and as her oppos, we had to help her feel better about herself.'

'That's lovely, Mum, but what are "oppos"?'

'Friends. We were Dorothy's closest friends, and we showed her how to make the most of herself. It worked, as well, because the next time we went to a dance, she and Alf became a couple.'

'Brilliant.'

'Mind you, she'd already impressed him and everyone else in a darts match, but that's a story for another time.'

'Oh, go on, Mum.'

'No, you've had two stories today, and the darts match is there to look forward to.'

Leah couldn't argue with that. 'You're right, Mum. Two war stories and an appointment are enough for one day.'

'Yes, it's been an appointment sandwich, really, and now that you're bolstered with good news from Mr Livesey and entertainment from me, you should be all set to help me with dance rehearsals for *Peter Pan*.'

23

PERSONAL QUALITIES

Freddy had taken the pirates into a classroom to work on their choruses, leaving the hall free for Sylvia's dance rehearsal, but it soon became apparent to Christine Wilkinson in her excitement that an empty space surrounded by people amounted to a performance area and a convenient audience. She began her display by somersaulting diagonally across the floor.

'Very nice, Christine,' said Sylvia, 'but we need to start the rehearsal.'

'I can do it backwards. Watch me.' Without waiting for consent, she demonstrated.

'All right, Christine. We must make a start.'

'Just let me show you this.'

'This rehearsal isn't just about you,' said Wendy, clearly a little embarrassed, being the one who'd recommended Christine for the part of Tinker Bell.

Christine reached the end of her demonstration and stood perfectly still, listening to neither Sylvia nor Wendy, but watching Leah, who was performing an effortless pirouette. After four rotations, she came to a dead stop and said, 'You see, you're not the only one who can do clever things.'

Still awestruck, the child asked, 'How do you do that?'

'If you're very good and do everything my mum says, I'll show you at the end of the rehearsal.'

Biting her lower lip unsurely, Christine asked, 'Who's your mum?'

'I am,' said Sylvia.

'You have to decide,' said Leah, 'whether you're going to join in with everybody to make this pantomime the best it can be, or whether

160

to carry on showing off and making everybody cross with you because they can't get on with what they have to do.'

Christine regarded her uncertainly, still chewing her lip. She asked, 'Who's cross with me?'

'So far, nobody is, but if you go on showing off and holding up the rehearsal, everybody will be very, very cross with you. Are you going to be good?'

Without hesitation, Christine nodded. 'Yes.'

'Good girl.' Leah took her hand and said, 'Come and sit with me until my mum's ready for you.'

'Thank you, Leah.' Sylvia was visibly grateful.

* * *

At the end of Christine's part in the rehearsal, Leah showed her, as far as possible, how to pirouette.

When Wendy had taken her home, Sylvia said, 'You handled that beautifully, Leah.'

'It was only common sense, really.'

'Even so, it's a fine line with amateurs, and particularly with children. We must have order, but we can't come down too hard on them.'

'No, that's my job,' said Freddy, joining them. 'Anyway, what did Leah do beautifully?'

'Little Christine Wilkinson wouldn't settle down. She was more inclined to show off to everybody, but Leah set her straight. I'm quite proud of our daughter.'

'So am I,' said her dad, 'and I wasn't there.'

A little self-consciously in view of their compliments, Leah said, 'I'm just glad I wasn't precocious and full of myself when I was little.'

'Nonsense,' said her dad. 'You were unsufferable at her age, a pain in the stern gland.'

'Don't be rotten, Freddy,' said Sylvia.

Leah took it in good part. She'd had more than seventeen years to get used to her dad's teasing ways.

* * *

Freddy told Walter about the incident while they were discussing fishing flies on the phone. 'We were quite surprised as well as rather proud of her,' he said.

'So you should be, Freddy. Leah has some remarkable qualities. I hope you're keeping a record.'

'A record of what, Walter?'

'The various ways in which she excels. They'll all stand her in good stead.'

That left Freddy thinking. 'You know, Walter,' he said, 'much as I love her and admire her ability, I wouldn't know where to begin.'

For a while, Walter was silent, and it was evident to Freddy, who knew him well, that he was formulating his argument. Eventually, he said, 'I read applications from school-leavers that are basically lists of projected exam results. They're very necessary, of course, but they tell me very little about the applicant. They don't tell me why they want the job, or what qualities they could bring to it. At least, they didn't. It's only recently that I've taken to wording the advertisements in such a way that they're obliged to address those questions.'

'One day,' said Freddy, impressed as usual by his father-in-law's insight, 'I'm going to write a book called "Walter's Wisdom".'

Walter laughed. 'I don't think it would find many buyers,' he said, 'but let's return to the subject of Leah's *curriculum vitae*.'

'Her what?'

'Her listing of information in support of her application. That's qualifications, experience and special abilities. From what you've told me, she showed particular ability in dealing with that little girl. She handled the job with firmness and sensitivity, and that doesn't come naturally to most people, especially to seventeen-year-old girls, or boys, for that matter.'

'No,' agreed Freddy, remembering something Sylvia had said at the time. 'Firmness is one thing, but sensitivity is very important in dealing with amateurs.'

'Exactly, and in listing Leah's remarkable virtues, let's not forget her greatest triumph.'

Freddy was lost again. Guessing, he asked, 'Do you mean winning the scholarship?'

'That was an achievement,' agreed Walter, but what about the way

162

she's dealt with the most crushing disappointment of her young life. A great many youngsters, I think, would be left empty and embittered, and who could blame them? Not Leah, though. You could say she's picked herself up, dusted herself off, and started... to do something different.'

Recognising a mis-quotation from a Gershwin song, Freddy grinned. 'It's quite fitting that the analogy's associated with Fred Astaire,' he said.

'I thought so too, Freddy, but isn't it admirable, how Leah's accepted second-best and decided to make a success of it?'

'It is. There's just a tiny fly in the ointment, and that's her modest nature. At least, she was always confident when she was dancing, but getting her to speak up for herself is another matter.'

After a pause, Walter said, 'Let me speak to Leah, Freddy. Maybe I can show her how to do herself justice without being too full of herself.'

* * *

Wendy hauled herself out of the swimming pool and wiped the water from her face. 'I still can't dive like you, Leah,' she said hopelessly.

'But you've improved no end. I've just been doing it longer, so I'm quite relaxed about it.'

'You're so graceful as well.'

Leah smiled sympathetically. 'That's down to ballet,' she explained, 'and that's basically expression and communication through body management.'

'I'm still impressed.'

'Okay,' said Leah, standing up, 'let's go in again, and try to keep your legs straight.'

'Oh, heck.' Wendy was watching a toddler who was running along the opposite side of the pool. She said, 'He's going to fall in if he's not careful.'

Leah scanned the length of the pool, looking for someone who might be responsible for the child, because clearly he was looking for someone. No one seemed perturbed by his behaviour, however, and he was still trying to locate the missing parent.

Leah said, 'I'll go round and stop him. Can you tell the

superintendent, Wendy? He can put a call out for whoever's supposed to be with him.' She'd taken two steps when the child seemed to trip over his own feet and fall headlong into the pool. At first, no one seemed aware, and two bathers expressed their surprise when Leah executed a shallow dive over their heads and struck out for the other side. The little boy was submerged and thrashing about frantically by the time she reached him; in fact, he managed to hit her across the face as she grasped him. 'You're all right,' she said. 'You're safe now.' He was still struggling, but she cupped his chin and kept his head above the surface, propelling him towards the steps at the deep end and trying to reassure him while he choked and cried. She reached the steps, where a woman helped her get him on to the side of the pool. 'Put him on his side,' said Leah. 'Here,' she said, 'like this.' She arranged him in the recovery position, where he continued to relieve himself of a quantity of chlorinated water.

The woman who had helped her called out, 'Has anybody lost a little boy?' As she did so, the superintendent put out a similar call on the public address system.

'You're all right now,' Leah told him. It sounded silly, but it was the only thing she could think of, and it was better than not reassuring him at all.

Eventually, a young woman pushed through the gathering crowd to ask, 'What have you been doing, Carl?'

Leah was about to make an unguarded remark, when the helper said, 'While you were gossiping, he was drowning. This young lass dived in an' saved his life.'

'I wasn't gossiping,' said the mother petulantly. 'It was an important conversation.'

'More important than your little lad?' asked Wendy, who had just joined them.

'Aye,' said the helper, 'instead of making excuses, you should be thanking this lass for saving his life.'

'I didn't know what he was doing,' she protested.

Leah contented herself with making sure the boy was properly recovered. 'Are you all right now?' she asked.

He nodded, still coughing tearfully.

'Well done, love,' said the helper. 'Somebody has to say it.'

There was a chorus of agreement from the bystanders, prompting the mother to say, 'Thank you.'

'You're welcome.' Leah and Wendy walked away.

'That woman's not fit to have kids,' said Wendy. 'If I had a little kiddie like that, I'd never let him out of my sight.'

'I think she's probably feeling a bit humble,' said Leah. The chorus of onlookers was now quite audible, and they seemed to be venting their feelings on the subject of neglectful parents. 'My only concern now is that the little boy could grow up terrified of water, because I don't think his mum has the sense to reintroduce him to it properly.'

'Not everybody thinks about these things, Leah. You're a bit special, that way.'

'Oh, I don't know. What shall we do now?'

Wendy looked up at the big wall clock, and said, 'What have we got time for? You're the one who has to work this afternoon.'

'Let's get changed and go into the new cafeteria for a cup of coffee and what my dad calls a "wad".'

'What's that?'

'A sandwich or a bun or something of that kind. He has lots of silly words that he uses. They've all got something to do with being an air-gunner and sitting in the after cockpit with his back to everything that was going on.'

'Okay, even though I don't understand a word.'

They went to their cubicles to dry themselves and change. Afterwards, they met outside the cafeteria.

'It looks all right,' said Wendy as they went in.

'It's a bit like the dining hall at school.'

'What's it like at boarding school, Leah?'

'It's difficult to say, really, because you get used to it after a while. Some of the girls are homesick at first, but the routine doesn't allow much time for that.' She laughed and then became serious. 'There's a tendency for some of the older girls to pour scorn on new girls who are homesick, and that must be awful.'

'Weren't you homesick at all?'

'A little bit,' said Leah, picking up a tray, 'but I tried not to show it. Most of all, I was conscious of being there to do the thing that meant everything to me, and that kept me on an even keel.' Suddenly, she laughed. 'I'm beginning to sound like my dad.'

'You could do worse.' Wendy picked up an egg mayonnaise sandwich and put it on her tray. 'This morning, you were more like your mum, except that I reckon she'd have told that woman how she felt about her neglecting her little lad.'

'Yes.' Leah laughed at the thought. 'My dad calls her "Leading Wren Charlesworth" when she gets stroppy, like the time she told Mr Shaw to mind his manners.'

'Apart from that,' said Wendy, 'you're a lot like your mum.'

'Oh, I don't know. That's a tough example to follow.'

They paid for their coffee and sandwiches and found a table.

'One thing that would really take some following,' said Leah, 'is my mum's sweet and generous nature, and another thing is her ability to put a smile on people's faces when they're up against it. She says my dad once wrote a song about that.'

'It wouldn't surprise me,' said Wendy. 'Anyway, there's a lot of your mum in you. You can't be exactly the same, but there's quite a lot of you that is.'

24

EACH TO HIS OWN

Walter had chosen an evening when his wife was at a meeting of the WI. Leah, who was far from naïve, knew he'd made the decision because he wanted to talk without interruption, although she had no idea what he wanted to discuss. Trusting him as she did, however, she drove to her grandparents' house in Leyburn, knowing that he would soon enlighten her. She arrived shortly before her grandma was due to leave for her meeting, and was treated to an enthusiastic report on the latest achievements of Bruce, Pauline and Andrew, her cousins. It was a familiar story; Auntie Audrey's children were a constant source of delight to their grandma, although Leah knew that her grandad would doubtless redress the balance in the next couple of hours. He usually did.

'As you're driving,' he said when they were alone, 'I shan't offer you anything alcoholic.'

'That's fine, Grandad. Have you any of that apple juice?'

'I have, and if that's what you'd like, I'll get you some.'

He went to the kitchen and returned with a glass of apple juice. 'I imagine,' he said, pouring himself a glass of cognac, 'you're looking for somewhere to study. Have you anywhere particular in mind?'

'One or two. The Cory School of Dance looks quite promising.'

'You have the advantage of me there,' he said, 'but you know what to look for. Now, what happens next?'

'When I get my mock results, I'll have to apply to the clearing house for university and college applications. I'll state my preferences and fill in the details on that.'

'I imagine there'll be a place on the form for supporting information, and presumably you'll have to attend an interview.'

'Interview and audition, yes.'

'Of course.' He paused for a moment, possibly choosing his words, and then he said, 'You're very much like your mum in many ways, Leah.'

She laughed. 'Someone else said that, quite recently. Hers isn't a bad example to follow, though, is it?'

'It's an excellent example, although I have to admit to being a shade biased. I think it's also fair to say that you've inherited some of your dad's qualities, too.'

'Do you think so?'

'I'm sure of it, Leah. One of his outstanding traits is modesty, and you have that in abundance. That's why I asked you to come here tonight.'

Now Leah was mystified. All she could do was wait for him to explain, which he did.

'Modesty is a worthy characteristic, but as I pointed out to your dad on Sunday, and he agreed with me, there are times when you need to make your achievements and qualities known. One such occasion is when you're writing an application.'

She nodded self-consciously. 'The Reverend Stapleton has told me I hide my light under a bushel. I don't know what a bushel is, but I know what he means. Even so, these places ask for the information they want, surely.'

'I'm sure they do, Leah,' he said, reaching for his pipe, 'but the kind of questions you'd encounter in making an application couldn't possibly help them obtain a whole picture. That's why they ask for supporting information. At least, I imagine these people will, and you'll certainly have an opportunity at your interview to tell them about your particular abilities.'

'What abilities?' It puzzled her that her grandad knew something about her that she didn't.

'One that occurs to me is the ability to correct someone's behaviour without causing offence.'

She stared at him uncomprehendingly.

'Just as an example, I happen to know that you performed a very useful service at the last pantomime rehearsal.'

'Oh, that. Honestly, Grandad, anyone could have done that.'

'I disagree. You're very good at lots of things that come so easily to you that you imagine everyone else must find them just as easy, and that's not the case.' He finished lighting his pipe and returned his lighter to the small table beside his chair. 'As I understand it, you persuaded a very young and enthusiastic child to stop showing off and to cooperate with your mum. You did that without offending the child or denting her enthusiasm. In fact, such was the relationship you formed with her, she spent much of the evening at your side. Have I understood that properly?'

'More or less, but she hung around because I'd offered to show her how to pirouette.'

'And she likes and admires you. Your dad suspects there may be even an element of – if you'll allow a masculine expression – hero-worship involved, even though you'd told her off.' He broke off to re-light his pipe.

'I can't see anything special in that. Little girls often get innocent crushes on older girls.'

'You don't see it as special because you do it so naturally. Listen, Leah, there are many people on this planet who can communicate, but there are many more who haven't a clue where to start. Between you and me, as a school governor, I know of several members of staff who'd benefit from just a little of the quality you dismiss so lightly. Let's look at this in broader terms. You have the ability not only to censure without causing offence, but also to form a bond with the person you've censured. The little girl is... how old?'

'I think she's seven.'

'But she might have been older, maybe the age of some of the people you will one day be required to teach. Won't that ability come in useful then? Just think about those temperamental performers, Leah, full of ambition but, if I dare say it, subject to the pressures and trials of... adolescence.' He smiled mischievously and said, 'I think that's the word. It's a phase of development that's become recognised since I was young, but I think I'm right.'

Leah had to laugh. 'Troublesome teenagers, like me?'

'If only there were more like you,' he said, 'but let's take a hypothetical case. Let's imagine a dance student who's just suffered a disabling injury.'

She grimaced at the idea. 'That's not difficult.'

'Of course it's not, but where could such a student turn for emotional support?'

Leah shrugged. The answer was obvious to her. 'It goes without saying that I'd do everything I could.'

'I know you would. You'd do that in the light of your own experience of having your dream set to nought, and then coming to terms with your loss, a mountainous task that you've performed superbly well. You've come out of it without a chip on your shoulder, and you're preparing yourself positively for what you might have regarded at one time as second-best. Yours is quite an example to follow, believe me, and you'd be an excellent mentor in such a case.'

Leah was almost squirming. 'Grandad, you're embarrassing me.'

'I'm afraid I am.' Picking up a notebook placed conveniently beneath his chair, he said, 'Let's have a go at expressing these qualities in a way that makes the point without sounding boastful, the kind of thing you might write under Further Information in Support of Your Application. I think that could be a useful exercise for someone as reluctant as you are to lift the bushel and let some light out. Don't you agree?'

It was good advice, and the longer Leah thought about it and referred to her grandad's notes, the less inhibited she became, at least to some extent, about describing her strengths. Mock exams would take place in February, and then she would write her application. In the meantime, however, she had agreed to help with the pantomime.

* * *

Peter Pan called for a great deal of choreography. The Darling Children, the Lost Boys, the Pirates, the Red Indians, Tiger Lily and Tinker Bell all needed dance steps that had to be rehearsed. It was during this time that Leah demonstrated her worth, taking one group into a separate classroom while her mother worked with another. The arrangement worked so well that Sylvia commented on it during a brief meeting with Freddy.

'There's a danger of taking Leah for granted,' she said.

'Oh?'

'If I ask her to take the Lost Boys and rehearse them, she simply goes off and does it. She doesn't need to be reminded about the choreography. Seeing it once is enough for her, and she brings them back drilled almost to perfection.'

'Amazing.' He was thinking about some of the characters among the Lost Boys, who might have tested the ability of an experienced dance coach. 'It's something else to go down on your dad's list.'

'Not only that, Freddy, she sometimes has to take Christine with her and keep her entertained as well. She's worth her weight in gold.'

'Oh well, I've always known that. I think it probably has something to do with the fact that she was conceived in an enchanted place.'

'Shh.' Sylvia put a finger to her lips, but her smile betrayed her pleasure at the memory of that special afternoon on Lady Hill.

More seriously, he said, 'What a blessing it is that she's prepared to put so much effort into the job. I'm sure she still misses ballet school, but she's being surprisingly grown-up about the way things have turned out for her.'

* * *

It was less straightforward for Leah. Although she was careful not to reveal the extent of her feelings, she did miss ballet school quite badly, but the hitherto central part of her life, now tragically absent from it, was her dream of becoming a professional dancer. To mope and sulk about it would be unforgiveable; more than anything, it would hurt her mum, who had shared her dream from the outset, and that would be too awful for words, so she had to do the almost impossible, to hide the greatest despair of her life. It was fortunate that there were distractions, one of which involved Martin.

* * *

On one of the rare evenings when there was no pantomime rehearsal, Freddy and Sylvia were passively watching University Challenge. They were actually waiting for the drama series that followed it; Leah was writing an essay, and Martin was finishing his homework.

Bamber Gascoigne asked, 'Which chemist presented the Periodic Table in 1869?'

'Dmitri Mendeleyev,' replied Martin without looking up from his work.

The student representing Jesus College Oxford gave an incorrect answer, so the question was offered to King's College Cambridge, who also failed to impress.

'No,' said Bamber Gascoigne, 'the answer is the Russian chemist Dmitri Mendeleev.'

'Well done, Martin,' said Freddy, who hadn't a clue what they were talking about, but who was nevertheless impressed by his son's knowledge.

A series of Physics questions followed, each of which Martin answered correctly, unlike the teams in the studio.

'That was good, Martin,' said Sylvia. 'Well done.'

He shrugged. 'They were easy.'

Conscious that November was the usual time for school prizegiving, Freddy asked, 'When's Speech Day, Martin?'

'Next Thursday.'

Puzzled, he said, 'We haven't seen a letter about it.'

Silently, Martin stood up and went upstairs, returning with a dog-eared envelope addressed to the parents of Martin Hinchcliffe. 'I forgot about it,' he mumbled.

'In that case, it's a good thing I reminded you,' said Freddy, taking the envelope from him. He opened it and took out the letter. '"Dear Mr and Mrs Hinchcliffe,"' he read, '"You are invited to attend our Speech Day at seven-thirty on Thursday, the fourteenth of November. I am delighted to advise you that Martin has been awarded the E. Spicer Mathematics Prize and the F.H. Burns Physics Prize. I hope to see you then." Martin, this letter is dated two weeks ago. Didn't you think it was important?'

Martin considered the question. 'They've given the Chemistry prize to somebody else,' he complained.

'It doesn't pay to be too greedy,' said Freddy. 'Was that what made you forget about the letter?'

'Yes.'

'Maybe someone did rather better than you in chemistry,' suggested Sylvia.

'No.' Martin's face was as expressionless as usual. 'They gave it to him because it would look bad if I received three prizes,' he said. 'Nobody's ever won three in one year.'

'Who told you that?' asked Freddy.

'Mr Newbould, the chemistry teacher.'

Freddy looked at Sylvia and it was clear they were equally baffled. 'Was the Chemistry Prize important to you, Martin?'

'Yes. There were three books I wanted. I'm getting two of them as prizes.'

'And you were expecting to get the other for chemistry?'

'Yes.'

'Tell us what the book is, Martin, and we'll get it for you. You've obviously worked hard for it.'

After a moment's hesitation, Martin said, 'Right.'

'What does Brian say?'

'Thanks, Dad.'

'What about me?' asked Sylvia, trying to sound neglected.

'Thanks, Mum.' Martin gathered his books together and took them upstairs. As he did so, Leah joined her parents.

'I think I know why Martin's not good at communicating,' she said.

'Tell us,' said Freddy, 'because we've been wondering about it for years and we still haven't a clue.'

'I think it's because he's so good at numbery things, like maths, physics and chemistry. People who do that don't use words if they can help it. When they do, they don't make themselves understood, and when they try to use letters, they get it all wrong, instead of leaving them to those of us who do know how to use them.'

Laughing, Freddy held out his arms and invited her on to his lap. 'You know, Leah, I think I can agree with your theory.'

'Well, it stands to reason, doesn't it? If a equals three, and b equals nine, why don't they just settle for being those numbers instead of masquerading as letters?'

'Each to his own, darling. They don't understand our world any more than we understand theirs.'

'Isn't it good, though,' said Sylvia, 'that Martin's won two prizes?'

In an ever-challenging world, it was worth remembering.

25

A SOLUTION AND A STRATEGY

The pantomime was finally coming together. Everyone was working hard, and all but the youngest of the children had developed a sense of urgency. Freddy still couldn't afford to relax, however. Indeed, had he done so, the shock might have been much worse when he received word that Jack Thornton, alias Captain Hook, was retiring sick and would be unable to take any further part in the production.

'He's got something called shingles,' said Freddy, 'whatever they are.'

'It's related to chickenpox,' said Leah. 'Bruce called into the supermarket today, and I asked him about it. Apparently, when someone's had chickenpox, the virus stays dormant in the body until it's reawoken by contact with someone else who has it, usually a child. Also, if someone touches the rash who hasn't had chickenpox, they can catch it that way.' She considered that briefly and said, 'I think that's what he said. I was trying to serve customers at the time.'

'Fascinating, Leah,' said her mum. 'What else did he tell you?'

'Only that it's very debilitating and it can be painful. You just have to take life easy until it goes away.'

'I'm sorry for the poor bug… chap,' said Freddy, 'but it leaves us with a problem.'

'Is there no one who could take on the part at this stage?' asked Sylvia.

'There's Stan Widdowson, who's playing Big Chief Dirty Face. He

174

and Captain Hook are never on stage at the same time, but I'm pretty sure he couldn't learn the part in three weeks, and certainly not without swearing. It's taking him all his time to learn the Chief's part.'

The problem hung over the household like a threatening cloud for the next hour or so, and then the phone rang. Leah answered it.

'Hinchcliffe Photo Services.'

'Dearest girl, how are you?'

'I'm fine, thanks, Bailey. How about you?'

'In the pink, I should say. How are the rest of the family?'

'We're okay, thanks, but we had some news, last night. It's bad news for the pantomime, I'm afraid.'

'Is it, by Jove? Go on, dearest, spill the beans.'

'Jack Thornton, who was to have played Captain Hook, has shingles, so he's out of it, and we can't think of anyone else who could do it in the time that's left.'

'My dear old soul. Poor old Jack, as well, because shingles is no joke. Listen, dearest one, will you ask your esteemed papa to come to the phone. I may just be able to lob a suggestion in his direction.'

'Yes.' Wondering quite what to expect, she called, 'Dad.' She handed him the phone. 'It's Bailey. He says he may be able to help with the Captain Hook problem.'

'Thanks, darling. Hello, Bailey.'

The remainder of the conversation was difficult to follow, as Leah and Sylvia were only able to hear one side of it, but when Freddy finally put the phone down, he looked very relieved.

'Bailey's going to do it,' he said. 'It'll mean extra work, but I know he's more than capable of it, and we know how professional he is.'

Leah asked, 'What have you seen him do, Dad? I can't remember anything.'

'It was before you were born, Leah.'

'Like everything else,' she said with an air of fatalism.

'That's right. After the war, Yoredale Players had about a pound in the bank, so they couldn't afford scores or a band. In the end, they let me write a musical about Wensleydale's Viking past. Your mum did the choreography and coached the dancers, the costumes and scenery were home-made, and the Dalesmen provided the band. We were just short of a leading man with a bass-baritone voice, and then out of the blue came Bailey. It was the first time I'd seen him since the war, and he was more than welcome.'

'We heard him singing in the bath when he was staying with us,' said Sylvia, and that, believe it or not, served as his audition.'

'I didn't know he could sing,' said Leah.

'In that case, you're in for a surprise. Around the time we were preparing the next show, Janice was born, and he retired from the stage to devote his spare time to parenthood. That's why it never occurred to me to ask him about Captain Hook, but he's confident he can find the time to learn the part, and I gather from the other conversation he was having while he was talking to me, that Elaine's agreeable. As you can imagine, Janice is also jumping up and down with excitement at the prospect.'

'He hasn't much time before it goes on stage,' said Leah, as fearful for Bailey's sake as for the pantomime.

'Bailey won't let us down,' Sylvia assured her. 'If all the cast were as dependable as he is, we'd do it in half the time.'

* * *

As expected, Bailey turned up promptly for the next rehearsal, when Freddy announced a change in the programme.

'I've decided to include "For I Am a Pirate King" from *The Pirates of Penzance*,' he said.

'Oh, good,' said Bailey, 'I know that one, and it should be easy enough for the chorus to learn.'

In the absence of scores, Freddy taught the chorus its lines by rote, and very soon, with Bailey's bloodthirsty solo, they had a set piece.

'I told you he wouldn't be a problem,' said Sylvia.

'He's unbelievable,' agreed Leah, who'd previously thought she knew all about her godfather's talents.

Freddy spent the rest of the evening taking Bailey through his lines while Sylvia supervised the galley scene between Dame Smee and Cedric the Cabin Boy, and Leah rehearsed the Red Indians and the Lost Boys. The only setback was that she found it impossible, at least for the current rehearsal, to communicate with Christine, so powerful was Bailey's stage presence, even at that juncture. Instead of practising

Tinker Bell's part, which admittedly, she knew pretty well, she stared, open-mouthed at this larger-than-life addition to the cast. Eventually, he had to reassure her.

'You mustn't be afraid of Captain Hook,' he told her. 'He threatens to do all kinds of things, but Peter and the Crocodile will put a stop to his tricks in the end.' Seeing that she was unconvinced, he asked, 'Can you keep a secret?'

She nodded a little uncertainly. 'Yes.'

'Captain Hook,' he whispered, 'is a bit of a softie on the quiet. Just see how he behaves when the Crocodile goes after him.' He treated her to a slow wink because only he and she knew the secret.

Leah, who had been watching, had long-since decided that she was in the company of a master.

*   *   *

On the following day, she took Nina for a long walk. She had no doubt Nina, now fully recovered from her operation, would appreciate it, but she was being a little selfish. The fact was that she needed time and space to think.

Everyone, it seemed, was ready to tell her how sensibly and courageously she'd adjusted to the knowledge that her dream was no more than a cruelly broken memory. They'd praised her for accepting the possibility of a career teaching dance, when the truth was that she saw the option as no more than a poor second-best. Now, it seemed, she could either disappoint her family and everyone who'd expressed their high opinion of her, or she could go on living a lie.

'Something's wrong, Nina,' she told her companion. 'I'm seventeen. That's old enough to drive, and almost old enough to get legless in a public bar – not that I want to do that – and I should be able to take charge of my own feelings. You understand that, don't you? You're not yet three, and you know how you feel about things.'

As is the way with dogs, Nina pricked up her ears on hearing Leah's voice, and wagged her tail, which was her way of saying, 'I haven't a clue what you're talking about, but I like you to talk to me, and I do care whether you're happy or sad.'

'Grandad told me I'll be able to help and advise anybody who suffers the same kind of horror that I did, but what could I tell them? "Stick with it. You'll still feel bitter a year later – at least – but people will say nice things about you." What kind of comfort would that be?' Her memory returned to her homecoming from hospital in London and the reception she was given when she arrived home. She thought about her grandad having her bed moved downstairs, and Martin bringing Nina to her and buying Charlie the Camel to stop her crying in the night. They were only a few of the kindnesses people had heaped on her. It was almost painful to think about them.

'And now I feel ashamed,' she told Nina. 'It's not that I'm ungrateful. I just move those things to the back of my mind when I'm feeling miserable.'

After a while, she remembered something that had emerged from one of her mother's war stories. She'd said that whenever she was feeling less than cheerful, she thought of her dad in Poland, and what he must be enduring. That was a lesson in itself. She thought about that for a short while, and said, 'Nina, I've made a decision.'

Nina took that as a cue to wag her tail.

'I can't make the accident less than the tragedy it was, but when I'm feeling sorry for myself, I can take a leaf out of my mum's book and concern myself with someone else's misfortune. Then, at the very least, I shan't feel quite so ashamed.'

Nina wagged her tail harder than ever, and that had to be an encouraging sign.

* * *

Her first opportunity arose that evening when Martin came as close as he ever did to venting his frustration with schoolwork. Although Leah was busy with her own work, she was mindful of her recent resolution.

'Wassup, Martin?' She ignored the parental looks of annoyance and joined her brother on his side of the table, where she could see a textbook open at a chapter on figures of speech.

'I don't know what any of this means,' he said.

'Similes and metaphors?'

'Yes.'

'All right. You know when people say that the night is as black as pitch, don't you?'

He studied the question briefly and said, 'It can't be as black as pitch. The night sky is dark blue.'

'Yes, well, some people tend to exaggerate.'

'But that's not exaggerating. Black and blue are two different colours.'

She tried a different approach. 'What they're actually saying is that the night is so dark it's scarcely recognisable as blue. In fact, it's so dark it might almost be black.'

'In that case, why don't they say so?'

Leah was beginning to feel sorry for Martin's English teacher. 'Lots of people exaggerate when they describe things, and sometimes, their descriptions are inaccurate. A example might be, "As honest as the day is long." Honesty can't be measured in hours or by any other system of measurement, can it?'

'No.'

They finally had agreement on something. 'They're actually saying that twenty-four hours is a long time, and the person in question is very, very honest, so they're comparing one extreme with another.'

'But time is relative, and compared with a century or even a year, a day is very brief.'

'It can feel long to some people, Martin.' The last few minutes had seemed interminable to her. 'Basically, a simile is a comparison that emphasises a description. To say that a man is as strong as an ox is silly, on the face of it. He can't be, but it simply means that he is very strong.' She was conscious that both parents were listening to the conversation, and she hoped they were following it more easily than Martin.

'I see,' he said. 'I know people who exaggerate.'

'I think we all do, Martin.'

'So that's a simile. What's a metaphor?'

Leah took a breath and said, 'Metaphors are even sillier, because instead of saying something is *like* something else, it's a way of saying it *is* that thing. Before he could interrupt her, she said, 'Instead of saying that someone is like a colossus, they say he *is* a colossus. Similarly, someone who is very greedy *is* a pig.'

He appeared to be assimilating that information. Eventually he said, 'I think I can do this, now. I have to say which of these are similes and which are metaphors.'

'Right, I'll go through it with you.'

He worked his way down the list, marking each one correctly. When he reached the end of the exercise, he said, 'Thank you for helping me with that, Leah. I couldn't have done it by myself.'

'Think nothing of it, Martin. It's what big sisters are for.'

'But I'm an inch taller than you.'

'Don't start that again, Martin, please.'

For a moment, he looked almost hurt, and then he collected himself and asked, 'What are you working on?'

'A poem by Goethe.'

'Haven't you got any maths or science you can't do? You always struggled with those subjects.'

'Yes, I did, but that's all in the past. I don't have to do them, now.'

'I see. I was going to say that if you were struggling, I'd help you.'

'That's a lovely thought, Martin. Thank you, but I'll be all right now.'

'Good. I'm going to bed, now. Goodnight, everybody.'

His parents wished him a good night, and Leah blew him a kiss.

When he was gone, her mother said, 'He just doesn't think like the rest of us, does he, Freddy?'

'I don't understand it. Was the milkman any good at similes and metaphors, SP? I'm sure he didn't get it from me.'

'Don't be rotten, Freddy. Anyway, it was kind of Leah to help him. Well done, darling.'

'I do what I can, Mum.' It seemed to Leah that keeping her new resolution was likely to prove onerous at times.

26

PANTOMIME AND TESTING TIME

Christmas 1968 was a different occasion from its predecessor. There were no crutches or plaster casts, and the nervous anticipation of the first hospital appointment was an unpleasant, but mercifully fading, memory. Another difference was that it took place at home, with Leah's grandparents as guests, this time, and the added excitement of a visit from the Bailey household.

Everything began on Christmas Eve, when Leah persuaded her parents to accompany her to Midnight Eucharist at St Jude's. Not surprisingly, Martin preferred to stay at home and listen to a radio programme about the latest development in computer science at the University of Washington. He was in bed by the time they returned.

As usual, the great excitement came on Boxing Day, which fell most conveniently on Friday, the twenty-seventh, when the popularity of the annual pantomime ensured that every seat at Easingthorpe Town Hall was sold.

The Dalesmen, serving in their *alter ego* as pit orchestra for the pantomime, played the *pot pourri* overture Freddy had arranged for them, after which the curtains opened on the Darling children's bedroom. There was some clowning involving Nana, the dog and prompting Janice's first visit to the loo – Elaine had reserved end seats to facilitate such excursions – and the next excitement came with Peter Pan's dramatic entry through the bedroom window. The gasps of excitement from the younger children were spoiled to some extent by the wolf-whistles of some of the older boys in the audience, but Wendy was too consummate a performer to be distracted by loutish behaviour. Instead, she made a hurried and urgent search of the room before sitting on Wendy Darling's bed and sobbing loudly.

With the reattachment of Peter's shadow complete, the children joined him in song and, now convinced of their ability to fly to Never-Never Land, exited in turn through the bedroom window to generous applause.

In the next scene, in Never-Never Land, one of the Lost Boys provided fresh merriment with his inability to keep in step with the others. It was just possible that most of the audience thought his antics were deliberate – certainly, they entertained Janice almost to the point of embarrassment – but Leah knew the truth. Something else she'd learned from working with her mother was that lack of ability was cause for neither recrimination nor fun-poking, and she'd been able to convince the boy in question that his contribution was entertaining in the nicest way.

Elaine had barely got Janice settled after the entry of the Lost Boys when it was time for Captain Hook to make his terrifying entrance. He was heavily made-up, bewhiskered and emitting the kind of blood-chilling laugh that might have been the envy of many a pantomime villain, but Janice wasn't fooled.

'Daddy!' she cried.

Bailey ad-libbed, saying, 'I told you it was our secret.'

There was a thrilling swordfight between him and Peter Pan until the Crocodile appeared, putting Hook temporarily to flight.

Another born performer was Christine Wilkinson, whose talent seemed to burgeon in front of an audience, so that a hearty cheer went up whenever she came on stage. As well as applauding her indisputably excellent performance, Leah hoped ardently that she wouldn't become spoilt and egotistical, like so many child performers.

The obligatory galley scene featuring Dame Smee and Cedric the Cabin Boy served as a distraction from everything that had preceded it, and Elaine had to bundle Janice out before it was over, much to her audible displeasure. It was as well she would be returning for the final evening.

Everyone knew, long before the performance was over, that the pantomime was a great success, and everyone associated with it received the audience's appreciation on the final evening, including Leah, who was embarrassed because she felt she'd contributed very little, and that there had been nothing remarkable about her efforts. By contrast, she now needed to put all her determination into the A level mock examinations.

* * *

Walter was also concerned about Leah's future, and with the trout season now last year's memory, he met Freddy for a drink at the Shearers' Arms.

He got the drinks in – he seldom allowed Freddy to buy a round – and they took a settle by the fire, acknowledging, as they did, Bert Whittaker, who occupied the settle opposite them. He seemed lost in his own thoughts, as usual, so Freddy respected his space.

Walter asked, 'How's Leah getting on with her studies?'

'She's giving it a hundred percent of her attention, as usual. She has an unbelievable capacity for work, when you consider all she has to do, and with the pantomime on top of everything else. It's just as well that's over and done with.'

'She's a worker,' agreed Walter, 'there's no doubt about that. I just can't help wondering if some of it is a distraction. By that, I mean a way of distracting herself. She shows every sign of having come to terms with the accident and the loss of her career, but it seems too good to be true. It's always been an awful lot to ask of her at seventeen.'

'Sylvia would be inclined to agree with you, Walter, and she knows Leah even better than I do.'

Walter laughed. 'Female intuition?'

'Maybe, and the fact that they have so much in common that they seem to think in the same way. To be honest, she's convinced me, but maybe that's been wishful thinking on my part.'

Walter nodded thoughtfully. 'Maybe it has,' he agreed. 'You know I spent some time with her talking about her application, don't you?'

'Yes, it was a good idea, Walter, because she'll never speak up for herself.'

'No. I've been wondering about that. Do you know who her referees are?'

'Yes, she's talked about that. There's the Principal of the Royal Ballet School, obviously, and I believe her second referee is Miles Stapleton.' Looking at Walter's glass, he said, 'I'll get them in, Walter.'

Then anticipating an argument, he said, 'I will, because I'm going to get one for Bert as well. Another pint, Bert?'

Bert Whittaker looked up for the first time since the two men had joined him. 'Aye,' he said, 'I'll get the next 'un.' He always said that, but Freddy found himself buying every round, although he was happy enough to do that, as Bert was permanently out of work.

He returned from the bar with three pints.

'Much obliged, Freddy,' said Bert. 'I'll get next 'un.'

'You're welcome, Bert.' Joining Walter again, he asked, 'What were we talking about, Walter?'

'You said Leah had asked Miles Stapleton for a reference. He's a good choice. Of course, I know him best as Chairman of the Governors at Yoredale High School. I believe he's the vicar at St Jude's.'

'The Rector, yes. He's tutored Leah in history, and they've come to know each other very well.'

'I believe you said she was going to church.'

'Yes, she's a regular attender. Of course, it helps that Wendy Albright's in the choir at St Jude's.'

Walter chuckled. 'That lass would be a good influence on the Archangel Gabriel.' More seriously, he said, 'I have it in mind to speak to Miles Stapleton. He'll have formed his own conclusions about Leah, but there'll still be things he should know about her.'

'That's very good of you, Walter.'

'Well, she's my granddaughter, after all.'

Perhaps sensing a natural pause in the conversation, Bert Whittaker looked up and asked, 'Are you keepin' all right, Freddy?'

'Right as rain, Bert. You know Walter, don't you? He's my father-in-law.'

'Aye.' Bert nodded in Walter's direction. 'Sylvia's dad. That's a grand lass you've got there, Walter.'

'It's good of you to say so, Bert.'

'Aye, we were at elementary school together, an' then Sylvia passed for t' grammar, but it made no difference to her. She still let on when she saw us, as friendly as ever.'

'I should hope so.'

Bert lowered his beer by a third and said, 'We're old mates, Freddy an' me. We were both PoWs, him in Poland and me in Burma. Were you?'

'No,' said Walter. 'I was in the Nineteenth Green Howards in the first war, but I'm pleased to say the Huns never caught me.'

'Be thankful for that, Walter.'

'I am, believe me.'

Presumably remembering that Walter was connected with Yoredale Players, he said, 'We came to t' pantomime, the missis an' me. That were a fair old treat. That lass that played Peter Pan....'

'Wendy,' prompted Freddy.

'She's got a rare talent.'

'We're lucky to have her,' agreed Freddy.

At the call, 'Last Orders,' Freddy said, 'Do you want us to see you home, Bert?'

'Aye, that'd be right good of you. I seem to have had more than I intended.'

Freddy forbore to point out that it was a regular occurrence. Instead, he and Walter helped him to his feet and supported him all the way to his house, where his wife was waiting.

'Thank you, Freddy,' she said. It was a routine event.

'This is my father-in-law Walter Charlesworth,' he said.

'Sylvia's dad? I'm pleased to meet you, Mr Charlesworth. Thanks for bringing Bert home. Come inside, Bert.'

As they left the house, Freddy said, 'Mrs Whittaker has the patience of a saint. Having said that, though, Bert's a pitiful character. You've got to feel sorry for him, permanently unemployed and haunted by his experiences.'

'It goes without saying,' said Walter, 'but how does he manage to get drunk on the dole?'

'He never buys a drink. He always says, "I'll get t' next 'un," but he never does.

'What a life, eh?'

'He makes me ashamed to complain about life as a PoW. You know how much Sylvia's letters meant to me, don't you, Walter?'

'I've a fair idea.'

'Bert told me they'd been in their camp in Burma more than a year when the first mail arrived.'

'No.'

'It takes some imagining. The worst thing was that they dumped all the mail in front of the prisoners and the commandant told them they hadn't worked hard enough. To punish them, he ordered his men to burn it in front of them.'

'That's sickening, Freddy. They should have hanged the bugger for that alone.'

'He escaped that. Instead, he was shot in a hotel room.'

'Good.'

They reached Freddy's gate, and he asked, 'Are you coming in, Walter?'

'No, I won't, thanks.' He looked at his watch. 'Jessie's not quite as understanding as Mrs Whittaker.'

'I imagine very few are. Good night, Walter.' They shook hands.

'Good night, Freddy. I'll speak to Miles about that other business.'

'Thanks.'

Walter drove away, and Freddy let himself in to find that Sylvia was still up.

'Have you been seeing Bert Whittaker home?' she asked.

'Yes, we thought we'd better.' Because he knew the knowledge would please her, he said, 'He enjoyed the pantomime.'

'Good, I'm glad. What else have you to report?'

'Only that your dad's going to speak to Miles about Leah's reference. He's concerned that she might be too modest for her own interests, and he's keen to see that Miles is in no doubt about her personal qualities.'

'Mm.' With that non-committal utterance, Sylvia gave the impression that she was deep in thought.

'A penny for them, SP.'

'I think Leah's working hard at her "A" levels because she genuinely enjoys the subjects she's studying. As far as the other thing's concerned....'

'Her application for a place?'

'Yes, I think she's going through the motions, but without enthusiasm. She's tried to convince us that she's keen without realising that we know she's not. Just reading between the lines, I think she doesn't want to disappoint us after all the support we've given her, and the awful thing is that there's nothing we can do to make her keener than she is. It's going to be a testing time for us as well as for her.'

'You're amazing, SP.' He felt like Dr Watson after one of Sherlock Holmes's brilliant deductions, except that they were fictional characters, and he and Sylvia were dealing with a real and sensitive situation.

'Have you only just realised that?'

'You know you never fail to astonish me with your insight, both you and your dad.'

'Oh.' She looked disappointed. 'Do I have to share the compliment with my dad?'

'Don't worry, SP,' he said, leaning towards her to kiss her. 'I've just thought of something you can't share with your dad.'

'How clever of you. Are you going to tell me what it is, or will you show me?'

'Come upstairs and I'll show you what I have in mind.'

'I can't wait,' she said, standing up. 'Let me bank the fire up first, though.'

Not for the first time, Freddy wondered about the secret, illogical world of the female sex, but not for long, distracted as he was by another matter that required his immediate attention.

27

FEBRUARY

MOMENT OF TRUTH

Leah continued to pursue her 'A' levels in the same determined way, even though she needed only two to matriculate and go on after dance school to take the Certificate in Education that would enable her to teach anywhere. History was always going to be an unknown quantity, although Miles Stapleton was pleased enough with her progress. She sat mocks in the other subjects, however, and awaited the results as patiently as she could.

First, the German results were made known. She had a projected 'B', which was very respectable. The other two took a little while longer, but the wait was worthwhile. She had projected 'A' grades in French and English Literature, and she could now make her application. More immediately, her parents organised a celebration dinner with the usual participants at the County Hotel in Northallerton. It was, in some way, to be a double celebration, as well, because the hotel had recently asked the Dalesmen to fill a regular spot.

'It was all thanks to you, Bailey,' said Freddy.

'My dear old soul, not in the least,' protested Bailey, 'but why are we arguing? We're here to celebrate Leah's latest success.'

'Projected success,' she corrected him.

'At all events,' said Walter, 'we're all very proud of you.'

'What has Leah done?' demanded Janice at a volume capable of penetrating every room in the hotel.

'She's worked hard and got some very good exam results,' Elaine told her.

'What are they? Can I have some?'

'I think you'd get bored with exams very quickly.'

'Why?'

'Because,' said Bailey, 'you'd have to sit on your own without talking, for three hours at a time.'

'I can't do that.'

'No,' he said soothingly, 'but don't worry. We'll make sure you don't have to.'

'Anyway,' she said, 'it'll all be the same in a hundred years' time.'

'So it will,' said Elaine. 'Leah, are you looking forward to going to dance school?'

'I suppose I am, really. It won't be what I've been used to, but it'll be dance, when all's said and done, and it's been missing from my life.' She didn't want to go as far as saying that it would be better than nothing, but that was nevertheless how she felt.

'Well, I think Leah's done remarkably well,' said Walter, 'to go from the classroom to studying at home, and then to make the change again to the classroom. All that, in fact, and to get the grades she got.'

'Projected grades, Grandad.'

'If you convert those into actual grades,' said her grandma, 'you'll have the same as Bruce got.'

'Really?' It was typical of her grandma that she remembered Bruce's 'A' level grades and probably everything else to do with his MBChB as well, but he was Leah's favourite cousin, so it didn't matter that he was also Grandma's favourite grandchild via her favourite daughter.

'Don't you wish you'd worked harder when you were at school, Sylvia?' asked Jessie, for whom comparisons were an enjoyable diversion.

'No, I don't. I achieved everything I wanted.'

'Oh?' In spite of Walter's discreet efforts to dissuade her, Jessie insisted on challenging her daughter's claim.

'I served my country in its hour of need, and much more besides.'

'She enlisted to "free a man for the fleet",' said Freddy, 'but she did much more than that. She mended a broken man, brought him safely home and made him happier than he'd ever believed possible, even providing him with two lovely children.'

189

'Well said, Dad,' said Leah. 'That was better than daffodils in December.'

'Yes, I agree,' said Walter, to his wife's surprise.

'Not just that,' insisted Leah. 'I've known some excellent teachers, including my dad, but my mum taught me to drive, to cook and to bake, better than anyone could.'

'I taught you swimming and ballroom dancing as well, darling.' Sylvia was flushed with embarrassment at being the focus of attention, but she was determined to hold her corner against her mother's biased testimony.

'That settles it,' said Bailey lifting his glass. 'Here's to Sylvia, whom we love and admire!'

The toast was taken up eagerly, and Leah, who knew the score as well as anyone, exchanged winks with both her parents.

'Everybody owes a lot to their mother,' said Martin a little belatedly, 'because mothers get all the hard work to do before and after their children are born.'

'Well said, Martin,' said Leah.

'Yes,' said Bailey, 'you got that one just right, Martin.' Holding up his glass again, he proposed, 'Mothers everywhere!'

Perhaps feeling that the accolade had become rather one-sided, Martin said, 'Fathers too. They do a splendid job.'

'Thank you, Martin.' Freddy was surprised but no less appreciative of his son's tribute.'

It was Leah's turn to propose a toast. 'Fathers everywhere!'

'This is getting silly,' said Jessie.

'And that's just the way we like it to be,' said Freddy.

'Hear, hear,' was Walter's energetic endorsement.

* * *

On the way home, Leah asked, 'What were Grandma and Grandad Hinchcliffe like, Dad?'

'Well, let me see. The last time I saw them was almost thirty years ago. How can I describe them? After a little thought, he said, 'Your grandma was always quite reserved. In retrospect, I suspect she was rather shy. At all events, she made sure that Catherine and I behaved with "decorum". That was one of her favourite words. At least, it seemed so to us.' Thinking again, he said, 'She probably had more to do with Catherine's upbringing than mine. In those days, you see, it was a mother's job to bring up her daughter.'

'I suppose it makes an old-fashioned kind of sense.'

'They were old-fashioned times, Leah, the nineteen-twenties. Your grandad was particularly old-fashioned, almost Victorian in his values, but he was born during Victoria's reign, so it was hardly surprising. Anyway, with two strict parents, it's little wonder I grew up to be such an upright citizen.'

'We hear you, Dad,' said Leah.

'Mr Turner keeps telling us to sit upright,' said Martin, 'but it doesn't makes us any better at Physics. I can do it just as easily and just as well round-shouldered.'

'You don't know when you're well off,' Freddy told him. 'We had to sit to attention in all our lessons.'

'You can read all about it,' Sylvia told them, 'in *Nicholas Nickleby*.'

The allusion was lost on Martin, who asked, 'Who was he, Mum?'

'A character in a novel by Charles Dickens.'

'Oh.' Fiction meant nothing to Martin.

Leah asked, 'What was... Auntie Catherine like, Dad?'

'She was four years younger than me, so I remember her mainly as a little girl. She was very skilful and inventive, I remember, with a skipping rope.'

'It's difficult for your dad to remember,' said Sylvia, 'and painful, most likely.'

'Yes, I'm sorry, Dad. I didn't mean to make you sad.'

'It was a long time ago, Leah, and it's a shame that I have no photographs I can show you. They were all destroyed with the house. Everything was.'

'Well, even bombs can't destroy memories. You'll always have them.' They were entering Easingthorpe, which was probably just as well.

Later, Leah lay in bed, unable to sleep. She was thinking of Grandma Charlesworth's insensitive utterance, and how little she knew her daughter. Finally, she thought of her dad and his five-hundred-mile trek through blizzards and freezing conditions, supporting Bailey all the time, weakened as he was after five years' near-starvation, and her mum, whose unstinting love had kept him going throughout that time. She had good reason to be proud of them both.

* * *

Unfortunately, it was her own qualities she had to address in her application, and it felt completely unnatural.

Pausing beside her, he mum asked, 'Are you finding it difficult?'

'Yes, it's this business of Further Information.' She tapped her grandad's notebook and said, 'Grandad put it much better than I could – I wouldn't know how to begin – but it still feels wrong, somehow, like boasting.'

'Do you feel as if you're baring your soul?'

'Yes.'

'And it feels unnatural?'

'Yes.'

'That's a legacy from your dad,' she told her gently, 'but it's possible to defy inhibition. Your dad did it just recently, at the County Hotel, when he spoke up for me.'

'I know,' she said, remembering the occasion, 'he was brilliant.'

'Well,' said her mum, giving her a squeeze, 'it's your turn to be brilliant. Just keep in mind the fact that these people need to know the best about you, and if you don't tell them, there's no way they can ever know it.'

Leah nodded, but with little conviction.

'It seems to me,' said her mum, pulling out a chair for herself, 'that your heart's not really in it. It's not what you want to do most, is it?'

As if on a long-awaited cue, Leah's shoulders began to shake, she bowed her head and sobbed helplessly.

After a while, she felt herself being helped up and taken to the sofa, where she sat, still sobbing, but with the familiar reassurance of her mum's arms around her.

Her dad must have come into the room at some time, because she heard him ask, 'What's the matter?'

'It's all right,' her mum told him quietly. 'We're having a moment of truth.'

After a while, her sobs subsided, and she heard her mum say, 'For a year now, you've been trying to convince everybody that you've come to terms with it, but anyone with any imagination must realise it was impossible. It would be hard enough for anyone, but at your age it was too much to ask.'

'I didn't want... to seem... ungrateful. Every...body's done so... much....'

'I know why you did it, darling. I'm not blaming you at all, but you've got to be true to yourself.' Taking a large box of tissues, she offered them to Leah with the advice, 'Mopping-up time.'

With a bundle of waterlogged tissues on the table, Leah struggled to control the shudders her sobs had left behind. 'I thought I was... being... sensible,' she said.

'Yes, you did what you thought was expected of you. In truth, we didn't know what to expect. I hardly need to tell you, it came as a shock to all of us.'

'It... must have.'

'What you have to fall back on now is common sense. You know you've been denied the career you always wanted, and nothing can change that. On the other hand, you can help a great many others find enjoyment and fulfilment through dance.'

'I suppose so.'

'Performers, dancers particularly, are vulnerable and sensitive people, Leah, as you know, and they can't always solve their own problems, or even find their own way forward. Bear that in mind.' Glancing at the form on the table, she asked, 'Can you get another application form?'

'Yes, they have them at Kit Calvert.'

Her mum smiled. 'Isn't it lovely that they named a technical college after a cheesemaker?'

'Yes, but why do I need a new form?'

'Because the one you were working on is smudged with huge teardrops. I don't think they'd put that down to passion and determination.'

28

MARCH

REALISATION

Within a very short time, Leah was invited to an interview at the Cory School of Dance. As it would be necessary to travel to London the day before the appointment and stay overnight, Sylvia elected to accompany her, assuring her that there was plenty for her to do in London while the interview was taking place.

'You'll buy up half of Oxford Street, if I know you,' said Freddy, 'but never mind, it's all in a good cause.'

Sylvia booked hotel rooms, reserved train seats, and made all preparations.

On the day, Freddy drove them to Northallerton Station, kissed them both, bought a copy of the *Times* for Sylvia and wished his daughter luck, being careful at the same time to sound confident.

'All the news seems to be about the lowering of the Age of Majority,' said Sylvia when they'd taken their seats. 'The Government say that if someone can serve his country in war at eighteen, he should have the vote. The Opposition say it's no more than a cynical ploy to capture the left-wing student vote.

'But when is it going to happen?'

'Not until later this year.'

'That's a fat lot of good. I'll be eighteen next week.'

'Bad luck, darling, but by the time you begin your studies, you'll be... oh... ages old, like me and your doddering old dad.'

The interview was seldom far from Leah's thoughts. 'I was

surprised,' she said, 'when they asked for a medical report from Mr Livesey. It must be all right, though. I mean they'd have cancelled the interview if they had doubts, wouldn't they?'

'That, and it was Mr Livesey's idea in the first place. I shouldn't worry, darling.' After some thought, she asked, 'Have you thought about what I said?'

'You've said lots of things, Mum.'

'About vulnerable dance students and their particular needs.'

'I've thought about it a lot. I'm still thinking, as it happens.'

'That's the spirit.'

For no obvious reason, other than that they were on yet another journey, Leah was reminded of an incident her mum had mentioned earlier, and it seemed a good time to remind her of it. 'Last time we went to the hospital,' she said, 'you were talking about Auntie Dorothy and Uncle Alf. I think it was about a darts match, of all things.'

'Oh, yes, when six of us went on a run ashore.'

'What?'

'That was what we called it when we went outside the main gate. You didn't have to be in a ship to go "ashore".'

'Weird.'

'Oh, we had to learn a whole new language – two languages, in fact. There was official navalese, which requires a dictionary in itself, and then there was Jackspeak, the language of Jolly Jack, the sailor.'

'Go on, Mum.'

'In those days, it wasn't considered respectable for a woman to go into a pub alone. In fact, it was only after the Americans came that women frequented pubs at all. Anyway, on this occasion, six of us went on a run ashore, as I said. There was Joyce, Dorothy and Alf; there was our leading telegraphist Will Hay, a most unpleasant Royal Marine called Norris, and me, and we all went to a pub called the Cinque Ports Arms because it was handy for us. I don't drink much, as you know, but it was a change of scenery, and that was a treat in itself.'

'Did the other Wrens drink?'

'Dorothy and Joyce drank very little. As I said, it was a novelty for us, in those days, to visit a pub at all.' She gathered her thoughts

195

again and continued. 'Well, I remember that Will told a dirty joke that the men found incredibly funny, but Dorothy and I didn't get it. We were both innocent and very naïve in those days.'

'Can you remember the joke?'

'Not after all these years, and if I could, I wouldn't tell it to you.' She smiled at the memory. Joyce had offered to explain the joke to them later, but it never happened, and it probably wouldn't have meant much to them, anyway.

'After that, the boys suggested a darts match. It was all very complicated, and we were divided into three teams, each consisting of a man and a girl, because we were deemed hopeless at the manly arts. Joyce and I were as bad as each other. Neither of us had thrown a dart in our lives, but at that stage, I didn't care.'

'What about Auntie Dorothy? Was she better at throwing darts than you were?'

'I'm coming to that.'

'Okay.' Leah waited patiently for the story to unfold.

'Alf was Hostilities Only, whereas Norris was a regular Royal Marine and an incurable loudmouth. He'd been teasing Alf quite unpleasantly. Alf was too good-natured for his own good, so he had little to say, but Dorothy surprised us all when she told Norris exactly what she thought of him. Clearly, something was developing between her and Alf, although the latter was unaware of it at that stage. Anyway, Dorothy and Alf won the first two rounds. Actually, Alf didn't do all that well. The star of the evening was Dorothy, who had no difficulty in putting her darts just where she wanted them, and after the first two rounds, Norris was getting quite nasty about her, saying it was all down to beginners' luck, and that sort of thing. Well, Dorothy, being Dorothy, put him firmly in his place. I seem to remember she told him it was to be hoped he was better with a rifle and bayonet than he was with a dart. Anyway, having sorted him out, she went on to throw the winning score. It seems she'd learned to throw darts at an early age. I suppose it came of having brothers.'

'Wonderful.'

'Yes, that was the start of the great romance between those two. It was a lovely thing to happen.'

'I can't imagine them not being together.'

Sylvia just smiled in recollection.

Conversation was easy the rest of the way to King's Cross. Sylvia took good care of that.

* * *

When they got off the train at King's Cross, Leah asked, 'Do you think you'll have time to show me where you and Dad met for the first time? I'd love to see it.'

'Yes, we can do it this afternoon. Let's book into the hotel and leave our luggage, and then I'll show you the place.'

They took a taxi, first to the hotel, and then Sylvia asked the driver to take them to Spring Gardens, WC2.

He asked, 'Are you thinking of joining the Navy, love?'

'No, I did that a long time ago, twenty-eight years ago, actually, but I want to show my daughter where it all happened.'

They left the taxi outside the Old Admiralty Building, and Sylvia explained that her place of work had been below ground. 'It kept us safe from the bombing,' she said, except that it was all over by the time I came here.' Pointing towards Trafalgar Square, she asked, 'Can you see the lion on the corner nearest us?'

'Yes.'

'Try to imagine the scene. When I came out of that door,' she said, pointing to the double door behind them, 'it was raining pretty hard, but I squinted through the downpour and saw a man standing beside the lion. I felt terribly nervous, because, although we'd written reams to each other, it was the first time we were going to come face to face. I didn't even know what he looked like, except that I'd been told he looked a bit like Len.'

'I suppose they are rather alike, really. Uncle Len's not quite as tall as my dad, but they've got similar features.'

'Very similar. On the other hand, your dad had seen a photo of me when he was staying with Grandma and Grandad, so he was at an advantage. Shall we walk over to the lion and pay our respects?'

'Yes.' The idea of being reunited with a lion appealed to Leah.

They waited for a lull in the traffic and crossed the road to the Square itself.

'Hello, Mr Lion,' said Sylvia, 'it's me again, Leading Wren Charlesworth, after twenty-four years. I married the man I met here, and this is our daughter Leah.'

The lion seemed unimpressed, but Leah looked about her excitedly. 'I can't believe we're actually here,' she said. 'What did he say when you met?'

'Who? The lion?'

'No, my dad, silly.'

'He said, 'Hello, Sylvia,' hardly the most romantic line ever uttered, but what else could he say? It was raining hard by that time, so we went to a café in Whitehall.' She peered in that direction and said, 'I don't think it's there any longer. It was only a quick meeting, you know, just to say, "Hello" and have lunch. Your dad had two lunches that day, believe it or not. That's how hungry he was after three years of starvation. Anyway, I only had a couple of hours before I had to get back on board, but we met again the next evening.'

'That was the time you told me about, wasn't it, when Bailey requested a dance tune for you?'

'That was no ordinary dance tune, Leah. It was "All the Things You Are", and you know how important that is to us.'

'I should, after all this time.'

'Yes, some things are sacred.'

'What was Bailey doing there?'

'Oh, he wasn't there when we were. He'd called in earlier and left the request. He left a note for your dad as well, explaining what he'd done and why he'd done it. He said it was for saving his life on the Long March, but you know about that, don't you?'

Still enchanted with the idea, Leah asked, 'When did you choose this place to meet?'

'It was a convenient place for me, because I was at the Wireless Station, but your dad first suggested it in a letter, much earlier. After all this time, I'm not sure whether he was in Poland or Germany at the time, but he thought it would be a suitably grand meeting place, not hackneyed, like the ever-popular "under the clock at Waterloo Station", but still with a touch of splendour. He called the event "The Immortal Memory and The Grand Romance".'

'I get the Grand Romance, but what did he mean by "The Immortal Memory"?'

'The Immortal Memory is up there,' she pointed to the top of Nelson's Column. 'He's a hundred and seventy feet in the air, but he's never been forgotten.'

'Wonderful.' Leah took in the imposing figure of Lord Nelson and said, 'I wish we could go to the other places you went to together.'

'And I wish we could afford them. I'm afraid the American Bar at the Savoy is rather beyond my pocket as well as the fact that you're under-age, and the night club's out of the question, but we'll find somewhere nice for dinner. I think we should, as this is a special visit.'

* * *

They spent a pleasant evening, during which Sylvia managed to distract Leah's thoughts away from the interview, but the time finally came, the next morning, for them to take a taxi to St John's Wood and the Cory School of Dance.

'The actual interview is this afternoon at two o'clock, Mum,' Leah reminded her.

'I know. I'll come back at about three and wait for you. Good luck, darling.' She kissed her and returned to the taxi, leaving her to find her own way into the building, a touch that Leah appreciated. No one wanted the embarrassment of a fussing parent at an interview.

She found the entrance and made her way to the nearest office, where she knocked on the door and waited. She could hear someone typing, but then it stopped, and a neatly-dressed woman of maybe forty or so, because Leah could never be sure of people's ages, opened the door.

'Good morning,' she said.

'Good morning. I have an appointment at ten-thirty.' The office clock showed that it was a little before ten-fifteen, but it was always better to be early than late.

'What's your name?'

'Leah Hinchcliffe.'

The woman smiled. 'If you like to come with me, Leah, I'll take you to a room where you can prepare yourself and wait.'

'Oh, do I have to change now?'

'I don't think so. Why do you ask?'

'I was thinking of the audition.'

'Ah well, that'll be up to Miss Winn.'

Leah caught her breath. 'Sarah Winn?'

'Yes.' She seemed amused by Leah's reaction.

'I saw her dance shortly before she retired. She was wonderful.'

The secretary chuckled. 'You might tell her that. It can't do you any harm.' She led Leah down a passage, past several studios, until they came to a small room lined with chairs. 'Wait here, and Miss Winn or someone will come for you. The usual offices are next door, by the way, in case you need them.'

'Thank you.' Leah wondered what the 'usual offices' were. The term was new to her, and it remained a mystery until she peeped round the corner and saw the doors marked 'Male' and 'Female'. Those labels, as well as the stick-figures beneath them, told her what she wanted to know, and they served as a helpful prompt, as well, when she realised that she needed to make a visit while she could.

She returned to the waiting room to find Sarah Winn waiting for her. 'Oh,' she said, 'I'm sorry. I'd just popped out to the loo.'

'That's all right, Leah. We're ahead of time, anyway.' She offered her hand and said, 'I'm Sarah Winn.'

'I know. I saw you in the Prokofiev *Romeo and Juliet*, oh, two years....'

'It's three years ago, now. I retired from the ballet stage shortly afterwards.'

'You were wonderful.'

'Thank you, Leah. It's very kind of you to say so.' Looking at Leah's drawstring bag, she asked, 'What have you got there?'

'A leotard, ballet slippers, *pointe* shoes, a towel and washing things.'

Miss Winn smiled and said, 'You're not going to need those things today.'

Confused for the moment, Leah asked, 'Won't I need to audition?'

'No, Leah,' she laughed, 'the Royal Ballet School sent us a glowing report about you, and we're not going to argue with them. All we're going to do this morning is show you around the school and answer any questions you may have. Your interview will be this afternoon, but first of all, shall we find some coffee and continue our conversation over that?'

* * *

The process was proving to be much less formal than Leah had anticipated. Her informal chat with Sarah Winn revealed that Mr Livesey's medical report had been supportive and that her application was already being viewed in a positive light.

'I'm afraid injuries are a fact of life, Leah,' said Miss Winn, 'although thankfully, not everything we have to deal with is on the same scale as your terrible ordeal.' As if she'd only just made the decision, she said suddenly, 'I'm going to take you to see a third-year student who's laid up, probably for two months. Like you, she was hit by a car, but only the bones in her lower leg, the tibia and fibula, were fractured. I imagine that sounds quite tame, compared with what you've suffered.'

'I suppose it is, but....'

'What?'

'I was thinking of my own feelings after the accident and before I learned that I'd never dance professionally. I was just coping with being immobilised and in hospital. Those things alone made me feel desperate enough.'

Miss Winn appeared to consider that before saying, 'Yes, I think a visit from you might be just what Carla needs.'

'Is that the girl with the broken leg?'

'Yes, Carla Daniels.' She consulted a timetable on the wall and said, 'If you've finished your coffee, we'll go and find her.'

They took a different route from before, which brought them to a classroom. Miss Winn opened the door and spoke to the person taking the class. 'I'm sorry to interrupt you. I wonder if I might relieve you of Carla, please, just for a few minutes.'

A slight, dark-haired girl tried to get out of her chair, and Miss Winn went in to help her. Leah held the door while the girl came through on her crutches. Her lower right leg was in plaster.

Miss Winn got a chair for her and invited her to sit outside the classroom. 'How are you feeling today, Carla?' she asked.

'Not bad, thanks, Miss Winn.' Clearly, she was still less than happy.

'This is Leah. She's being interviewed today.' When the two had shaken hands, she said, 'I wanted you to meet Leah because she had a devastating accident some time ago. Would you like to tell Carla about your experience, Leah?'

'Yes, of course. I was hit by a car in Oxford Street. It was more than a year ago. My left leg was broken in three places, my hip was fractured right up the middle, and my right leg was broken in two places, but the worst injury was to my right knee. It was well and truly mangled.'

Carla's mouth had fallen open at the catalogue of Leah's injuries, but she remained silent, possibly in her shocked state.

'I was very lucky with the third surgeon I saw. He was the second one to operate on me. He repaired my knee as far as he could, probably as well as anyone could, given the mess inside there, and gradually, through hours of physio and mile upon mile of swimming, I'm... well, I'm very much better. I can do forty *pliés* before it becomes uncomfortable, and I intend to improve on that in time.'

Carla was shaking her head, possibly in disbelief, although it was impossible to say. A tear ran down her cheek, and she said, 'I feel so ashamed now.'

'Why?'

'Because what I've got is nothing compared with what you've been through.'

Leah was very much aware that she was an interviewee talking to a third-year student, but there were things that had to be said. 'Don't feel ashamed, Carla. That won't do you any good. Leave it behind you and start looking forward again. Your fractures will heal, and you'll have to get back into your routine gradually, because that's the only safe way to do it. Instead of being ashamed, though, be determined to succeed in your training. I am, even though I know I'll never dance professionally.'

'Leah was being groomed at the Royal Ballet School for a future as a prima ballerina, Carla,' Miss Winn told her.

'Oh, that's awful.' Carla began to sob, and Leah knelt beside her on her good knee. 'It's all right, Carla,' she told her, putting her arms around her. 'It really is. I stopped crying a long time ago.' It wasn't strictly true, but she felt that circumstances granted her some allowance. 'Even if you have to come back and do a resit, you'll get through, and this

202

experience will stand you in good stead.' She wasn't sure how useful it would be or in what way, and she didn't care as long as Carla felt better. As she thought about it, she became conscious that her mum's words were beginning to make more sense than ever.

'Thank you, Leah,' said Miss Winn. 'Do you want to tidy yourself up before you rejoin your class, Carla?'

'I'll help you to the loo, if you like,' said Leah.

'Two doors along the passage,' Miss Winn told her helpfully.

* * *

The interview panel consisted of two people: Miss Winn and a man called Robert Fenner. All Leah knew about him was that his background was in musical theatre. His first question was about the reference from the Reverend Stapleton.

He asked, 'What is your relationship to the Reverend Miles Stapleton, Leah?'

'He's Rector of St Jude's, where I live, and he's tutored me for "A" level History since I had to leave ballet school.'

'I see. He knows an awful lot about you, about your part in the local pantomime, for example, and the way you brought your special skills to bear on that.'

It sounded very much as if there'd been some collusion between the Rector and her grandad, but Leah just said, 'He takes a close interest in local matters, and I suppose the pantomime is an important tradition for the whole community.'

'Of course.'

'Actually, the pantomime is more important than you might think. It grew out of something that began the year before I was born, when my dad wanted to do something that would lift everyone's spirits after the war. My dad writes it and conducts it, and my mum does the choreography and dance coaching. They also produce an annual show that my dad sometimes writes. I just helped with it because I was at home. It was quite useful, really, working in modern and jazz, for a change.'

'You sound like an enterprising family,' said Mr Fenner.

'Well, we do what we can.'

'I imagine working with amateurs of all ages and levels of ability can be quite testing,' said Miss Winn.

'I suppose so. Sometimes it calls for a balance of firmness and encouragement. They're taking part for their own enjoyment, and we must always remember that and not be too critical or demanding, but I never had any difficulty with it. The people I've worked with have all been very cooperative.'

Miss Winn smiled, very likely at something in the reference, and said, 'One of your chief characteristics, apparently, is that you're quite dismissive about your own qualities, and I suppose that makes you something of a perfectionist. How do you balance that against the, sometimes, more modest qualities you see in others?'

'Well, I suppose we're all individuals with various levels of ability. I'd certainly never belittle other people's strengths and achievements, just as I'd be horrified if anyone took that line with me.' She was beginning to wonder just what the Reverend Stapleton had written about her. Thinking quickly, she said, 'It's like this morning with Carla. She could be accused of making a drama out of a relatively minor setback, something that's going to improve in time, anyway, but the way I see it is that she's in the middle of her difficulty and unable to see it from the outside, and certainly not in perspective. She simply needs help to find her way forward. There's no shame in that, and I was happy to give her what help I could. I hope I did her some good.'

'You did,' Miss Winn assured her. 'Dance students are vulnerable people, as you know.'

'Oddly enough, my mum said that quite recently.'

'Your mother does the choreography and dance coaching for the pantomime and the musical, doesn't she?' Mr Fenner consulted his notes. 'Has she worked professionally?'

'No, she's what I'd call a gifted amateur. She's also very good with people. That's why she said what she did.'

'How did that come about, Leah?' asked Miss Winn. 'I mean what led her to say that?'

Being a basically honest person, Leah decided to tell the truth. 'I was so heartbroken at seeing my dance career go up in smoke, that for some time, I viewed the prospect of teaching dance as a poor second best. That's what my mum was talking about.' She could see that she had the close attention of both interviewers. The next bit was going to be decisive. 'That was how I saw it, but since then, I've come to realise where my purpose lies.' They didn't need to know that the realisation had only crystallised that morning, when she met Carla. Speaking confidently, she told them, 'I'm never going to dance on the professional stage, and I've accepted that, but – and I think this is just as important – I *can* help others realise their ambitions and help them through the trials and... pitfalls, I suppose... on their way. Dance students are vulnerable, as you said, Miss Winn, but I can see myself teaching and supporting them. I mean to say, I know how it feels to be on top of the world, because I've been there. I've also been in the pits of despair, so if I don't know how a student feels when things are truly wonderful or when they go disastrously wrong, who does? Anyway, that's what I think, and it's what I want to do if I can.'

The interviewers looked at each other and smiled. Miss Winn said, 'Have you any questions you'd like to put to us, Leah?'

'I don't think so. I spent a lot of time finding out about the Cory School of Dance before I applied, and we had a very useful conversation this morning, so I'm quite satisfied, thank you.'

'In that case, would you like to go back to the waiting room while we have a conference? We'll tell you when we've arrived at a decision.'

'Of course.'

Leah looked at her watch as she left the room. It was almost two-forty, so her mum was most likely waiting outside, or she would be, soon. It was good timing. She found the waiting room and sat down to read some of the printed information she'd been given. She hoped she hadn't been too open about her earlier doubts, but no one could possibly criticise her for telling the truth.

She'd only been waiting a few minutes when Mr Fenner came to say, 'Will you come back to the interview room, Leah? We'd like to talk to you.'

She followed him back and took the seat she'd vacated only a few minutes earlier.

'Thank you for coming to talk to us today, Leah,' said Miss Winn. 'We'd like to offer you a place subject to your gaining grade "E"s in any two subjects.'

'Really?' Leah was completely thrown. 'But grade "E" is just a scrape-through, isn't it?'

'Yes, it is.' Laughing at her response, Miss Winn said, 'Having said that, you did more than scrape through your interview, so basic matriculation is all we're demanding.'

'That's wonderful. Thank you very much.' She shook hands with her interviewers.

'You're very welcome, Leah. We look forward to seeing you in September.'

Leah took her leave of them and found her way back to the main entrance, where her mother sat waiting for her. 'Oh, Mum!' she said, drawing her into a celebratory hug.

The End

AUTHOR'S END NOTE

It will be apparent to most readers that Leah's brother Martin was affected by autism spectrum disorder. It was known for some time as Asperger syndrome, but in 1967 it must have been a mystery as well as a worry to most parents and siblings, and a great many children must have suffered at school, as Martin did, because the condition was yet to be recognised. I remember a boy at the primary school I attended, who displayed characteristics which, in retrospect, were consistent with ASD. He had a difficult time, and then he suddenly disappeared. We were told in a reverential whisper, that he'd gone to a special school where they took 'children like him'. I hope he fared better at that place, and I used to think about him, years later, when I was teaching children with ASD to play the piano. We have come a long way since the late 1960s, when this story is set, and hopefully we shall become even better informed.

Janice, on the other hand, had a recognised condition, now referred to as trisomy 21 anomaly. It was previously known as Down's Syndrome, because it took its name from John Langdon Down, the paediatrician who first described it. Some of those with the disorder have also suffered in the past from the insensitivity of an uninformed population, and in some cases, they still do. I was fortunate as a youngster growing up in the 1950s, because my mother encouraged me to play with the girl who came to visit her grandmother, our next-door neighbour. She explained that Cynthia had 'something a bit wrong with her' that meant she didn't learn as readily as most children, but that she was a lovely girl for all that. In my seven-year-old innocence, I saw nothing unusual in her flat features and almond-shaped eyes. She was just Cynthia, a very likeable girl. My mother had worked as a nurse in a mental hospital at the time when the care of educationally disadvantaged children was the responsibility of the Health Service, so she had a head start, but that was in the 1950s. Seventy years later, there is still room for enlightenment.

After all that, Leah's difficulty, whilst devastating, was purely accidental, and I hope you have enjoyed reading about the way she survived it and found her way forward.

RH

www.ingramcontent.com/pod-product-compliance
Lightning Source LLC
Chambersburg PA
CBHW020839260626
47169CB00003B/1067